UNEXPECTING

UNEXPECTING

A Novel

Jen Bailey

WEDNESDAY BOOKS

NEW YORK

First published in the United States by Wednesday Books, an imprint of St. Martin's Publishing Group

www.wednesdaybooks.com

Designed by Jen Edwards

Library of Congress Cataloging-in-Publication Data

Names: Bailey, J. Leigh, author.
Title: Unexpecting : a novel / Jen Bailey.
Description: First edition. | New York : Wednesday Books, 2023. | Audience: Ages 13–18.
Identifiers: LCCN 2022060139 | ISBN 9781250780942 (hardcover) | ISBN 9781250780959 (ebook)
Subjects: CYAC: Teenage fathers—Fiction. | Gay men—Fiction. | Family life—Fiction. | Friendship—Fiction. | LCGFT: Novels.
Classification: LCC PZ7.1.B3243 Un 2023 | DDC [Fic]—dc23
LC record available at https://lccn.loc.gov/2022060139

Our books may be purchased in bulk for promotional, educational, or business use. Please contact your local bookseller or the Macmillan Corporate and Premium Sales Department at 1-800-221-7945, extension 5442, or by email at MacmillanSpecialMarkets@macmillan.com.

First Edition: 2023

10 9 8 7 6 5 4 3 2 1

This book is dedicated to Michael Marr, who has shown me every day for more than thirty years what it means to be a parent. From the day you married my mother, you've demonstrated that step is just a word and family is more than blood. Thank you, Mike, for all the things you've done for me, small and large. You taught me how to drive, how to change a tire, and how to make a budget (sticking with a budget is a different story, and that's all on me). Thank you for all the handyman projects, the hours of walking, and the bangers and mash. Thank you for cheering me on, supporting me, and most important, believing in me even when I didn't believe in myself. Thank you for choosing to be the father you didn't have to be.

UNEXPECTING

CHAPTER 1

"Mom, there's something I need to tell you."

Everything about this moment is eerily familiar. Like I did two months ago, today I sit facing my mom and stepdad, hands hanging between my knees, fingers clasped.

"Another big announcement, Ben?" Mom asks with an awkward chuckle.

Though she's making light of it, she's closer to the truth than she could ever imagine. She too recognizes the similarities to the last time I initiated such a conversation. And, like last time, Mom and Roger, Stepdad #3, watch me with a combination of worry and confusion.

I can't make myself look her—or Roger for that matter—in the eye. Instead of meeting her gaze, taking a deep breath, and saying "Mom, I'm gay," this time I take a deep breath and brace myself for the shitstorm I'm about to unleash.

I stop to swallow. My mouth is dry and anxiety is throwing a pool party in my gut.

"Mom, I'm going to have a baby." *Crap crap crap*. Wrong word choice. My having a baby is a physiological impossibility. "I mean, I'm going to be a dad."

She stares at me for a really long time.

Roger glances between Mom and me like a spectator at a tennis match. Back and forth. Back and forth.

I bring my hand to my mouth, tugging a sliver of thumbnail between my teeth. Why is this so hard? I'd thought coming out to my mom and my new stepdad was going to be tough. It wasn't bad, just supremely awkward. But this . . . this is so much worse.

A beam of late-afternoon sunlight sneaks through the gap between the two halves of the front window's navy-blue curtains, spilling over me. I sit on the center cushion of the worn suede couch, but it might as well be center stage at the school's auditorium given the spotlight treatment and Mom and Roger's scrutiny. Even though I requested this conversation, I've never felt so exposed.

The coppery taste of blood hits my tongue and I cringe. I've chewed my thumbnail down too far. I shove my bleeding hand under my thigh, brushing past the thick packet of papers I've crammed into my pocket. My knee immediately starts bobbing. Up and down. Up and down.

Okay, so things could definitely be worse. I mean, she isn't laughing at me. There's no screaming or tears. All she does is fall back into her matching suede chair, hand covering her mouth, which is her "I'm thinking" pose. Roger scrunches his face up, which is his "I'm thinking, but I don't quite know what's going on" pose.

Finally, Roger asks, "How is that possible?"

Roger's a nice guy, and he's great to me and Mom, but sometimes his common sense comes to the party late.

"Well, I had sex with a girl."

"But aren't you gay?"

I look to Mom. Does she seriously expect me to answer that? She's still got her thinking pose going on. I'm not sure she's even paying attention.

I shrug. "I wanted to make sure."

Roger scrunches his face again. I decide to let him work things out on his own, and look back to Mom. She stands. "Well, it sounds like we've got some figuring out to do."

We move our discussion from the living room to the kitchen table. Important conversations happen in the living room. Plans of attack happen in the kitchen. I don't know why, but it's always been that way. Mom tells me she's going to get married? Living room. When Mom and Stepdad #1 get divorced and we have to divide the assets and find a new place to live? Kitchen. Tell Mom I'm gay? Living room. Identifying the next steps of a soon-to-be teenage dad whose experiment in heterosexual relations has a serious side effect? Kitchen.

Mom sets a cup of tea in front of me. I don't like tea, but since she's just found out she's going to be a grandma when she's not yet forty, I accept the drink without comment.

"Who's the girl?" Mom asks after she settles in across the table from me.

"Maxie."

Mom nods as though the answer doesn't surprise her, as if this conversation is completely normal. Her hand trembles as she stirs sugar into her tea, so maybe it's not so normal after all.

"I thought you two were only friends. Is it more than that?"

I shake my head. "It isn't like that. We . . ." The words get caught on my tongue. I can't get into that right now. I need to deal with the forms burning holes in my pocket and psyche. I pull out the sheaf of papers and try to smooth the creases. God, I hate these papers. The stupid papers that started this whole thing. Papers giving away my parental rights so the baby can be put up for adoption.

"Can I see?" Mom gestures at the papers. Her face is impassive. Neutral. Mom is rarely neutral around me.

Even looking at that stack has my nerves jittering and nausea roiling through me. I pass them over.

While Mom reads through them, I watch her face, desperate to catch her thoughts. My knee starts to jump again. I want to shout at Mom, *What are you thinking?* I'm not always good at reading emotions on people, but Mom is usually the exception. Not today.

I've read and reread those pages a hundred times since my friend Maxie gave them to me on Tuesday. Over the last forty-eight hours I haven't been able to think. Not about school. Not about anything. I haven't even been able to fully process the bomb Maxie dropped in my lap. I've been living like one of the projects my high school robotics club creates. Following the basic programming, moving from one task to the next, without thought or plan. I need time to think, time to wrap my head around the impossibility of . . . everything. But Maxie's parents want these forms returned by the weekend.

It's as if finally passing the documents to Mom broke the automation I've been relying on over the last two days. Everything I've been holding back, every thought and emotion that I've suppressed, crashes into me in a whirling, swirling, chaotic mess.

Maxie's going to have a baby. A baby she's putting up for adoption. My baby. A baby she—or more likely her parents—assume I'll want nothing to do with. Like I'll be fine with the whole thing. But it's not okay. I'm not fine with it. I'm being sucked into a black hole and I can't breathe, can't think. I'm consumed by unfamiliar and overwhelming emotion. I'm suffocating and I can't figure out why no one else is suffocating with me.

Mom doesn't say anything. I want—*need*—her to say or do something to make this okay, to make things better.

Mom flips to a new page in the document.

"*Say something!*"

Roger jumps in his seat, and Mom's head jerks up. Crap. I close my eyes, count to ten, and try again. "Sorry. I just . . ." The words get caught in my seizing throat. I need Mom to understand. To recognize what I can't even put words to myself.

Mom sets the pages down. I think she sees some of the panic on my face. Her expression softens, becomes less neutral and more compassionate. Mom is a compassionate person by nature. She's always picking up strays, usually men who are emotionally broken, and fixing them. She helps them heal, and then they move on. I never wanted to be one of the broken men she had to fix.

Roger, Mom's current fixer-upper, fidgets, clearly out of his depth. But he's present, he's trying. Pretty sure he didn't sign up for all this drama when he and Mom decided to get married.

"I'm not sure where to start." She tucks a wild orange curl behind her ear. "This," she says, gesturing to the paperwork in front of her, "is not something I ever expected to have to deal with, especially after our conversation two months ago.

"This is a big deal, Ben. A lot to process."

"No shit." I didn't mean to say it out loud, but luckily Mom is too distracted by more important matters to worry about me cussing.

"A lecture on safe sex seems too little, too late at this point. Though, I reserve the right to revisit the topic at a later date." She trails a finger over a block of black text on the papers in front of her. "How did this happen, Benny?"

I know she isn't asking the same question Roger did. She isn't confused about how a gay kid got a girl friend (two words—Maxie has been one of my friends for years, but definitely not a *girlfriend*) pregnant. She wants to know how I, socially awkward and too smart for my own good, ended up in a situation where a girl got pregnant. It's a small but critical difference.

I need to tackle it like a science report. Details without the emotion. I think it's the only way I'll make it through this discussion. And, added bonus, it will give me a couple more minutes to figure out how I'm going to break the rest of my news to her.

Unfortunately, the explanation needs a bit of a foundation, and I have to go back a ways and delve into uncomfortable self-discovery BS. "I've suspected that I'm gay for a few years now."

She acknowledges this, so I continue. "Last June, while the guys and I were at Camp Galileo, we were playing Truth or Dare"—because apparently that's what you do when you're at camp and there are no adults around, even if you're a bunch of STEM-focused geeks—"and I chose truth." It hadn't occurred to me to lie about it when they asked. The guys (and I call them *the guys*, even though there are two girls in the group, including Maxie) don't care about stuff like that.

They asked. I answered. *I think so.* Mo, my best friend, had leaned forward, real curiosity in his eyes, and asked, "You don't know?" I'd shrugged and told him the truth: I'd never been interested in girls that way, so it seemed likely, but I'd never put it to the test or anything. Then Maxie asked if I was interested in any guys that way. I'd shrugged, said *I think so* again.

Mom interrupts my story with a laugh, an incredulous, not-really-amused laugh. "Benny, Benny, Benny. You really were trying to make sure. Let me guess, you had sex with Maxie as a scientific test."

I shrug. She's pretty much dead-on. "It seemed like something I should make sure of before I made any announcements."

"And that is what Maxie wanted?"

I jerk my head up at the suspicion in her voice. She can't think I'd pressured Maxie, can she? Or that I'd force her? "She was doing an experiment of her own. Some kind of TikTok social experiment thing."

Mom's face went pale. "Jesus, Ben, you didn't record yourselves—"

"Of course not. How could you think that?"

"I don't know, Ben. This is a lot to take in. I never thought you'd get a girl pregnant, either."

Since I couldn't exactly argue with that, I didn't try. I'm not sure Mom would understand. Both Maxie and I had hypotheses, and neither of us could report any conclusions until we'd tested the hypotheses and analyzed the results. That's how the scientific method works, and we were at science camp. It seemed very logical at the time.

There's another question or some other worry behind her eyes, but I can't decipher it. Finally, she says, "So you and Maxie had sex."

"Yeah."

Roger speaks up for the first time in a while. "Not to put too fine a point on it, but if you're not . . . interested . . . in girls, how did you . . ." He waves his hand to finish the question. "I mean, you had to have"—another hand wave—"for her to be pregnant."

I remind myself he's really a good guy and he means well. "I'm sixteen. It doesn't take much for me to—" I stop and copy Roger's gesture, suddenly understanding the hand wave thing. Some things shouldn't be talked about in front of your mother. But, yeah, despite the rather inevitable conclusion, I have no doubt about my orientation.

Orientation. I hate that word. It makes me feel like a compass or map or something that can be twisted or turned to point in the right direction. Like I'm something that needs to be altered to follow the right path. Or maybe I'm overthinking meaningless details in an attempt to avoid the bigger issue.

Roger's eyes widen in understanding, and he blushes. Maybe he remembers what it's like to be sixteen? He's several years younger than my mom, so sixteen maybe doesn't seem so long ago to him. I close my eyes. More meaningless details.

Mom shuffles the papers, drawing our attention back to them. Those damn papers that would mean my child won't know his dad. My guts twist into greasy knots again. My dad—my biological father—is only a name on a piece of paper and a face in a photograph. I hardly know anything about him, and I've never had a relationship with him. He died before I got the chance. I can't do that to a child—*my* child. I just can't.

"Did you read these?"

I nod.

"And you understand them?"

I nod again. If there's one thing I'm good at, it's research.

Then she asks a question to which a nod isn't an acceptable answer. "This is what Maxie wants?"

I blink for a moment, letting the question process. "I mean, yeah. She gave me the forms, right?"

Mom sighs. "And you, Benny? What do you want to do?"

My throat seizes again, and I struggle to breathe. Again. *I don't know.* That's the answer I want to say, but it's not altogether true. I do know what I want to say, but I don't know how to say it.

I swallow. I open my mouth. Still the words don't come. Words can't be spoken if your mind doesn't even let you think them.

Mom seems to understand. "Before we decide anything, I think we need to ask for a paternity test to make sure you really are the child's father. I'm not sure what the rules are for that. We might not be able to get that until after the baby's born. We'll have to check. If we can have everything confirmed before the baby's birth, that would be best. It's important to know before you agree to anything."

"I am the father," I say. "Maxie wouldn't lie about that."

"I know you believe that, Ben. I believe it, too. But it's for your protection."

"Yeah, okay." I lick my lips. This is good. A logical step. Having a goal—even a simple one like a genetic test—eases some of the pressure in my chest. It's a first step. Once we have a first step, we can come up with a second step. Enough small steps, and we have a plan. I don't need the test to prove the baby is mine, but it makes sense to do it.

Mom scans the papers. "We should probably have a lawyer look at this before you sign it. I'll call James."

James Christianson, Stepdad #1, is a family law attorney, so that makes sense too. I haven't seen him since first grade, and my memories of him are hazy, but like the paternity test, it's a step.

"Everything looks reasonable," Mom says. "Seems aboveboard to me, but still, better to be safe. There's nothing here about financial assistance or medical costs or anything."

"Mom," I try to say, but the word gets caught in my throat.

"Dodged a bullet there," Roger says. The words echo around me.

But that's not the point. Not at all.

"Mom." The word comes out in a croak. *"Mom,"* I say again, this time with more force.

She looks up from the last page in the packet.

"I don't want to sign."

She stills.

Roger is back at the tennis match, shooting his gaze between Mom and me. Back and forth. Back and forth.

"Benny?"

I fist my hands, take a deep breath. If I don't say it now, I don't know if I'll ever be able to.

"I don't want to sign. I want to keep the baby."

Shitstorm unleashed.

CHAPTER 2

Mom says she needs time to think about everything.

I get it. I do.

She says we'll talk about things after dinner, after she's had time to wrap her head around everything.

It's a lot. I guess I can understand that. It's a lot for me to wrap my head around too.

She goes to her bedroom. Our house is kind of small, so there's not really a good place for her to find privacy besides her bedroom. Roger looks a little lost, sitting across from me at the table. He opens his mouth once or twice, but he doesn't speak. He taps his fingers against the wooden tabletop, his eyes darting from me to the hallway leading to the bedroom. He bites his lip.

He so obviously wants to be there for Mom, but also wonders if he should be there for me. He really is a good guy and I probably should give him a chance. It's tough, though, because if history is anything to go by, he'll get his shit together, not need Mom or me anymore, and move on. It's easier, maybe, not to get attached.

I head to my room, partly to make Roger's decision easier, but mostly, if I'm being honest, because I need time to figure my own shit out.

I shut the door behind me before closing my eyes and pressing my forehead into the jamb. I expected to be relieved once I got this first, major step over with. I'm not. I don't know what to do with that.

The scrape of tiny claws against wire pulls me away from the door.

Sonic, my pet hedgehog, bounces in place, recycled-paper bedding shifting under his tiny feet.

"Hey, buddy." I open the hatch of his four-foot enclosure and reach for him. I'm careful, of course, because those spines along his back aren't for show, and because his little bones always seem so fragile. He nuzzles my thumb, his legs scrambling in a swimming-like motion while I carry him across the room. I'll refill his water bottle and release a couple of crickets into his cage before dinner, but right now I need the cuddle.

Maxie and Mo got together to give me Sonic as a birthday present two years ago. *Maxie*. Maxie and I have been friends for so long, and now things are weird between us. Having sex hasn't changed our relationship. At least not until now. I'm afraid things between us are going to be irreversibly altered now.

Like me, Maxie approached the whole encounter like an experiment. She's started a research project—on her own, not for school or anything—deconstructing things she's deemed social constructs. One of the social constructs she's attempting to dismantle is virginity. Virginity, she said, was a tool used by the patriarchy to dominate and control female behavior. I don't quite understand all of it—social and philosophical queries are not my strong suit. Ultimately, she told me the pressure and expectations surrounding a girl's virginity were ridiculous, and she'd rather get it out of the way. And she knew and trusted me not to be a dick. She explained all this while we snuck into a maintenance shed behind the camp's main lodge.

We got the data we sought. I concluded girls really didn't do it for me, and Maxie got more data to add to her "life is a social construct" hypothesis. It really wasn't a big deal.

Except now it's a huge deal. And our relationship is . . . altered.

I look at the photo frame above Sonic's cage. It's the only picture I have of my father—my biological father. It's an army portrait taken sometime before his deployment to Iraq. Taken before I was born, it's also the photograph that was used when the paper ran his obituary when I was only six months old.

It's that picture—and the father I never had the chance to meet—that pushes me to make the decision I have.

I lie back on my bed and cradle Sonic to my chest. He snuffles at my neck and chin. I run a finger along his pointed snout, teasing his whiskers. He snorts, which is the most adorable sound in the world, then curls up into a ball on my shoulder.

It's a small house with thin walls, so I hear it when Mom starts to cry.

I hear Roger's comforting murmurs.

I close my eyes tight, wishing I could turn off my ears too.

I don't know if I'm doing the right thing, but I do know I can't imagine doing anything else.

A little bit later, while Sonic munches on a cricket in his cage, Mom, Roger, and I sit down to dinner. It's delivery pizza, because, let's face it, no one is in the mood to cook.

Mom's face is pale and her eyes are red, but she's resolute. She's got a plan and if I'm going to do this, if *we're* going to do this, she has some guidelines. And since we're at the kitchen table, she lays out our plan of attack, complete with rules.

CHAPTER 3

I manage to avoid Maxie at school the next day. Or maybe we manage to avoid each other. It's like there's this new distance between us, a barrier or force field separating us that has never been there before. I hate this distance. We need to talk. There is *so much* we need to talk about, but I don't know what she wants. I mean, she won't be able to hide the pregnancy forever, obviously, but I don't know if she wants anyone to know *now*. Has she told anyone? Is she, like me, waiting until some decisions have been made before sharing?

The last few days are a haze. I don't know what we've covered in any of my classes. Mo's been giving me odd looks, and I missed two obvious answers on a calculus quiz earlier in the week. Talking to Mom last night changed things. *I* have changed. But I need today to be as normal as possible, so I can avoid thinking about tonight. So I try really hard to act like it's normal. Well, except for the Maxie thing.

I don't know what to say to Maxie right now. There's too much to say, too much I can't say yet. So much hinges on tonight's dinner with our families. So, avoidance. In the classes we have together, it's easy enough to focus on the lesson rather than her. At lunch, she is conspicuously absent. The final bell brings me to the one place where I have to interact with her: the robotics workshop.

Maxie is part of the Benjamin Franklin High School competitive robotics team with me. And since we're each other's backups on the team, she and I are supposed to be reviewing the programming strategies to prepare for our next battle. Which means Mr. Rose—the team's advisor and my favorite teacher of all time—expects us to interact with each other like nothing has changed. As if a baby—my baby—isn't growing in Maxie as we sit there.

Like every time I've seen Maxie after Tuesday's news, I immediately fixate on her abdomen. I can't see any change yet. She wears a lot of leggings with *Star Wars*–themed T-shirts and weird baggy cardigans she probably steals from her grandpa. The T-shirts, like the sweaters, are always two sizes too big, and manage to overwhelm her body. I don't know if I should be able to see signs of the baby yet. I pull out my phone and add a line in the Notes app, to remind myself to research pregnancy stages and fetal development.

"Ben? Earth to Ben . . . Don't make me call you Benji."

I jerk out of my lost thoughts to face my best friend, Mo. Mohammed Bhatia and I have been friends since kindergarten. We fought over the proper placement of Thomas the Tank Engine's track, then abandoned it when we found out it *only* went in a circle, which was ridiculous, because trains went all over, not just in circles. Instead, we dove into the K'Nex and built a space station, complete with loading docks and shuttle launches.

Eleven years later we still build things together.

He slides onto the stool next to me, dumping his backpack on the long table in front of us. He waves at Maxie, who's got her nose buried in a copy of *Mastering ROS for Robotics Programming* at a table on the other side of the room. She's not actually reading it. When she concentrates, she's completely oblivious to anything and everything that happens around her. Today her back's stiff and her gaze keeps darting my way.

"Check out my new soldering iron." Mo pulls a narrow case out of his backpack. His grip slips, and the plastic container crashes to the tabletop.

Maxie jumps, head jerking in our direction. Her face is pale, making her dark freckles and blue eyes stand out more than usual. Our eyes meet and she averts her gaze immediately.

This is weird. We've been friends since third grade. She meshed seamlessly with Mo and me when she moved to town with her family. Now she watches everything and everybody, Mo and me included, like she's waiting for the apocalypse. I hate seeing her like this, but I don't know what I can say. She's probably panicking because my mom made an appointment to discuss things with her family, and I'm avoiding her when she expected me to simply return the papers she gave me.

"What's the deal with Maxie? She's been a total flake lately." Mo keeps his voice down as he opens his new soldering iron kit, the one he convinced his father to buy since the school's version doesn't, in his words, "work for crap." "And this morning in third period, she totally puked her guts out. In front of the whole class."

I busy myself with straightening the already neat stack of papers in front of me. Yeah, I heard all right. Now the whole class thinks Maxie, who has blown the curve in almost every science class she's ever taken, can't handle dissecting a grasshopper. A grasshopper, for crying out loud. We did that same experiment in eighth grade. I have no idea why the new teacher thought our AP Biology classes need the refresher.

"Probably something she ate," I say. "If she was already queasy, the smell of the preserved grasshoppers might have taken her over the edge." I could hardly blame morning sickness, could I?

Because I can't quite keep my eyes away from her, I see her shoulders relax. She's listening in on our conversation. Does she think I'd tell Mo about it? Well, maybe she does. He's my best friend; I don't usually keep secrets from him. I've never lied to him before. The thought makes me sick to my stomach. I'm lying to my best friend.

I can't tell him. Not yet. Not this.

He won't understand. I mean, he knows Maxie and I had sex, but beyond a slightly quizzical look the next day when he asked if I'd confirmed whether I was gay or not, he's never brought it up.

I have to concentrate on something else, something normal, for a while. I've been accused of having tunnel vision when it comes to robotics and engineering, and right now I need that narrow focus. For the next hour, I'm going to keep my brain occupied with something—anything—else. Taking a page from Maxie's book, I pull out my own copy of *Mastering ROS*.

Mr. Rose strides in, his tablet glowing in his hands. I swear he's more connected to his devices than any teenager ever is. I've seen him walk into walls because he's so focused on his screen. "Change of plans," he declares, not even bothering to look up from his tablet. The other three members of the team—Percy, Anna, and Mitch—trail after him, mouths tight, expressions grim. Mr. Rose is the most organized person I know. I've never known him to deviate from a plan. To change one now means something is seriously off-kilter.

"What change?" Mo asks.

Percy, half a step behind Mr. Rose, his hands full of spare electrical panels, curls a lip at Mo's new soldering iron kit.

Technically, Percy is the club's president. He's a senior and this is his third year on the team. We elected him because of his time on the team, rather than his skill. He's not bad, but he thinks he's better than he is. He's a good builder, but his programming skills are only average, and he's terrible at the written portions of our competition. He resents Mo, I think, because Mo is twice the builder Percy is. Unfortunately, this makes things awkward when we plan projects and divvy up the work.

Anna Su and Mitch Black, the other two senior members of the team, lean against the wall, their bodies nearly hiding the poster-sized retro cover image from Isaac Asimov's *I, Robot*. They adopt matching stances, all folded arms and hunched shoulders. Yeah, something is definitely up.

"Scoot up. Time to confab." Mr. Rose gestures to the big workbench in the center of the room.

Mo and I exchange glances. My gaze slides to Maxie, and her vacant stare makes me wonder if she's even paying attention. But she stands when Mo and I do, pulling her stool to the center table too.

Mr. Rose sets his tablet on the workbench. He shoves his reading glasses up his head, kind of like he's using them for a headband. Since he's bald as a brown egg, they don't keep any hair back. He does this a lot. In ten minutes, he'll forget he did it and start searching for them. He scrubs his hands over his face, stopping to massage his temples for a second. Usually Mr. Rose is hyper, snapping with energy like a high-voltage wire. Not today.

Everyone except Anna and Mitch park on stools next to the workbench. Those two keep their silent vigil against the wall. People think Mo and I are attached at the hip, but we're nothing compared to Anna and Mitch. They act like some sets of twins I've seen, where they're so in tune with each other they don't need anyone else. In fact, if a five-foot-nothing girl of Korean descent and a six-foot-two blond-haired, blue-eyed boy who looks like he just stepped off a dairy farm could be twins, I would totally think they shared a womb.

"I've got good news and bad news." Mr. Rose drums his fingers on the dinged and chipped surface of the workbench. *Tap-tap. Tap-tap.*

I look around the room at all the grim faces. Only Mo, Maxie, and I seem to be out of the loop. Percy, Anna, and Mitch technically are the team's executive board, but it isn't usual for Mr. Rose to meet with them separately from the rest of us.

"What's going on?" Mo asks.

Mr. Rose purses his lips. "We just got out of a meeting with the school financial director and the activities director. There is talk about disbanding the robotics club next year."

"What? Why?" I sit forward. What the hell?

"There are several factors." Mr. Rose pinches the bridge of his nose. "Almost all the extracurricular groups are seeing budget cuts."

"Probably not football," Maxie mutters.

I grunt in agreement.

"Outside of that," Mr. Rose continues, ignoring our byplay, "our low membership numbers and high costs make us a target."

Yeah, robotics clubs aren't cheap. The tools, equipment, and supplies add up pretty fast. "They don't feel like they can justify our budget with only six team members. And without the donations brought in by Miles's family . . ."

Last spring, four members of the team graduated, taking us from a team of ten to a team of six. One of those graduates was

Miles, whose father owned a metal fabrication company, and who supplied the team with a lot of the pieces we needed to build the mechanical frames. He also donated a bunch of tools and equipment. Unfortunately, none of the current members have the same kind of connections.

"The school is trying to build their reputation as a top STEM high school in Wisconsin, but they're willing to cut the only engineering-related club?" Percy sneers, but anxiousness is heavy in his voice.

"I don't understand it, either," Mr. Rose says.

"What are we going to do?" Maxie asks. "I mean, is there anything we can do to change their minds? Or, you know, prove our worth?"

"What if we win?" My brain is filtering through streams of possibilities and scenarios.

Six sets of eyes focus on me, urging me to continue.

"Seems to me, if we do well, bring some of the prestige to the school in an area that supports one of the administration's goals, we can make a case to keep our funding, and keep our team next year."

Mr. Rose's mouth angles into a pleased smile. "Keep going."

"You said next year, right?"

Mr. Rose nods.

"When are the budget decisions confirmed?"

"March."

"Well, sectionals are in November. If we qualify for the state competition in April, they'll know we're serious. Especially since it would mean we'll have a shot at regionals next summer. That's got to mean something, right? Maybe even enough to keep the team. The more we win, the more prestige we bring the school. And, as Percy said, the school is trying to build its reputation as a top STEM school. If we make it to state, they'll have to seriously consider keeping the team."

Mo claps me on the back. "Hell yeah!"

Anna speaks up for the first time. "You think we can win sectionals with only the six of us?"

"Teams have won with as few as five," Percy says. The fervor in his voice is a little terrifying.

"But most of the teams that make it to the state competition have twenty or more," Anna counters.

"That just means we have to be better." Percy rubs his hands together like a cartoon mad scientist. Normally I would roll my eyes at his drama, but right now I agree with him. The six of us are talented enough. With a little hard work and a few extra hours a week studying and practicing, we should be able to succeed.

"We should do some recruiting, too," Maxie says. One of her hands strays to her abdomen. "Not only to build the strength of the team in general, but, you know, to provide backup in case something happens."

My heart stutters, a sickening *bah-boom*, at her words. Is she thinking about herself? Is she worried about something happening, or does she plan to quit the team as her pregnancy progresses? I stare at her, but she doesn't meet my eyes.

"Definitely," Mr. Rose says. "We need to strategize some serious recruiting for the next few weeks."

"What was the good news?" Mo asks.

Mr. Rose's brows knit. "What was that?"

"You said you had good news and bad news."

"Right! The sectionals board emailed the challenge specifics for November."

I sit up. We weren't supposed to get the specifics until Monday. This means we can have all weekend to brainstorm. This will be our first major battle of the year, and given our new circumstances, we have a lot to prove.

"Soft robotics," Mr. Rose says, waving his tablet at us.

"No way!" Mo breathes. "That's so freaking awesome."

The news cheers up the team, and we spend the next half hour going over the guidelines for our first competition of the year and splitting up the research and schematics duties.

I try really hard not to notice that Maxie is quieter than usual.

I try really hard not to think about *why* Maxie is quieter than usual.

I try really hard to pretend tonight's dinner isn't less than two hours away and that I'm not going to be facing the parents of the girl I got pregnant at science camp.

I try really hard, but I fail.

CHAPTER 4

Of course Mom picks Greco's.

I'm not real sure why Mom wants to meet the Jacobsons for dinner in the first place. Like soup and a salad will make the conversation we are going to have less awkward.

No, I remind myself, not soup and salad. Probably linguini arabiata or gnocchi in vodka sauce. Greco's does great Italian food, but that's not why Mom wants to go there. She's counting on the private dining alcove and her relationship with the owner, Paolo Greco—Stepdad #2—to make things less traumatic. Neutral ground, she calls it, but with a slight home-court advantage to us.

Mom makes me wear a button-down shirt and a tie like I'm going to a wedding. Or a funeral. "You need to present yourself as responsible and respectful to Mr. and Mrs. Jacobson."

"They've known me since I was eight," I say, loosening the strangling knot. "I've always been responsible and respectful around them."

"That was before you got their teenage daughter pregnant."

The noose-like pressure around my throat doesn't have anything to do with the tie.

The car ride to Greco's takes place in awkward silence. It might be October in Milwaukee, a time when it should be relatively cool, but I'm sweating through my undershirt. Roger looks equally uncomfortable in the driver's seat. Even as I watch, he hooks a finger under his collar and tugs. Mom shoots him a sidelong look and he stops, smoothing his hand down his blue-and-green-paisley tie. I notice we're wearing the same tie. And the colors of our ties coordinate with Mom's teal blouse. We look like we're going to pose for a Christmas family portrait.

Mom spends the ten-minute drive with her face glued to her phone. She's touched base with James—Stepdad #1—and gotten some pointers for the discussion with the Jacobsons. She's probably memorizing the email he sent her this afternoon.

The tension in Roger's ten-year-old Ford Escape builds until I don't know why the windows don't shatter from the strain. I'm 87 percent sure my ribs are cracking under the pressure of my pounding heart and immobile lungs. I suck in a breath, my hand creeping to my tie again.

"So, what's the plan?" Roger asks, breaking the weirdly heavy silence.

"We're going to go in, be respectful, and discuss our thoughts with Maxie's parents. Open communication and authentic dialogue will be crucial."

Sometimes it's easy to tell Mom is a guidance counselor. She's all about open dialogue and personal narratives. She works at the middle school, thank God, so I don't have to deal with her every day at school and at home. But sometimes she still breaks into counselor-speak.

Roger turns into the parking lot and we all take a fortifying drag of air.

"You need to understand," Mom says, turning in her seat to look at me, "the Jacobsons have the upper hand when it comes to decisions for the baby. They can make things very difficult, even impossible, for you if they decide to fight this. Tonight, you are doing them a courtesy by letting them know your intent."

She says this very deliberately, like there's some kind of subtext I need to be aware of. But I don't always get subtext.

"What happens if they decide to fight me? Fight us?" I swallow past the lump in my throat.

Her eyes, nearly the same blue-green as my own and made brighter by her teal blouse, are grave. "It will require legal action, court hearings, and petitions for you to gain custody. And as a sixteen-year-old boy, the courts could very easily find you unfit, or unable to provide a stable, healthy home for a child. The burden will be on us to prove that a child will be better off with us than with an adoptive family. It will be made harder if they already have an adoptive family chosen."

I press a white-knuckled fist to my chest, a useless act to lessen the stabbing pain in my sternum. "That's . . . a lot."

She nods, and I notice tiny lines between her brows, a sign of aging and stress I've never seen before. "It is. Which means we need to be very sure of our next steps before we commit to anything."

I lick my dry lips with my equally dry tongue. I can't tell if she's cautioning me to be on my best behavior or hinting that she thinks I should back off. "Right." Because what else was there to say?

I don't have time to think about it. Headlights flash past us and the Jacobsons' late-model Acura pulls into the parking spot across from us. We all freeze when we recognize the other car's occupants.

Six car doors open and we all step out.

Six car doors shut, echoing dissonantly around us.

We six face off across the painted white line separating the parking spaces.

Mrs. Jacobson and my mom must have read the same how-to manual for this kind of scenario. Maxie stands behind her mom, wearing a knee-length black skirt and magenta sweater. I don't know if I can remember the last time I saw Maxie in a skirt, at least a skirt that isn't covered in superheroes and meant to be worn with leggings. The outfit she's wearing looks like something she'd be required to wear to Midnight Mass on Christmas Eve. And her mom is wearing a nearly identical sweater over black slacks. Mr. Jacobson is dressed like the tax attorney he is.

"Wow, more Christmas card portraits," I say.

Mom hisses, glaring metaphorical daggers at me, even as her lips turn up in a Barbie doll plastic smile I've never seen on her before.

Maxie, on the other hand, blinks, then grins as she takes note of Roger's and my matching ties.

That grin melts the icy manacles that have been holding my guts hostage after Mom's little warning.

Mom, Roger, and the Jacobsons make adult-themed small talk as we cross the parking lot. Maxie and I trail behind them. I edge closer. "Hey."

She tugs at the knit sleeve of her sweater. "Hey."

When we reach the portico of Greco's, I turn in front of Maxie so she has to stop when I do. She scrunches her face at me, cocking her head.

"I . . . I want to say something real quick before"—I wave my hand at the restaurant's double doors—"all that."

She bites her lip and I hate—*hate*—how awkward things are between us. But I need to say this. It's past time, and it isn't fair to Maxie to not address it. "I'm sorry I've been . . . off . . . all week. To be honest, I've been kind of in shock. It's a lot to process."

She ducks her head and stares at her feet. "You're telling me."

"I'm sorry I've been so . . . awkward."

"It's not like I blame you," she says, peeking up at me for a second before averting her eyes.

I grab her hand. She stills. We're not normally the kind of friends who touch. Well, except for that one time. There was definitely some touching then. "Well, I blame me," I say. "I want you to know I'll try to do better. Be a better friend."

Another flicker of a smile. "Okay."

I'm still holding her hand when we follow our parents into the restaurant.

When I swing the door open, I'm accosted by two things, one amazing, one . . . not.

I could bask in the scent of garlic, oregano, and marinara day in and day out. When that first aromatic wave swells over me, it's a happy, comforting hug.

But that comfort, that happiness, immediately crashes at the sight of Giovanni Greco grinning at my mom, wrapping his lean arms around her waist, squeezing her into a mighty bear hug. Mom is laughing, her pleasure in seeing her former stepson obvious.

I haven't seen Gio Greco since school started. We're only a grade apart—he's a senior—but we have no classes in common. I'm on the advanced STEM track, and he's focused on athletics, and weirdly, food and nutrition classes. Not that I'm keeping tabs on him or anything. But, you know, our parents were married for a few years, so it's only logical that . . . Fine, I may have done some digging when the semester started and I hadn't seen him. But only to make sure he was okay. For Mom's peace of mind.

Not even I buy my excuses.

I've been half in love with Gio Greco since I was thirteen. Which, to be clear, was *after* our parents got divorced. He's gorgeous, charming, athletic. He's one of the nicest guys I've ever met. So, basically, he's everything I'm not. He's even an out and proud bisexual. He's already light-years out of my league, but at least I don't have to admit to crushing on the straight jock. I'm not that much of a cliché.

"It's great to see you, Eliza." He steps away from Mom but keeps his hands on her arms. "Pops said you'd be coming by. He saved the table for you."

Mom grins, cupping his cheeks. "Look at you. I can't believe how grown-up you are. Why aren't you still the gangly twelve-year-old I remember?"

He flashes a smile. "That's what happens. Time goes by, we grow up."

"Well, I wish you'd stop. It makes me feel old."

"Never!" He looks at the six of us. "Are you waiting for anyone else, or should I take you back?"

"This is us." Her smile dims as she seems to remember that our dinner has an ulterior purpose.

"Hey, Benji. How's things?"

I bristle at the nickname. Pretty much everyone else in my life has graduated past that stupid name. I've grown out of the dog jokes. My aunt Shannon is the only holdout in my family, and she does it because, to use her words, "You take yourself too seriously, kid."

I can never tell if Gio is teasing me when he calls me Benji, or if he still thinks of me as the eight-year-old little brother he'd gained when our parents got married. Neither option is particularly pleasant.

"I'm fine," I say more curtly than I intend.

His eyes flick to Maxie's and my joined hands. "Maxie."

Mr. and Mrs. Jacobson, who have stood silently throughout this whole interaction, notice our joined hands too. Mrs. Jacobson's back goes iron-post stiff, and Mr. Jacobson scowls. Maxie pulls away, fisting the hem of her skirt in her newly freed hand. I tuck mine into my pocket because I don't know what else to do with it.

Gio raises a brow at the stilted atmosphere but doesn't say anything. He grabs a stack of menus, then gestures us to follow him.

The dining room of Greco's is busy, it being a Friday night and all. Couples and families sit around tables, smiling and laughing while they dip fresh-baked Italian bread into puddles of olive oil or twist strands of spaghetti around forks. The maroon walls, the flickering candles, the white shirts of the waitstaff, create a dizzying kaleidoscope of color and lights. It's happy and chaotic, and so totally doesn't match the mood of my dinner party.

Gio leads us to a small room at the other side of the dining room. It's one of two private dining areas. It's the small one, designed for intimate dinners—rumor has it more Bay View residents propose in that room than any other place in the Milwaukee area. A table for eight is set, candles lit, napkin-wrapped breadbasket already situated at the center.

I'm not sure this is one of Mom's best ideas. We look like we're about to sit down for a romantic, or at the very least celebratory, dinner. It doesn't look at all like we're going to sit down to talk babies and teenage parenting and court hearings.

"Mrs. Ferguson," Mr. Jacobson begins.

"We've known each other for eight years, Dave. That whole

time you've called me Eliza." Mom is smiling her uber-polite, forced-cheer, look-at-us-aren't-we-being-pleasant smile. "Recent events," she says, "don't change the relationship we've had."

"Recent events?" Maxie's mom—Maureen—folds her hands on the table in front of her. Her fingers are kind of short and stubby, with trimmed, unpainted nails. They're the same as Maxie's, and I don't know why I've never noticed that detail before. In fact, Maxie's hands are folded in front of her, a mirror image of her mother.

Mom and the Jacobsons face off from opposite sides of the table. None of them seem to be looking at me or Maxie, which I guess is a good thing. It keeps us from being the awkward center of attention. On the other hand, having a conversation about something that so absolutely revolves around us without acknowledging our presence feels a little wrong.

I wonder if the use of the phrase *recent events* is the parents' way of actively not mentioning the pregnancy.

My teeth break off a tiny sliver of nail. I pull it out of my mouth, hoping no one sees. I then have to find a way to dispose of the remnant. I tuck it into my pocket until I can find a trash can. My mouth is dry, likely a result of the anxiety and tension here at the table. I'd give almost anything for the water glasses at the place settings to be full. Not only would something to drink take care of the dry-mouth problem, it would give me something to do besides bite my nails.

"I think we can all agree that things have changed," Mr. Jacobson says, looking at Mom and Roger. He never glances at me or Maxie. Is that weird? Significant?

Looking back, I realize I don't really know much about Mr. Jacobson. Sure, Maxie and I have been friends for years, and I've been to their house a lot. Maxie's mom was always in the background, a friendly adult presence. She works at the public library, and her schedule usually meshes with Maxie's school schedule, so if Maxie is home, chances are good her mother is too.

But Mr. Jacobson, he's another story. He's a tax attorney and holds some kind of position with a local professional networking organization. I don't really know what all that entails, but he's rarely around when I am. Maxie says he works long hours, even a lot of weekends. So maybe it's no surprise that I don't know much about him. My impression of him has always been of a stuffy man who, while not disapproving of Maxie, is a bit distant.

"I'll be honest, I don't understand why we're here," Mr. Jacobson says. "The signed papers could have been returned without all this." His gaze sweeps the dimly lit alcove.

"I thought it important that we talk." Mom's fake, uber-polite, forced-cheer smile is still in place, but it's cracking a bit around the edges.

"There's nothing to talk about. It was a mistake, and one we are dealing with. There's no need to make this into something it's not." He still doesn't look at Maxie or me.

"It's the how we're dealing with it that we need to talk about." Mom puts her best guidance counselor voice on. "This is a serious situation with serious consequences. It's important that everyone is on the same page."

I appreciate that she doesn't use the word *mistake*. I mean, yes, it was a mistake, but there's so much judgment inherent in the word.

"It's the consequences we are attempting to mitigate," Mr. Jacobson says. "I will not have one careless act ruin my daughter's future. This situation is unfortunate, Maxie will deal with the inconvenience, then we'll move on."

"Inconvenience?" Mom isn't pretending to smile anymore. She stiffens in her seat, shoulders going back. "This is a child you're talking about."

He flinches. "It doesn't matter. The point is we all must deal with the temporary repercussions. There's no need to make it a bigger issue than it already is."

Mom glares at him.

Maxie hunches into herself.

Roger looks like he'd rather be anywhere else.

Maxie's mom squeezes her folded hands so tightly the knuckles glow white.

Me? I'm pissed. Pissed because the pieces are shifting together, clean as a blueprint. He still hasn't looked at Maxie. He's trying to play this off like it's a sprained ankle rather than a baby. I may not be the best at social or emotional cues, but suddenly I know exactly what's going on. "If you don't want to deal with the *repercussions*, why adoption? Why not abortion? That would have taken care of things, right? It'd make it that much easier to *move on*."

Maxie's mom hisses in a breath.

Mr. Jacobson's face goes red. "Is that why we're here? You want to persuade Maxie to terminate the pregnancy? The sanctity of life—"

I shake my head. "You're a hypocrite."

"Ben." Mom places a cautioning hand on my shoulder.

I shrug off her hand, ignoring the warning. "You sit there, talking about the *sanctity of life*, but refer to the baby as an inconvenience, a thing to be dealt with until it can be forgotten. Where's your respect for the sanctity of that life?"

"I do not need to listen to the delinquent who took advantage of my daughter speak to me this way." Mr. Jacobson scoots his chair back.

Mom bristles at the insult to me, but I'm not done, so I rush in before she can get a word in. "Don't pretend this is about Maxie. You don't give a shit about her, either. If you did, you'd actually acknowledge her presence. You're punishing her."

"That's ridicu—"

"Why else force her to go through the pregnancy? And even if Maxie would refuse to get an abortion"—I honestly don't know what her thoughts on it are, beyond knowing she's an avid female reproductive rights advocate, but I seriously doubt Mr. Jacobson asked her one way or the other—"you still go out of the way to shame her."

"I do no such—"

"That's why you made her bring me the paperwork at school."

"He's right," Mom says. "Legal paperwork, including documents granting consent to the termination of parental rights, are not passed in school hallways like notes. And since the actual paperwork will have to be filed with the courts, I, and my *lawyer*," Mom says, stressing the term, "couldn't figure out what your game was. But Ben is right. It really was about punishing Maxie."

Mrs. Jacobson shifts in her seat, lips pressed into a thin line. Does she recognize the truth of our theory, or is she just uncomfortable with the whole situation?

Maxie is staring at the white tablecloth as though she's verifying the thread count. Her face is nearly as pale as the fabric.

Mr. Jacobson's already red face darkens more. "Without consequences, children do not learn from their mistakes."

I can't help it. I snort. "She's sixteen and pregnant. Do you really think she's ignorant of the consequences?"

Mom reaches over and squeezes my knee. "We're straying from the point."

"Which is what, exactly? I've had enough of this farce."

For all her good intentions, Mom must realize the futility of her plan. She faces Mr. Jacobson dead-on. "Fine. The point. Ben won't be signing the papers."

Mr. Jacobson rears back. "What?"

"I'm keeping my baby."

All three Jacobsons gape at me. Mrs. Jacobson gasps. Maxie squeaks. Mr. Jacobson erupts out of his seat. *"Ridiculous!* I don't know what game you and your delinquent son—"

Mom surges to her feet, leaning forward so that she and Mr. Jacobson are nearly nose to nose. "That's twice now you've called Ben a delinquent."

"What do you expect? I shouldn't expect anything different, not with the revolving door of men in your life—"

"Dave!" Mrs. Jacobson clutches at her husband's arm.

"Hey!" Roger pushes his chair back.

This is escalating quickly. I lean forward. "Stop. None of this is the point."

They cease shouting at each other, but no one looks at me. I raise my voice. "The point is, it's my baby and I'm keeping it."

Crash.

Silence descends immediately, and we all turn to stare at Gio. He stares at me with wide eyes, his mouth a gaping O. His arm is raised, elbow bent as though he still held the water pitcher that crashed to the floor. Ice cubes and glass shards are strewn in all directions.

Shit. I was so caught up in our little drama, I didn't see him come into the room.

"But I thought you were gay."

CHAPTER 5

Even twelve hours later I can feel the impact of that moment. I can see the way Maxie slumped in her chair, looking away. I can see the disgust on Mr. Jacobson's face and the humiliation on Mrs. Jacobson's. There was no recovering after that. We didn't stay for dinner. We didn't have a pleasant chat. Mom said something about getting in touch again when tempers weren't so high, and Mr. Jacobson sneered at us. We packed up our stuff and filed out of the room, passing a confused Gio.

But I thought you were gay.

It won't be the only time I'll face that, but God, I hope I'm more prepared for it next time. I tell myself it's no one's business but mine. And maybe Maxie's. I tell myself I don't care what others might think of my decision. I tell myself all this, but I know it's significantly more complicated. It *is* my mom's business, and I *do* care what Mo thinks, for example.

I slump in my seat at the kitchen table, eyeing the half-eaten toast sitting on a square of paper towel. My stomach clenches around the three bites I managed to choke down a couple minutes ago. I wonder vaguely if a dollop of strawberry jam would make the scraps more appetizing. But since it's anxiety, not lack of flavor, that's killed my appetite, no amount of sugary fruit spread will make the food easier to keep down.

I pinch the corner of a thumbnail between my teeth and tug.

Mom shuffles into the kitchen, a fuzzy purple robe covering her from shoulders to toes. I have a memory of huddling at her side, tugging at the long belt of a similar purple robe when I was seven and James drove away after packing up all his stuff. I hadn't understood why Mom had been so sad. At least not until days later when I realized he wasn't coming back.

She waits until the Keurig dispenses a cup of her favorite breakfast blend before sitting across the table from me.

I bite through the nail, the pop of incisor puncturing keratin oddly satisfying. Mom flicks her fingers at my hand. "Stop."

I drop my hand into my lap. Mom hates it when I chew my fingernails, always has. But now the ragged edge is going to drive me crazy until I can even it out or file it down. I tuck my thumb into my fist, hoping out of sight, out of mind works on fingernails.

"So," Mom says after taking a sip of coffee from the mug cradled in her palms.

I tuck my fist—the one with the half-chewed nail—into my armpit. Knowing that the micro-focus on the annoyance of a ragged nail is nothing more than a way to distract myself from more important issues doesn't alleviate the clawing need I have to finish the job I started.

"So," I say, echoing Mom's matter-of-fact tone.

"You need to find a job."

I nod. That was one of Mom's criteria for moving forward on

getting custody of the baby. "I'll help you, Benny, and support you in this, but I'm not going to do it for you," she'd told me. "Babies—children—are expensive. You have to be ready to take care of a child."

I hadn't expected anything else. The words, calm and practical, hadn't fazed me at the time. Now, the idea of looking for a job, interviewing . . . I swallow hard. Interviews mean questions. Questions from strangers.

"Have you thought about where you're going to look?" She traces the ceramic rim of the coffee cup with a fingertip. The fingernail making laps on the mug showcases a ragged nail, bitten down to the quick. In fact, her hands resemble mine, with short, nearly nonexistent fingernails. Her eyes, too, show dark smudges that speak of sleepless nights and stress.

"There's that grocery store near the school," I tell her, my knee starting to bounce. Close to the school would be good. I haven't spent as much time thinking about logistics of things like an after-school job, but I know it has to be within walking distance of the school or the house. I don't have a vehicle of my own, and both Mom and Roger work all day, so getting a ride to and from a potential workplace would be inconvenient, to say the least.

Mom lifts her coffee in acknowledgment, taking a sip, before setting it aside completely. She folds her arms across the table and leans forward. "I spoke with Paolo."

I shift back, hands dropping to the table with a smack. "You didn't tell him—"

"I explained to him the situation, yes. He's said he can always use reliable bussers."

My knee resumes its bounce. "But what if he tells—" I cut myself off this time. Gio. What if he tells Gio? But that doesn't matter, because Gio already knows. My stomach drops again and the three bites of toast in my stomach creep toward my esophagus. I drop my head to the table, barely missing the cold toast.

I don't understand this reaction. I'm not ashamed. I'm not. Not really. And eventually everyone is going to know that Maxie is pregnant and that I'm the father. So, okay, there's a little bit of shame there. I guess I haven't really thought about what it means that others will eventually know. As soon as word gets out, people—kids I go to school with, teachers, neighbors—are going to wonder about me. About the gay boy who got a girl pregnant at science camp. There'll be judgment, sure, but mostly it's going to be speculation about me and Maxie and sex.

I don't want anyone thinking about me that way, but I especially don't want *Gio* thinking about me having sex. With a girl. With Maxie.

That's the rub, though. If I were a regular, heterosexual boy in this situation, it would all be condemnation over the carelessness or the irresponsibility, or about smart kids doing stupid things. But I'm gay, so now it's really all about the sex.

But I don't say anything about this to Mom.

I don't want her to know about the stupid crush I have on Gio.

I don't want her to know, or even suspect, that I have doubts about any aspect of this situation.

So I fall back on the one thing I'm good at. Logic.

"I don't think Greco's will work. It's too far away. By the time I take the bus to the nearest stop and walk the rest of the way, I'll have eaten up an hour and a half after school."

"That's the benefit of knowing the owner. And the owner's son."

I tilt my head, eyeing her. She sounds way too smug, like she's worked out all these details already. Which means, as far as she's concerned, this is a done deal.

"Paolo is willing to work out the schedule so that you work the same shifts as Gio. Gio has a car and can take you to work after school and even drop you off at home if Roger or I can't pick you up."

My eyes bug out at this. "Wait. What? You want me to *carpool* with Gio Greco?"

"I don't understand why you're reacting this way. I'd have thought you'd be more comfortable working with people you already know. And since he knows what's going on, Paolo will be more flexible with the schedules than a random company."

"But . . . but . . ." I rack my brain, searching for a viable, logical reason this won't work. "I don't know anything about Italian cooking."

Mom rolls her eyes. "You'll be a busser, Benny, not a chef. I think Paolo will have that part of things well in hand. You'll pick up dishes and wipe down tables, not roll pasta by hand. Also, Paolo will pay better than the grocery store."

Unless I can come up with a good, solid, irrefutable reason not to, I'll be working at Greco's. I sigh and bang my head back onto the table.

"Great," Mom says, with a completely unnecessary clap of hands. "You'll start this afternoon. You're meeting Paolo at three to go over the paperwork."

I peek up at her, not quite lifting my head from the table. "But I'm meeting Mo to work on the specs for the sectional meet. He thinks he's found a way—"

Mom looks pissed for a moment, then the expression morphs to sadness. "Being a parent often means prioritizing responsibilities. You have a new top priority, Ben."

Damn. She called me Ben. Which means she's serious. Something in her voice tells me she believes this is only the first of several sacrifices I'll have to face.

"Fine," I mutter, closing my eyes and swallowing back the toast I'm still not 100 percent sure will stay down.

My cell phone explodes with texts as I fill out paperwork at an out-of-the-way booth in Greco's dining room. Mom dropped me off, promising to come back in two hours to pick me up. I haven't seen Gio yet, but Paolo, who I haven't seen in at least two years, greeted me with a bear hug and a pat on the back powerful enough to send me to my knees. Five minutes later, I had a stack of forms and a glass of Coke.

My pen skitters along the job application as my phone vibrates in my pocket again. The zero in the zip code now looks like the Nike swoosh. Mom's voice in my head tells me it would be inappropriate to deal with texts at work, even if all I am doing is filling out a job application for a position I've already been told is mine.

"Formalities," Paolo said before he headed back to the kitchen, muttering something about a late seafood delivery.

My phone buzzes again.

I glance around the room to make sure I'm alone, and then slip my hand into my pocket. I pull the smartphone out far enough to see the screen full of texts from Mo. With another glance around the room, I tap the screen. *Cant talk. Will call soon*

I didn't even stop to correct the punctuation. No matter how uptight people (Mo and Maxie) say it is, I detest sending texts without proper spelling, punctuation, and grammar.

"Don't make a habit of that. Pops has a rule about phones on the job. Basically, the rule is *don't*."

I squeak and drop the phone as Gio plops into the seat across from me, grinning in a way that absolutely does not make my insides squirm. I snatch the phone off the booth next to me and shove it back into my pocket.

"I was, um, you know, trying to—" I snap my mouth closed.

"No worries. I mean, you definitely need to keep the phone off during work hours, but you're in the clear right now." Gio leans back, spreading his arms across the top of the booth. The white T-shirt he's wearing stretches with the movement and I'm again reminded how far out of my league he is. Over the last year or so, he's really grown into his frame. He now has muscles my skinny body could only dream of.

These are the most words we've exchanged in years. We've barely acknowledged each other since our parents' divorce, let alone stopped to chat. Come to think of it, even when our parents were together, we barely spoke. Due to a complicated custody schedule, he stayed with us three out of seven nights a week. Whenever we were both at home at the same time, he played video games or kicked around a soccer ball with his friends, and Mo, Maxie, and I were buried in at-home science experiments.

Basically, this means we've never really gotten to know each other. That doesn't mean I don't know anything about him. In fact, I know way too much. Like borderline stalking. Though I prefer to think of it as scientific observation. For years, I have watched him, wanting to be like him. People swarm to him. They like him. They like to be around him. And he's comfortable in the crowd. No one looks at him through narrowed eyes because his interests lean a little too much toward steam engines and computer programming. They don't talk around him in group projects. They don't roll their eyes at him when he corrects their math calculations.

I wanted to know the trick of it, the knack that allowed people to be so comfortable around him.

So I watched. I observed. And I yearned.

I didn't just want to be like him, I *liked* him.

He smiles. He laughs. He teases with affection rather than meanness. He may not be science and tech smart, but he gets good grades and belongs to at least six different after-school clubs that I know of. He's maybe a little arrogant, but most of the time I call it confidence.

Since our parents' split, we have even fewer reasons to engage with each other. I am still a science nerd and he's still a jock. And now it looks like we're going to be coworkers.

I've been staring at him mutely for a ridiculously long time. What are we talking about? Oh yeah, no phones while on the clock. I clear my throat. "Good to know, thanks." I blink and look at the Nike swoosh on my paper. I carefully retrace the zero a few times so it's clear what it's supposed to be.

I glance up at him through my lashes, trying not to be obvious. It doesn't matter. He watches me with the same intensity I use to examine an unknown chemical equation. His head is slightly cocked, and I can practically see scenarios and variables running through his mind.

"What?" I lift the pen from the form in front of me.

"Look, I know it's none of my business—"

My breath hitches. I try to cover my reaction by going to the next field in the application. Here it is. He's going to ask me about Maxie. About the pregnancy. I brace to tell him that, no, it really isn't any of his business.

"The guy with your mom last night. That her new husband?"

"That's none of your . . . Wait, what?" I blink, trying to redirect my thoughts. "Roger?"

"Is that his name? Seems kind of young for her, but given the scene last night, I figured it had to be serious." There's a soft note in his voice I have trouble identifying. Kind of wistful, maybe.

"Uh, yeah. They got married about a year ago. He's a few years younger than her, I guess."

He slides deeper into his side of the booth. "I guess I'd always . . ."

"Always what?" I ask when his voice trails off.

His dimples make a brief appearance even though his smile is a little wry. "You'll think it's weird."

I set my pen down and lean forward. "No, I won't. Promise."

He bites his lip, gaze sliding away from me for a moment. He shrugs. "You know, I always sort of hoped they'd get back together. Our parents," he clarifies.

"But it's been years."

"Sure. I know. But your mom is great. She did so much for us. And she still keeps in touch with me, even though she's not with Pops anymore. It was nice, I guess, to have a mom who was so . . . mom-like."

"Oh. I see." What am I supposed to say to that? I know on some level his relationship with his mother is a little dysfunctional, but I don't know any details. Really, I only picked up on a few things his dad let slip to my mom when I was younger.

"It was a silly dream." He flashes his smile again, this one a hair less genuine than usual.

"Wait a couple years. You'll have another shot eventually. She never keeps them for long." The words escape before they've even registered in my brain. And they sound so damn bitter.

Gio straightens and glowers at me. "Dude. That's harsh."

And instead of apologizing and backing off, I try to explain. "No, it's not that. It's just that she's been married four times already, and in two other serious relationships since I was born. None of them last more than a couple years. The evidence, the pattern, is there. Enough to hypothesize future actions with some degree of accuracy."

He snorts, pushing up from the table. "Nice. That's your mom, Benji. Not a freaking science project. Hypothesize. Seriously?" He stands next to the table, hands planted on his hips.

"No . . . I . . ." I sputter, trying to find the words to dig me out of the hole I've landed myself in.

"Whatever. You start on Monday, right?"

I sigh, giving up on explanations that clearly make things worse. "Yeah."

"Meet me at the main entrance after the bell. Don't be late. We'll start your training at four."

I nod.

He turns and leaves.

Awesome. He's totally disgusted with me. And we're going to be carpooling coworkers. Freaking awesome.

CHAPTER 6

I tell Mom to drop me off at Mo's house after she picks me up at Greco's.

"How'd things go with Paolo?" she asks, taking a left at an intersection, heading toward the Bhatias' place instead of turning right toward our home.

"Fine." I scroll through the twelve texts from Mo. Each is a version of *Where are you?* Three came after I'd sent the message about calling him later.

"Care to expand?"

I resist rolling my eyes. "It was fine. What else do you want me to say?"

I'm not usually this snappy with my mom—with anyone, really—but I can't stop thinking about Gio's disdain and Mo's impatience. And Maxie's humiliation last night. And Mom's verbal battle with Mr. Jacobson. Each one a tiny needle jabbing me. Irritating at first, but with each concurrent and repeated sting the pain to my battered psyche is almost too much to deal with.

"Try again," Mom says. I can practically see icicles forming on the words. I chance a glance to her side of the car. Her mouth is pressed into a firm line, though her gaze is fixed on the street ahead.

I deflate. "Sorry." Rubbing my eyes, I say again, "Sorry. I mean to say things went well. All the forms are filled out and I start on Monday." Mentioning Gio's comments about hoping Mom and Paolo would get back together might be a distraction, but I don't know if Mom'll find it sweet, bittersweet, or just plain bitter.

Mom pulls into a Walgreens parking lot. Letting the engine idle, she says, "If this is going to work, I need to know you're taking this seriously. I can't afford—*you* can't afford—to be casual about this. Having a child means facing some unpleasant responsibilities. Getting a job is the least of it. If you're not ready to face this one piece—one of many—how do you expect me to trust that you're ready to face the rest? 'Cause, kiddo, this is nothing."

"No, it's fine. Really. I'm . . . I'm still processing."

She turns the ignition off. "Okay. Real talk. And maybe I should have picked a better place for this, but I think we need to get some things out in the open."

"Okay, but, um, does it have to be now? Can we maybe do it tonight?"

"I think it's better to do it now. At least start it now. I know you. You'll want some time and space to pick things apart in your brain. We'll come back to it tonight."

She does know me, and she's right about needing time to process. But—"We've already talked about most of it, right? We sat at the kitchen table and worked out details, and the rules, and logistics."

She reaches over and rests her hand on my knee. "Logistics,

yes. Details, yes. But not the emotions, the feelings, and the motivation."

I tense. More phantom needles prick my skin.

Mom smooths a thumb over my brow, which is scrunching. "I know this makes you uncomfortable."

Understatement.

"But it's important that we get this out of the way."

I take a deep breath, trying to shake away the pins-and-needles sensations talking about emotions always bring with it. "And it has to be now?"

Mom's mouth quirks. "Consider yourself a captive audience. No better time."

I shrug. It's fine. It's okay. Or at least it will be. If I'm going to pursue teenage parenthood I need Mom's help more than I need to be comfortable. I'm too smart to assume otherwise. Not that it makes it any easier to face. "So, feelings?"

"Motivation," Mom says.

I cringe. Feelings would be easier. I mean, I feel anxious. I feel resolute. I feel a hope for the future and attachment to something that is new to me. It's different than the hope of getting into a good college, or of moving on to a stimulating and lucrative career. It's a softer kind of hope, one that fills my chest, my soul, to almost uncomfortable levels. Though it's not really my style, I can talk about these feelings.

Motivation is harder. I don't know how to explain to Mom the driving need I have to be the father I never had. The despair of potentially leaving a child to experience the same. How do I tell her that, and have her not face regret? I mean, if it wasn't for her, I wouldn't have had to meet, get to know, and start to rely on half a dozen different father figures only to have them leave. How can I tell her that without sounding like I judge her?

The thing is, I do kind of blame her. And while I'm not completely fluent in emotional reactions, I know that will hurt her more than anything else.

"Why, Benny? Why is this so important to you?"

I search for the words. But I can't tell her the truth—at least not the main truth—so I go with a lesser truth. "It's mine. The baby is mine. The actions were mine, the consequences are mine."

Mom reaches out, curling her fingers around mine. She waits until I look up. When I do, her expression is grave. She shakes her head. "That's not good enough."

The words are a slap. I try to pull my hand away. I open my mouth, but my tongue freezes at the intent look on Mom's face. "No, Ben, I know that sounds harsh, but it's the truth. That child cannot be a consequence or a punishment. I need you to hear this. If you go into this with that kind of thinking, you're going to end up resenting your child. And that's not fair to either of you."

"I wouldn't—"

She looks away, the briefest twitch of her eyes. "I don't think you know what you will or will not do. You can't. Nobody could. You have no idea what you'll be sacrificing, what plans you'll end up abandoning now that your priorities have changed."

"I don't get this. You said you're okay with this." My temples throb.

Air whooshes out of her lungs. "I am, but I'm not. Benny, I'm never going to be okay with my sixteen-year-old son becoming a father. No one is excited by teenage pregnancy."

I slump in the seat, my insides going cold.

"But even though it's happening years earlier than I would have wanted, I will love and cherish any child of yours."

"But you think I should let Maxie allow the baby to be adopted by strangers," I say flatly.

"I think we have to consider what's best for the baby." Mom speaks slowly, choosing her words carefully. "I think regret and resentment are not good for any child."

I cross my arms over my chest, pulling away from her hold on my hand.

She scrubs at her eyes. Another big sigh, then, "I haven't told you much about my parents, have I?"

I blink at her, some of the resentment fading. "Um, no." Mom has always been strangely cagey about my grandparents. They're both alive as far as I know, but they've never been a part of my life.

"It was a different era, when I was a baby."

She acts as if she'd been born in the forties or something instead of the eighties. "Okay," I say.

"My parents had to get married," she explains, rubbing the edge of her thumb against the insignia at the center of the steering wheel. It's a random gesture, I'm not even sure she knows she's doing it. "My mom got pregnant with me when she was eighteen, just before her high school graduation. Both her family and my father's agreed that the two of them needed to 'do the right thing.' The actions had been theirs, so too were the consequences." She raises her brows for emphasis.

"But, what does—"

"So they did the 'right thing,' got married, had a baby. And I'm glad, obviously, since I wouldn't be here otherwise, but they weren't happy. Not together. Not with me. But they were stuck together because of some kind of antiquated societal norms."

"But no one is saying I should marry Maxie." Which, thank God. Wouldn't that be a catastrophe?

The absent motion of her thumb against the plastic silver logo on the steering wheel increases in speed and my knee bounces at the same tempo. Back and forth. Up and down. Back and forth.

Up and down. I have a vague inkling of where this conversation is going, and my anxiety ratchets up a notch or two.

"No. No one is pushing marriage." She licks her lips. "My dad was smart. So smart. You remind me of him, in fact. He had a mind that understood numbers in a way that most people can't even imagine. He was set to go to an Ivy League college. Had dreams of getting into aeronautics or even NASA."

I've always assumed my analytical brain came from the father I'd never met. Strange to think I have so much in common with the grandfather I also have never met.

"He was forced to give up his dreams. He had a wife and child to support. He got a job as an electrician because the pay was decent and there was a pension." Mom shifts in the seat, turning more fully toward me. "Benny, not a day went by that resentment didn't eat at him. He hated being tied to a family he didn't want. He resented and, I think, blamed me for it. He made sure I understood every day of my life that I was a mistake, one that cost him his dreams."

Eyes shining, she cups my face, making it impossible for me to look away. "I would not wish that on anyone. Being unwanted sucks, to be frank. It seriously sucks. Better a baby be raised by parents who love and want her, than stuck in a miserable situation because someone made a mistake and had to deal with the consequences."

I have no words. None. No wonder she doesn't have a relationship with her parents.

My eyes burn and I realize I haven't been blinking. So I blink. I still have no words. I know I'm supposed to say something. Something reassuring. Something to acknowledge her story. If my motivation is what I stated, then her words should absolutely have me reconsidering my stance.

"Can you drop me off at Mo's now?"

Mom closes her eyes and wilts into her seat. I think she's going to say something, but she only shakes her head and turns the key in the ignition. "Think about it, Ben."

Mo greets me at the door with a scowl. "What the hell have you been doing? And why do you look like someone fried your robot because they put the battery in upside down?"

He means to make me laugh—we saw something like that happen to some poor team at an invitational last year—but I'm not in the mood. I shrug. "Just some stuff with Mom."

Mo's hair sticks up on one side in oddly squashed peaks, a sure sign he's been clenching his fist in the thick mass, something he does when he's faced with a particularly thorny problem.

"And what's the deal with all the texts? What part of 'Can't talk now. Will call back later' don't you understand?"

He rolls his eyes. "Uh, the part where you said 'Can't talk now.' Dude, you were supposed to be here at two. Then you go all no-show on me and don't answer your texts? Unless you were on a date, there's no excuse." He pauses, eyeing me with sudden interest. "You weren't on a date, were you?"

"Yeah," I drawl, rolling my eyes. "I was on a date."

"Then why'd you blow me off?"

And here I pause. Once again, I debate between telling Mo the truth or telling him something less true, but more convenient. And the choice—the fact that I actively consider lying to my best friend, *again*—nauseates me. I hate myself for the liar I'm becoming, so I go with something truth-adjacent. "I got a job. Had to fill out the paperwork."

He looks at me as though I'm spouting Mandarin. "A job?" He somehow manages to make the word *job* sound as foreign as Mandarin. "A job," he repeats, testing the feel of it on his tongue. "What the hell for?"

Again, the choice between the truth or convenience. "I need to start saving money."

Mo nods sagely. "Yeah, I suppose we should be thinking about tuition. MIT isn't cheap, even if we can get some decent scholarships." We've been planning to go to MIT together since we were in sixth grade. At the time, the reality of a school whose annual tuition costs more than my mom's house hadn't hit us. Now that we're getting closer to that reality, the money definitely means something.

We make our way past the Bhatias' living room and through the pristine kitchen. Mo detours to grab a couple of juice boxes from the fridge—organic, no-sugar-added apple juice. His mom is a nutritionist, so nothing carbonated, caffeinated, or artificially sweetened is allowed in their house. Healthy drinks in hand, we head to the basement, where Mo's makeshift workshop is located.

The Bhatias' basement is only partially finished. Half the space is taken up by a laundry room and storage area. Mo's family isn't wealthy, but they have enough space to dedicate a small workbench and a few shelves to Mo's special projects. I love working here with him. My house doesn't have the space for anything like it. I had to move my dresser into my closet to make room for Sonic's cage; there's definitely no room for a workstation I could dedicate to my robotics work. Heck, even my homework gets completed at the kitchen table more often than not.

Mo plops his butt on a stool and reaches across the counter, dragging a wide-gridded sketchbook out from underneath a pile of abandoned sketches. "I've got some ideas for the SHORT competition, ways to construct the soft materials frame to strengthen it without the normal metal or hard plastic components. But I'm afraid I'm overcomplicating it." He flips the sketchbook open to a page near the back.

My phone chimes half a second before Mo's does. I shift the

juice box from one hand to the other so I can reach into my jeans. Mo mirrors my actions.

It's a message from Percy in the robotics team's group chat, calling an emergency meeting on Monday.

"Emergency meeting?" Mo flashes his screen at me, eyebrows arched. "What is a robotics emergency? Like, did that AI program Mitch thought he could replicate actually work and the bots are taking over the school? 'Cause, dude, that would be kind of awesome."

We're already meeting on Tuesday. Outside of some kind of AI takeover, what can't wait an extra twenty-four hours? "Do you think it has anything to do with the funding thing we talked about yesterday?"

"You know what I know." Mo starts tapping at his phone. "It's Saturday, it's not like he could have learned anything new. Probably just Percy being a drama queen."

My phone chimes again. This time it's a response to the group from Mo. A thumbs-up and a GIF of a cartoon starfish rubbing his hands together saying "I'm in."

A couple more dings as the rest of the group indicates they will be there. Mo looks at me expectantly. I stare at my phone. He cocks his head.

Crap. He's watching me, and I can't put if off anymore. I have to tell him. This sucks.

"I can't." The words come out weak.

"What do you mean, you can't?"

"I start work on Monday."

"Tell them you have to start another day."

"I can't do that on the first day. How would that look?"

"But this is an emergency." He tosses his hands in the air, a dramatic gesture worthy of Percy.

I roll my eyes. "Didn't we agree that this is probably Percy overreacting? How's that an emergency?"

"I haven't ruled out an invasion of free-thinking bots taking over the school."

I snort. Mo snickers. Sighing, I slump onto one of the stools next to the workbench. "I can't bail on work on the first day. I just can't."

"This whole job deal you've got going on is a pain in the ass. It's only been a couple of hours and you're already flaking out on us."

Shame and a hazy shadow of regret burn in my guts. I try to act like it's no big deal. "I already told them I wasn't available on Tuesdays and Fridays, and I gave Paolo the tournament schedule, so he knows when I'll need a little extra time off."

"Fine." Mo crosses his arms over his chest. Accepting, but not happy about it. Then his eyes widen. "Wait a minute. You said Paolo. Do you mean Paolo Greco, your former stepdad? That's who you're working for?"

"Um, yeah. Mom set it up for me, and well, we knew he'd be cool about—" I almost slip and say *the baby*, and I quickly change what I'm saying. "—robotics stuff."

"Let me get this straight. You're going to be working for your former stepdad, which means you'll be working with Gio. That's awkward."

"Awkward? Awkward how?" Sure, I know *I'll* find it awkward, but Mo doesn't know about my stupid crush on my former stepbrother.

He gives me an *are you kidding me* look.

"What?"

"You've been in love with the guy since you were twelve years old."

I sputter. I can't help it. "I haven't . . . I don't know what . . . I do not . . ."

Mo shakes his head like I'm being an idiot. And, well, maybe I am. But how could he have known?

"You've been mooning after him for years. Why else would you drag me to all those football games?"

"Uh, school spirit?" The implied *duh* I'd intended is completely hidden by the unfortunately timed crack in my voice. Now I sound a little desperate. Which I'm not.

Mo rolls his eyes. "Uh-huh, sure. We'll go with that. And last spring when you lost ten pounds because you spent the entire lunch break spying on him and the other popular jocks instead of eating your lunch?"

"I was in the middle of a growth spurt. And the school lunch program is not as nutritionally sound as they want our parents to believe."

"You brought your lunch from home."

I let out a pained sigh, covering my face with my hands. "Oh man. Does *everyone* know?" I can't face everyone knowing I was that obvious.

"Nah, Ben, mostly Maxie and me. And only because we know you best."

Maxie. A chill, one I can't blame on the Bhatias' air-conditioning system, runs across my arms. She and Mo do know me best. And once people find out about Maxie and me, and then find out about the baby . . . Shit. Nobody's going to care that I have a crush on my former stepbrother.

Mo claps my shoulder. "Relax. No one suspects a thing. Of course, that means you'll need to watch what you say and do around him. Or maybe you two could re-create that moment in

Lady and the Tramp with the spaghetti." He waggles his eyebrows at me.

"Jerk." I shove him.

He manages to keep from falling off his stool by grabbing hold of the counter.

Yeah, no one suspects anything. *Yet.* Mo means Gio, of course, but they don't know about anything else yet either. But then again, there's this emergency meeting. It can't be related, right?

Our phones chime again. Another text from Percy.

Has anyone heard from Ben? Need him to confirm Mon. mtg.

I rub at my eyes in an attempt to ease the sudden pressure behind them. With a fortifying breath, I key in my response. *I can't make it. I'm starting a part-time job Monday.*

The barrage of messages that come next are full of exclamation points, question marks, and WTFs.

"People have jobs," I tell Mo. "Why are they acting like this is a huge deal?"

"Well, you didn't have a job on Friday, and now you do. We're about to start a campaign to save the club, and now your availability is compromised."

I almost want to make a joke about Mo sounding like we're launching a military occupation, not an after-school club, but more pings erupt from my phone.

Mo adds, "They just weren't expecting it. Not from you, of all people."

I grunt, scanning the new messages. There are shocked replies from everyone on the team. Everyone, that is, except Maxie. In fact, when I look at the list of members in the group chat, Maxie is not listed at all.

CHAPTER 7

My brain is still a chaotic mess on Monday. My homework is done, but I have no idea if I spent Sunday working on chemistry, English literature, or gym class. My mind has been frantically rotating between the stress of the new job with its frequent interactions with Gio, the worry of the "emergency" robotics club meeting and Maxie's missing name, the parenting classes my mom told me she expects me to start taking, and the conference call we have on Thursday night with James to start the legal process of claiming my parental rights. So, yeah, there's a very good chance my essay on "The Knight's Tale" from *The Canterbury Tales* will include a mention of Dalton's law of partial pressures.

It takes me longer to swap out my books between classes than it should because the jumbled thoughts seem to jumble everything else too. Colors don't make sense, and letters swirl and morph on the book covers. Every bang of lockers around me, every squeak of tennis shoes on polished floors, every raucous burst of laughter grates on my nerves. Even the soft cotton of my T-shirt feels gritty and rough. It's something that happens when I'm stressed, this getting sucked into sensory overload on all fronts.

I flinch when the locker next to me slams shut.

This is ridiculous. This tension, this anxiety, this needling, itchy pressure is ridiculous. I'm being ridiculous. I should have called Percy yesterday to find out what the "emergency" meeting was going to be about. Heck, I should have called Maxie yesterday to see what was going on. Or even to check in and see how she's doing. I mean, crazy as Friday night was for me, it had to be even more traumatic for her.

But every time I pick up my phone, I see the links to the parenting classes offered in the area. Just my luck, the closest one is held here at the high school. Mom is pushing me to register for one of the upcoming sessions. Heck, she wants me to actually attend with Maxie.

"But she doesn't want to be a parent. Why would she go to parenting classes?" I asked at dinner last night.

Apparently, a big piece of the curriculum seems to be geared toward the mother, the pregnancy, and the childbirth process.

"It'll be good for you, and for her to know she has a partner in this."

The bell rings, causing me to lose hold of my backpack. It lands on the floor, sending pencils and pens rolling. I squat down to grab them up, nearly getting trampled by the other students heading to class. At least three separate colors of Converse shoes land on my hands. One red one manages to kick my lucky mechanical pencil, the expensive metal one my aunt gave me that I use at all the robotics competitions, skittering down the hallway. I curse and scuttle after it.

I reach the pencil at the same time as a Vans high-top pins it to the floor. Gray fabric skater shoe. Newish. Knot and bow tied slightly off center. I squeeze my eyes closed, hoping I'm wrong. I follow the edge of the shoe up, where a hint of white athletic sock peeks out. Above that is golden skin covered in a smattering of dark hair, a muscular calf, and then the hem of glossy basketball shorts. And there, on the kneecap, is a little star-shaped scar. Identical to one Gio Greco received in a skateboarding accident when he was eleven.

I crane my neck to verify that, yes, my suspicions are, in fact, accurate. Gio Greco looms above me, wicked smirk twisting below those completely unfair dimples.

I close my eyes and wish that a portal to another realm would open below me and transfer me far, far away. It doesn't matter where it sends me, as long as I don't end up in a world where I'm scrambling on all fours in front of *him*.

Gio reaches down to pick up the pencil. His breath fans across my face and I'm in hell. *Why why why?* I clear my throat and try to play it cool. I rise until I'm at least kneeling instead of crawling, and hold my hand out for the pencil. "Thanks."

Instead of giving me my pencil, he grabs my wrist and hauls me to my feet. He's strong, so even if I don't want to be standing, I have no choice. I gasp out a breath and squeak out, "Thanks."

There are like six inches between us, and the jittery needle pricks of anxiety that have been plaguing me subside a little, and tension of another kind creeps in. My breath catches. Then I remember he's disappointed in me. *Then* I remember he's one of the few people who know about Maxie and the baby. And we're at school. If he says something . . .

I grab his forearm. "I need you to do me a favor."

"Something more than giving you your pencil? It must be a special pencil to have you voluntarily crawling on the floor. God knows what's on it."

"Seriously, Gio."

His humor melts away, replaced by concern. "What do you need?"

"What you heard on Friday." I lick my lips, looking for his reaction. There's not much. Maybe a slight widening of his eyes.

"Yeah?"

"Can you . . . can you not mention it to anyone? I mean, nobody knows and it'll be better if no one finds out."

He doesn't say anything for a few seconds and it terrifies me. Shit. He's already told someone? I'll need to find Maxie . . .

He shakes his head, and there's a hint of that disappointment from Saturday. "Why would I tell anyone? It's none of my business."

"Right. That's good. Good." After a second, I add a belated "Thanks."

I snatch the pencil—I'm not sure I'll ever be able to call it my lucky pencil again—and dash across the now deserted hallway to my backpack. I focus on zippering the necessary pockets before turning around. Gio's gone, which relieves and disappoints me.

Mrs. Stubbs, the vice principal, rounds the corner. She makes a point of staring at her watch. "Don't you have somewhere to be, Mr. Morrison?"

"Oh, um, yeah. Yes, I mean. I'm going now . . ." I swing the bag over my shoulder and practically run to my first-period class. It's only as I slide into my desk, babbling apologies for being late, that I realize I didn't grab the right books. I look at the AP Chemistry text in my bag. Maybe Chaucer really did have an aptitude for chemistry?

.   .   .

Mitch and Percy corner me in the hall after lunch. "Explain to me why you won't be there this afternoon?" Percy growls. Mitch hovers behind him, scowling.

I hitch my hands under the straps of my backpack. I've been trying to avoid him today. I don't have it in me to deal with any more intense emotion, and Percy is the definition of intense emotion. "Like I said the other night, I got an after-school job."

"Yeah," he says, crossing his arms over his chest. "So you said. But what I don't understand is why you'd do that. And why you didn't say anything on Friday at the meeting."

Mitch lurks behind him, quiet and stoic as a scarecrow.

I shrug, pretending to be way more casual about it than I am. "I didn't want to say anything until it was official. It became official on Saturday."

"I can't believe this!" Percy throws up his hands and starts to pace. "First the budget meeting, then Maxie, and now you. At this rate, we might as well close the club."

My brain stutters for a second. I grab Percy's arm, ignoring his continued shouts. "What do you mean, *then Maxie*? What's this about Maxie?"

He spins around to face me, propping his hands on his hips. "Maxie's why I called the meeting."

"But why?" What do they know? Have people found out about her? About Maxie and me? About the baby?

"She quit. Maxie dropped out of the group with no warning. She sent an *email*," Percy says, sounding scandalized. "No explanations, no discussion, just an 'I quit.'"

"She . . . what? I can't believe . . ." But I can believe. I *do* believe. Didn't the same thought cross my mind Friday? I don't know much about pregnancy, but at some point it is going to get in the way of one of our projects. "What are we going to do?"

"You need to talk to her. Make her come back."

"Me?" I gape at him. "Why me?"

"You're her friend, aren't you?"

"Yeah, but—"

"Look, you need to get her back." Percy can't seem to stay still. He starts pacing again. "We need all hands on deck. We need people to recruit, and we need people to train the new members. And while all that's going on, we still need to plan our upcoming competition projects. We can't do that with four and a half team members."

I blink at Percy, momentarily distracted. "Half?"

He narrows his eyes.

"Oh, I see." I'm the half member.

"We've got sectionals next month, and you and Maxie have point on the programming. As much as I hate to admit it, no one else on the team can code like you two. And we don't have time to train some theoretical new person in time for the competition. So, yeah, we can't compete without her. And this job situation is going to be a problem, too. Why'd you have to go and get a job now? Dude, your timing seriously sucks."

Percy's complete and utter drama queen routine aside, he's not wrong. To win the competition—not to mention save the team— we're going to have to work twice as much. Which in turn will mean additional club meetings every week, probably even on weekends, and more than a little work to do at home. And that's *with* Maxie on the team. Without her, it'll be so much worse. Strange, but when I think about the robotics club, every thought, every memory, in- cludes images of moments with Mo and Maxie. The club without Maxie seems . . . wrong.

So, yeah, Percy's definitely overreacting, but he makes some valid points. Recruiting, training, and prepping for sectionals will eat up a lot of time. "I can talk to her, but it probably won't help." No *probably* about it. I doubt anything I have to say will change her mind.

"Good." Percy nods sharply. "While you're at it, see if you can figure out what her deal is. She's been acting weird lately, and this tops it. She needs to get her head on straight."

Mitch dips his head in agreement.

"I'll see what I can do." Another futile promise. It won't matter what I say—her plate is going to be beyond full until the baby is born. Maybe I can convince her to stick it out through the sectionals? Or maybe help train the new people we still have to recruit?

"Good." Percy swings around, and he and Mitch head toward the English wing.

The bell rings, and I jump, heart skittering in my chest. Too much change in a short period of time always makes me twitch, and right now I'm twitchy as hell.

CHAPTER 8

I spend the drive to Greco's alternating between biting my nails, bouncing my knee, and watching Gio watch me. He doesn't say anything. He doesn't ask any questions. After a few minutes of no conversation, he turns up the radio, letting his head bounce along to a song I don't recognize.

I don't even know what to worry about at the moment.

Maxie? The job? The birth and parenting classes that I need to sign up for?

"What's got you so twisted up?" he asks as one song fades out to be replaced by the next on his playlist.

"Nothing. I don't know what you mean. I'm not twisted up."

"You've bitten your nails down so far they're bleeding, and the knee-bouncing is shaking the entire car. Classic anxiety symptoms for you. Something to do with Maxie?"

"Of course not," I snap, arms crossing over my chest.

"Uh-huh, right." Even though his eyes don't leave the road ahead of us, I feel like he's staring at me, judging.

"Yes, right," I insist. "It has nothing to do with Maxie." I look around the car, searching for inspiration. My gaze lands on my backpack. "It's robotics stuff."

I push past the fear into logical problem solving. "The competition next month is going to be something we've never done before. And we're too small as it is. We need more people. Lots more, to be honest."

"And that's got you all twitchy?" He arches a single brow, something I've always assumed doesn't happen in real life.

"It's not only the recruitment. The competition is going to be harder than anything we've done before. We've got to create a soft robot."

"Soft?"

"Oh, um, yeah, it means that it's made of soft materials. No metal. Malleable stuff only."

"And that's harder?"

"Well, this is the first time our team has been faced with creating a functioning mechanism without metal frames, or gears, or any rigid materials, really. I mean, the actual project is pretty simple—collecting and stacking hockey pucks. We did the same thing in middle school, but with standard materials. The challenge, of course, is agreeing on the actuation system. Mo is obsessed with making the robot move through the use of electric fields. Which, sure, would be cool, but creating and sustaining high-voltage electricity long enough to complete the task is a problem. No, I think pneumatic pressure is the way to go."

"Right," he agrees. I can't tell if he agrees with my thought process or is simply saying one of those things people say to acknowledge that you're talking. Either way, my brain is running full speed ahead to figure the problem out.

I pull out my notebook and begin to sketch out my ideas while

I talk. "Maybe a round base, flat like a dinner plate? And arms. Pincers or suction to retrieve the pucks. Probably pincers, which would give us more control."

"Lobster."

I blink up at Gio.

"Excuse me?"

He dips his chin toward the notebook on my lap. "Looks like a lobster."

I squint at the combination of lines and curves. Huh. Look at that. "I guess it does."

"So you're going to create a big lobster out of soft materials and air pressure to gather hockey pucks."

I shrug. "Maybe." I see the maroon awning of Greco's, so I jam my notebook back into my bag.

Gio pulls his car around the restaurant and parks between a Greco's catering van and a dumpster. "Staff parks in the back," he says. "Parking lot's for the customers." There are a handful of other vehicles back here, and even as we step out of Gio's car, a bright yellow VW Bug swings around the side and comes to a quick stop on the other side of the van. A wide grin breaks out over Gio's face as a tall Black woman with a shaved head erupts from the yellow car, babbling greetings and apologies even as she tries to button up the black vest she wears over a maroon button-down shirt.

"Relax, Monica, you're not late yet. And even if you were, it's not like Pops would dock your pay."

"You're not the boss yet, Gio Greco. And on time is—"

Gio rolls his eyes. "On time is late, I know, and early is on time."

"How early do you have to be to be considered early?" I ask.

The woman—Monica—grins at me. "Half hour, minimum." She reaches Gio's side and ruffles his hair. The thick dark curls

immediately fall back into place. She really is tall. At least as tall
as Gio, who's easily six feet. Which means I have to look up at her.
"And who are you?" she asks, smiling down at me.

"Oh, right!" Gio gestures to me. "Monica, this is Ben Morrison,
new busser. Ben, Monica Grant is the front-of-house manager."

"Front of house?" I've never heard the term before.

"Basically, I manage the dining room—the waitstaff, hosts, bartenders, bussers. Paolo runs the kitchen and kitchen staff."

"She's your boss," Gio clarifies. "And mine, for that matter."

"And as your boss," Monica says, tapping the smart watch at
her wrist, "I'm telling you to clock in so we can get going. Once
you're punched in, Gio will give you a quick tour and run you
through the basics of bussing. You'll shadow him for a while, then
after the dinner rush has slowed, we'll let you run solo for a bit."
She pulls open the back door, which leads to a small hallway, and
gestures us in.

The kitchen and a storage room with a couple of big stainless-
steel doors are on the right, and on the left, there's a restroom
and an office. Straight ahead, the swinging door has a small
window, through which I can see the dining room. A cloud of
garlic and oregano, edged a bit with something chemical, like
a cleaner or disinfectant of some kind, explodes around me the
moment I step in. The scents are familiar. The noise is not. I
don't know why, but I expected the back of the restaurant to
sound like the front. Maybe a little conversation, the occasional
clink of plates or cutlery. Instead, the rush of running water,
the clang of pans, the *snick-snick-snick* of knives chopping, and
shouted conversations and orders surround me.

There's a click of a latch and the *shoosh* of something large
moving behind the wall.

"Careful," Gio says, reaching for me.

I pivot toward him, my shoes slipping on the tiles. I fall forward, grabbing his arms to keep from falling on my face. Then I jerk back because I'm clinging to Gio—*Gio!*—like a baby koala bear, which, no way.

A blast of cold air rushes over me, and I spin again, just in time to see the big stainless-steel door arc open.

Instead of taking the extra step to put some distance between me and Gio, while at the same time avoiding the now-open door to a walk-in cooler, my feet get tangled together, and I lurch to the side, immediately crashing into someone.

I catch a blur of white apron and black plastic before I grunt under the impact of a large tub of fresh vegetables jamming into my chest.

I twist back, instinctively grabbing for the tub. I pull it my way, the guy on the other end jerks it his way, and the large eggplant balanced precariously on the mound of produce hurtles toward the ground. I drop the tub in a desperate attempt to catch the purple fruit. But I don't have the reflexes of an athlete, so my swinging hand knocks into one end of the eggplant, flipping it in the air like a juggler's bowling pin. The other guy and I both lunge for it and manage to bash our heads together. Then, because the whole moment isn't enough of a slapstick comedy routine, we both spring back and he loses his grip on the tub.

Tomatoes, onions, carrots, more damned eggplants, bundles of herbs, and a few things I don't recognize tumble to the floor. So what do I do? I step on a carrot, which rolls under my shoe, sending me to the floor. My legs tangle with the other guy's. He and the now-empty tub collapse on top of me. Something cool and soft squishes against my chest, liquefying and soaking through my T-shirt.

It takes my dazed brain a second to kick in and start to calculate the effects. I didn't hit my head—a plus. I landed hard on my ass—not so good. My butt's going to be sore, but not un-manageable. No twinges at my ankles or wrists, so bonus. The ache and pressure on my chest keeping me from breathing fully—concerning. I can't tell if I knocked the breath out of my lungs in the fall, or if it's the weight of the dude on top of me.

The guy rolls off me, scowling. "What the hell, man?" He turns his glare from me and redirects it to Monica. "This wasn't my fault. I'm not taking the heat for this." He pushes to his feet, bracing his hands on his hips, and stares down at me.

I still can't breathe, so I don't push up yet.

Gio and Monica are so tall it looks like they are looking down at me from miles above, not roughly six feet.

With the cranky produce guy out of the way, Gio kneels next to me. "You okay, Ben?"

"Fine," I gasp out. "Just . . . need a second."

"Take your time," Monica says, crouching to gather the vegetables that lie scattered around us. "How about you, Matt? You okay?"

"Fine." With an irritated sigh, he bends to grab the now-dented eggplant before tossing it into the tub.

The tightness in my chest eases, so I sit up.

Gio snorts. "Ben, dude, you look like someone shot you."

I look down at my chest. Pulpy, reddish liquid stains my shirt. On the light-blue fabric, it looks darker and grosser than it might have otherwise. My face heats and is probably as red as the mashed tomato on my front.

Monica sighs. "Gio, take him back and get him a shirt."

"Oh, but—"

"The shirt is part of the dress code. We'll send you home with a few of them. Before your next shift, we need to get you into some no-slip shoes, too." She tosses the last rogue onion into the bin and hands it to the guy in the apron, who she'd called Matt. "Toss these, write down the waste, and pull needed product again before Paolo wonders what happened to you."

Matt, still scowling, takes the tub.

"I'll find you in a bit to fill out the report. You too, Ben."

"Report?"

"I don't know that I've ever had to write up an accident report for someone on their first day before," she says.

"Oh, but—" Of course. Day one on a new job, and I've already screwed up. I hope they don't make me pay for all the produce they have to throw away. Mom will kill me. "I'm so sorry!"

Monica waves it aside. "It could have happened to anyone. Matt should probably have been more careful coming out too. It's a health-and-safety thing. All accidents and near misses have to get documented."

I bite my lip.

"Don't sweat it," Gio says. He reaches down to help me up. I ignore his hand and push myself to my feet. I need to prove to someone—myself, him, Monica—that I can do something right.

Monica heads through the door to the dining room and Gio leads me to a small office. There's a bag on the desk with my name written in dark ink. He tosses the bag to me. "Waitstaff and bartenders get button-downs and vests, bussers get T-shirts."

I peer into the plastic at the maroon fabric. There are three shirts folded neatly with the Greco's logo facing up. Maroon is going to clash horribly with my red hair, but that probably doesn't matter.

Gio drapes a matching T-shirt over his shoulder. I remember his button-down from last Friday. "You're not a busser, right?"

"Nah. Mostly I host and fill in as waitstaff when needed. I don't mind bussing, though."

"And you'll be training me?"

"Yep." He nods.

"Why you?" I ask. I don't know a lot about restaurant work, but it seems to me that bussing is near the bottom of the hierarchy.

"Why not me?" Thankfully he continues before I have to figure out what to say. "Pops thought you'd appreciate working with someone you know at first. I don't mind."

"Oh, okay." I don't know how to feel about that. Part of me wants to pick apart the many reasons he doesn't mind. He doesn't mind training a newbie? He doesn't mind working with *me*? The other part of me is irritated that Paolo thinks I need a familiar face. I'm not completely lost in new situations.

"We'd better get changed." He indicates the hallway with a tilt of his head. "There's a staff restroom where we can change. I'll also see if I can find you a bag or something to put your dirty shirt into while you get ready."

So it isn't the best start to a new challenge. It's going to be fine, though. I'm smart. I'm capable. I can certainly handle something like bussing tables. And focusing my attention on not screwing up at Greco's will ensure I don't focus my attention on Maxie and the baby, or the extra pressure from the robotics team.

As I change into my clashing new T-shirt, I mentally outline my expectations for the evening.

Do pay attention to the job training.

Do keep the end goal in mind.

Don't mess it up.

Don't mess it up, I repeat to myself. At this juncture, every little thing I do has huge, far-reaching consequences. I can't afford to drop any balls. Or eggplants, for that matter.

I open the door, preparing to juggle for all I'm worth.

CHAPTER 9

By the time I clock out four hours later, the muscles in my arms are trembling, my shirt is covered in marinara and alfredo sauce, and I've managed to break three water glasses, two appetizer plates, and a coffee mug. One dropped ball after another, over and over again.

"I'm terrible at this!" I declare, sliding into Mom's car. I slouch into the seat, snapping the safety belt into place and not making eye contact.

"Rough night?"

"I don't get it. I'm smart, right? I know stuff. And what I don't know, I can learn."

"Of course," Mom says, pulling out of the staff parking lot.

"And bussing's not rocket science, right? I mean, it's clearing and setting tables, filling water glasses, delivering bread baskets."

"Right," she agrees, drawing the word out.

"So why is it so hard?"

"Couple of things, Benny. First, it's your first day. You need to give yourself a break. No one is perfect at something on the first day."

"But—"

She holds up a finger. "Second, just because the job functions are not complicated, doesn't mean the work isn't hard. We shouldn't look down on a job—or the worker doing the job—because we think it is somehow less than another job. That kind of elitism and classism is why there is such a labor gap in our country right now."

"It's not about elitism or classism, Mom. It's that I suck at it. I can probably design a robot to bus tables for me, and I can calculate equations that would challenge college-level engineering students. I should be able to do something this . . . basic."

"What does Paolo say?"

I shrug. "I didn't really get to see Paolo. He was in the kitchen the whole time, while I was in the dining room. I worked with Gio and the front-of-house manager, Monica."

"And what did Monica say?"

"Monica said I'm doing fine, and that it can take a while to get into the swing of things."

"She'd know, right?"

"I guess." I bite my thumbnail and watch the vehicles pass in the other lane. A black Toyota something or other merges in next to us.

"Crap!" I shout, yanking my thumb out of my mouth. "I have to go back."

"Back?"

"I left my backpack in Gio's car."

She glances at the time display on the dash. "Can't you get it from him in the morning?"

"I have calculus homework. And another chapter to read in *The Canterbury Tales* for English."

She sighs and makes a right-hand turn at the next intersection, heading back to Bay View.

My plan is to try Gio's car first, before having to seek him out inside. After the debacle of my first night as a busser, I would rather avoid him as much as possible. Nothing like having the guy you're crushing on see you fail miserably at something that comes so easy to him. The plan will only work, though, if he's still at the restaurant. It's only eight o'clock, but his shift was the same as mine. What will I do if he's left already?

When we reach Greco's, I direct Mom around the back to the staff parking lot. Gio's car is still slotted between the catering van and the dumpster. Turns out I'm not going to have to check his locks or chase him down. He's leaning against the trunk of the Toyota, ankles crossed, my backpack dangling from one hand.

Mom's headlights illuminate his smug grin when he recognizes us. He walks to the driver's side—of course he goes to Mom's side first—the grin not fading, even as the smugness does. Mom lowers the window and pokes her head out. "Hello, Giovanni."

"Eliza." He leans in and kisses her cheek. It's a sweet gesture that makes me want to sigh at how adorable it is, and cringe at the thought of how awkward I would look trying it. Gio glances over Mom's shoulder and meets my gaze. "Figured you'd be back for this." He hefts my bag up.

"Yeah, thanks." I reach for the door handle. If he's over there by Mom, I guess I'll have to go to him to get my books.

"So how do you think Benny did for his first night?"

"*Mom!*"

"Oh, hush, Ben. Gio, you've been working at the restaurant

since you were practically a baby. You'll probably have some insight for Ben."

"Not bad." His stupid dimples flash. "We've definitely had worse first days. Though Pops would probably appreciate it if he didn't damage any more eggplants. Apparently, the vendor's supply is a bit limited right now."

"Eggplants?"

"Later," I tell Mom. "It was this whole . . . thing."

"You should come in sometime," Gio says, nodding at the restaurant. "I know Pops would love to see you again. Especially since your last visit ended the way it did."

"Now that Ben works here, I might have to. No one does a vodka cream sauce like Paolo. Has he gotten you in the kitchen yet?"

Gio laughs. "Nah. As much as he'd love to see two generations of Greco men behind the stove, I don't see that happening anytime soon."

"Don't like to cook?"

It might be the effect of the limited evening light or the inconsistent yellow glow from the safety light at the restaurant's door, but I think his normally charming smile stiffens a bit at the ends.

"No, I love to cook. I'm just not sure I want to do it for a living. I'm going to UW next year, and Mom's really excited about their journalism program for me."

Mom covers his hand where it rests on the doorframe. "I for one am sure you will be successful at whatever you choose to do. I also know your father is proud as can be of you, and that's not going to change, no matter what your plans are."

Now his smile wobbles. "Thanks, Eliza. That means a lot."

I don't understand what's happening here. I mean, on a surface level, I comprehend their conversation. But I'm missing something. I'm missing information, or context, or subtext. I don't know what exactly is missing, but because of its absence, I feel like I've started watching a movie at the halfway mark—a little lost and uncertain.

"Mom, we should get going. I have a lot of homework tonight." My statement seems to break the strange tension. "You must have a lot of homework." Gio lifts my backpack. "This thing weighs a ton."

Crap. I had been about to leave without my bag. Again. I slip out of the car and round the hood. Gio passes the backpack to me. "We'll have to remember to store this in the office on the nights you work so you don't forget it again."

"Sure," I say. I clutch the bag to my chest and scurry back to the passenger side of the car.

"See you later. Next shift is Wednesday." With a last look at Mom, Gio heads back to his own car.

Mom puts the car into gear and drives back out of the lot. "I feel for him sometimes," she says.

I narrow my eyes at her. "What? Why?"

"You know I don't like to talk bad about anyone, but his mother is a piece of work."

"His mother?" I think back to the days when Mom and Paolo were married. Neither Gio nor his father had much to say about her. Gio spent half his time at her house—an almost daily back-and-forth that seemed hard to track at the time—but other than that, I don't recall anything in particular about her, or Gio's relationship with her.

"She's got very particular ideas about Gio's future. She's always pushed him in ways I don't think are good for him."

"Like what?"

Mom hesitates before admitting, "She always seemed jealous

of the time he spent with Paolo, even as a little kid. She resented any hint that Gio might prefer Paolo or the life he could give Gio."

"Like the restaurant."

"Like the restaurant," she agrees. "She'll probably continue to push Gio at any career path that keeps him from cooking, even if Gio's heart is not in it."

"You don't think Gio wants to go to UW and study journalism?"

"I don't think he *doesn't* want to go that direction."

It takes me a second to untangle the double negative. "So you think he's going along with it because he doesn't care enough one way or the other not to?"

"Something like that. He probably doesn't know exactly what he wants to do. He's young yet. Also, I'm assuming a lot based on what I knew about him, Paolo, and his mother from years ago. Things may have changed."

"But you don't think so."

"It's not fair for me to speculate."

We drive a few more minutes in silence.

"Did you talk to Maxie today?" Mom asks.

I shift in my seat. "No."

"Why not?"

I fidget with the strap of my backpack. "Things are kind of weird right now."

"I expect they are."

"She quit the robotics team."

Mom sighs. "That's too bad. I'm not surprised, but it's got to be tough."

"No kidding. Now Percy's in some kind of crisis-management mode. He's freaking out and—"

"It's got to be tough on Maxie, Ben. I'm sure it's a bit of a blow to the club, but I'm more worried about her."

Hunching my shoulders, I look away from my mom. "Yeah, I suppose so."

"Ben." Mom uses her "pay attention" tone.

Reluctantly I turn back toward her.

"You need to be careful with Maxie. She's going through a lot right now."

"What do you mean *careful*? And she's not the only one going through a lot."

"Just don't put any additional pressure on her, okay? You will never understand what she's going through emotionally, physically, mentally. If she dropped robotics, you need to leave it alone. I know what that organization means to her, to you all, so if she feels like this is a step she has to take, you have to let her. No blame. No resentment. Support her decisions. Be her friend."

I swallow hard, and then look away. We don't say anything else the rest of the ride home. Roger greets me with a question about my first day on the job when we walk into the house, but I ignore him. At this point, my calculus homework is about the only thing I feel I have any control over. I slide past him and lock myself in my room. Homework now. Everything else, later.

CHAPTER 10

Roger dangles his car keys in front of my face. "C'mon, kid."

"Huh?" It takes a minute for the words to break through the strings of code running through my brain. Sectionals are less than three weeks away and I haven't finalized the coding for our bot. Construction plans are mostly set, but we can't test the prototype until I finish the coding. While we've found a couple of people to fill in our numbers for the team, I'm still the primary coder. None of the others are quite competition-ready, and without Maxie in the picture, it falls to me to make sure all our i's are dotted and our t's are crossed.

Speaking of . . . I click on one of the six active applications on my computer to pull up the preliminary written statement. Mitch dropped it in our shared files last week and he's been waiting for me to read through it and sign off on it. Problem is, Mitch is only a so-so writer, and can't spell to save his life, so I'll need to really be able to focus on getting it polished up. It was due two days ago and I haven't gotten past the purpose statement.

Roger clears his throat.

Crap. He said something, right? I look up from my computer monitor and blink to clear my vision.

"You need to get some driving hours logged in, right?"

"I'm kind of busy right now." I turn back to my monitor.

I'm sitting at the kitchen table. It gives me the most room to spread out. Next to my ancient laptop I have two stacks of books—Chaucer is buried under my copy of *Mastering ROS*, and another pile consists of a calculus textbook, *What to Expect When You're Expecting*, and half a dozen spiral-bound notebooks that have years' worth of robotics notes and tips.

It's been more than a month since Maxie broke the news about the baby. I swear, every day Mom or Mr. Rose or my teachers add something new to my to-do list. For the first time in my life, doing homework is a struggle. Not because the concepts are difficult, but because my attention is divided into a thousand different directions. Between preparing for sectionals, working nearly twenty hours a week at Greco's, and baby research, I'm left with barely any time to focus on homework.

Take today, for instance. As soon as I finish the next section of coding for the Lobster—a name the robotics club adopted as soon as I shared Gio's observations—I must finish my paper on the roles of microbes in waste recycling for my biology class. Then I have to head back to Greco's for an evening shift. The last thing I'm worried about is logging my driving hours.

"Don't you want to drive? When I was your age I couldn't wait to get behind the wheel."

"Sure," I say absently, digging through my pile of notebooks. I think the green one has my notes on Java syntax for pneumatic programming. Or is it the blue one?

Roger lays his hand on top of the pile, stopping my shuffling.

"Look, your mom asked me to take you out today. You need to keep practicing if you intend to take the test. And after the last time you went out, well, she thinks it's better for me to take you rather than her."

I flinch. Yeah. Last time Mom let me drive, things got . . . rocky. Literally. I still don't know why there was a big-ass boulder in the middle of an empty parking lot, or why I didn't see it before running into it. Lucky for us, I'd only been going about ten miles an hour, so the front bumper only got a small dent. Mom had been edgy and reactionary before that. After, well, let's just say I've never seen her so tense and irritable.

"I get that," I say, "but does it have to be today?" My knee starts to bounce, and the rapid motion shakes the table, knocking *What to Expect When You're Expecting* to the floor. I don't have time for this. I feel every second that passes like a screw being tightened into my chest, pressing me to do more, to be faster.

"We can't go at night, I'm working tomorrow, and if we don't do it now, we won't get another chance until next Saturday."

I think about what it will mean to have my license. I think about all the time I spend either waiting for other people to pick me up and drop me off. I think about sitting in the car with Gio every day. I think about Mom and Roger having to pick me up after each shift at Greco's.

The screw turns another rotation.

"Fine," I say, saving my code and shoving my laptop away from me.

Five minutes into our drive, Roger clears his throat. "So, Ben . . ."

Roger and I haven't really had much one-on-one time. Almost all our interactions have been buffered by Mom's presence. In fact, I can count on one hand the number of solo conversations we've ever had. Is that weird? It feels weird. I don't remember getting particularly close with James or Paolo or any of the men Mom dated, but it seems like there's an added level of distance between Roger and me.

"Yeah?"

"How are things?" His gaze is fixed forward, but I feel the weight of his regard anyway.

"Things?"

"Yeah, buddy. There's a lot going on for you right now. Just . . . how are you processing everything?"

I grimace. "Please don't call me *buddy*."

He chuckles weakly. "Yeah, no. I mean, you're right. Felt wrong as soon as I said it."

I squint at him. "Are you trying to *bond* with me?"

Slumping into his seat, he shrugs. "Well . . . yeah, kind of. I know I'm not your dad, but I want you to know I can be there for you. You and your mom are kind of a package deal, you know. Not that it's a problem. Wow. Just realized that makes it sound like I'm being forced to put up with you."

True, it really does. But it's also true, so it doesn't hurt my feelings or anything.

"You don't have to, you know."

"Don't have to what, put up with you?"

"That too. But I meant you don't have to try to bond with me, or whatever. Mom likes you, and that's what matters. I don't really need a dad, not anymore."

"It's not . . . I'm not necessarily trying to be your dad. But I'd like to be your friend. I want you to know I'm here for you. You know?"

I don't know, but I nod. "Sure."

"Seriously, Ben. I know I'm not James with the family law stuff, and I'm not Paolo with the job options. I know I don't have as much to offer you and your mom with all this." He waves one hand in the air, presumably encompassing me, my situation, Mom. Maybe Milwaukee in general. "But, hell, I can listen, and you can bounce ideas off me, or I can play chauffeur. Whatever you need, okay?"

"Okay." My voice lacks conviction, but it will be fine.

Ten more minutes later I stare at the iron sign arching over the entrance to Vickerson's Cemetery. "You've got to be kidding me."

Roger smirks at me, and the thought crosses my mind that this is how a lot of horror stories start out. I haven't noticed a particularly evil streak in Roger before now. He's always been sort of blandly nice. But sneaking me off to a cemetery while my mom is spending the day with friends? If not a horror movie, then it definitely lines up with some of those true-crime podcasts Mo is fascinated by.

"Do you have to visit a dead relative or something before we get started?" I ask, knowing I should feel at least a little bit of shame for how hopeful I sound. Dead family should never be the optimistic choice.

"Nope," he says, pulling into the small parking lot just through the entrance. "We're going to practice driving here."

He sounds serious.

"In a graveyard?"

"It's not like you can kill anyone here."

At my bald look, he chuckles and unbuckles his seat belt. "Come on. We'll switch places. This cemetery is good for practice driving. It's got wide lanes, lots of curves, and very few people. This is actually where my dad taught me to drive." He smiles fondly at the mention of his father.

I have a vague recollection of meeting Roger's parents when Roger and Mom got married. They live in Arizona, I think. My impression of Russel Ferguson, Roger's dad, is he's an older version of Roger, just as blandly nice, and he talked a lot about golf. His wife, Miriam, did something with art.

Most of my memories from the wedding—which was basically a courthouse appearance followed by dinner at some restaurant—are muted and indistinct. Roger's parents were there, as well as my aunt Shannon, and a handful of Mom and Roger's friends. I kept to myself, mostly, messaging Mo and Maxie throughout the evening. One moment is clear, however. Russel stood up and toasted the happy couple. He'd been beaming, eyes shining, as he wished Mom and Roger a happy future, while welcoming Mom and me to the family. There'd been such a look of pride and love on his face, I had to escape outside. It was easier to run away from the complicated emotions squeezing my throat than acknowledge them.

"I didn't know you grew up around here." Of course, I've never asked. Asking questions, getting answers, means getting to know him. Getting to know him better just makes it harder when he inevitably leaves. It isn't worth it.

"Yep. Went to school at Nicolet."

I grunt, unsure of what to say.

"Swap places with me." He opens his door and steps out. I do the same, only slower.

My gut churns and I watch Roger warily. What's even the point of this? I can't afford a car, let alone the insurance, or gas, or any of it. Not with every dollar I make at Greco's getting stashed away for baby-related stuff. I looked up the price of a crib the other day. Yeah, that's a lot of table-clearing.

The couple times I've driven with Mom have been rough. Even taking the stupid big boulder in the parking lot out of the equation, it hasn't been a good time. For some reason, her tension and anxiety infect me, making me forget all the information I've memorized to pass the written test to get my learner's permit. Doing this with Roger seems like a disaster waiting to happen.

I settle into the driver's seat and slide the seat belt into place. I shoot a quick glance at Roger, trying to get a feel for why he's doing this. Mom asked him, clearly, but how does he feel? He doesn't look impatient or resentful, which I guess is a good thing. He sits in the passenger seat like he's got nothing else to do or anything else to worry about.

We're in Roger's Escape instead of Mom's Corolla, so the controls and dash look foreign to me. Roger is taller than me, so my toes barely reach the pedals. I reach below the seat for the button to bring me closer so I don't feel quite so small and unprepared. I fumble my way through adjusting the mirrors and checking the placement of the turn signal. I hit something, causing the windshield wipers to flap wildly over the glass, squeaking with each rapid pass. I jab at switches and buttons until the wiper blades still. If only it were that easy to slow my heartbeat.

"Relax, Ben. Take a deep breath, then walk me through the steps."

I flex my fingers before placing my hands on opposite sides of the steering wheel. Of course, then I have to take my right hand off the wheel so I can turn the key. "Foot on the brake. Wheel straight. Start the ignition." I repeat each step as it appears on my internal check-off list.

"We're going to follow the road until it branches off. At the first fork, take a left."

"Left at the branch. Right. Okay," I say. I don't know if Roger actually wants me to tell him about the motions, but the recitation keeps my brain focused. "Side mirror. Check. Passenger-side mirror. Check. Rearview mirror. Clear. Side mirror one more time. Still clear. Lift your foot to gas pedal and accelerate."

Roger is completely relaxed, and his calmness settles my nerves. He's not grabbing the oh-shit handle or stomping on an imaginary brake like Mom does. As I maneuver the SUV along the paved lanes of the cemetery, he quietly points it out when I pull too close to the grass on his side, and gives me little tips.

"You want to look farther ahead, not at the space directly in front of you. You'll be able to get the full picture of what's ahead of you, while still being able to adjust your steering as necessary. My dad called it aiming high."

He keeps his voice quiet. No urgency. No panic. Just a soothing reiteration of instructions that aren't new to me, but that have escaped me at some point in my anxiety.

"Loosen your grip, Ben. You're doing great. You've got this."

By the time we've gone up and down every lane in the sprawling graveyard, my turns are smoother, and when I brake, I don't give anyone whiplash.

Roger claps me on the shoulder. "Nice job. You're getting the hang of this." He directs me to a particularly curvy stretch of pavement. "We've got a few more minutes before we have to get back. Let's try backing up. Try and keep the same amount of space between the tires and the edge of the grass as you go."

It's not until we get home fifteen minutes later that I realize the awkwardness, the barrier between us, has disappeared.

CHAPTER 11

"I think Percy is going to puke," Anna whispers behind me. Mitch grunts.

I sneak a peek at our team president. He definitely looks a little gray. He purses his mouth as his eyes jump around the busy convention center.

"I hope not," Mark, one of our two newest members, whispers to Jay, the other new recruit we picked up. He sounds a bit winded, but to be fair he and Jay are stuck pushing the team's massive rolling toolbox down the corridor. "I'm a sympathetic vomitter. If he throws up, I will too."

Last year, Mo and I had to push the toolbox. It's the cost of being the new guys. Mo and I had been stuck as the "new" guys for the last two years. Whenever we complained about it last year, Maxie would volunteer to take a turn. We never let her, and when Mo had the audacity to say it was the polite thing to do because Maxie was a girl, she made a point of dogging us about it at every competition.

While I'm happy to pass that particular duty on, it feels weird to not be bickering with Maxie over it.

"No hurling until after we get the truck unloaded," Mo says, weaving past the two freshmen, arms loaded down with bulging tote bags full of even more parts and tools. He juts his chin toward the competitors' entrance of the convention hall.

I trudge behind Mo with two laptop bags slung over my shoulder and across my chest bandolier style and a packed six-inch binder in my arms.

The rest follow behind, loaded down like covered wagons on the Oregon Trail.

It's always the noise that hits me first. Competitor voices—almost always shouting—echoing under the high ceilings, the whir and roar of tools, the clank of metal, the cheering crowd. Even now, when the robots are not powered up and engaged, the volume of the room is enough to rattle the bones.

I used to get stressed out around loud, unpredictable noises. I still do, if I'm being honest. But something about the energy and purpose of a robotics competition supersedes the anxiety. Now these sounds energize and excite me. My blood thrums in my veins, my brain buzzes with determination, and my fingers itch.

Percy stops at the entrance to fish a folded piece of paper out of his pocket. He doesn't seem to notice that Mitch, or more importantly the cart of air tanks and tubing he's pushing, nearly crashes into his ass. The paper turns out to be a diagram of the convention center. "Nice! We're in spot A3, which means we're on this side of the hall, and close to the first arena."

Muscles sagging under the weight of computers and binders, I cheer up at this news. I remember having to walk what felt like miles at the regional competition last year.

We find our workstation with a table placard with BENJAMIN FRANKLIN HIGH SCHOOL printed on it and immediately start to organize the equipment.

Percy and Mitch leave the setup to the rest of us. They head to the convention center's receiving area to sign for the robot, which we shipped to the event per instructions a couple weeks ago.

Anna and I move to one end of the table to set up the electronics. I will be the lead programmer for this event, and technically Mark is my backup, but we haven't had time to go over much. There's always some little thing that has to be adjusted on the fly, but there shouldn't be anything I can't handle. Anna is the lead driver. It's a role that a lot of people want to do. It's seen as the exciting job, steering and maneuvering the robot through the challenges using an Xbox controller. Anna and Mitch are evenly matched when it comes to driving, but Anna is a little better with timing on the pneumatic operations.

I power on the first laptop and pull up the code files. The date on the saved files is from two weeks ago. I know I've worked on it since then. Didn't I? My days kind of blur together, so maybe it has been that long since I've done any tweaking? At the last meeting we ran through the challenge and it worked okay, right?

I skim through the code, trying to see if anything stands out. It seems okay . . .

"Hey, Ben, can you help us?" Percy calls. They've arrived with the shipping box that houses the Lobster.

"Yep, just a second." I do a quick Wi-Fi test to see how strong the signal is. It's crazy how many teams run into problems with the communication between the CPU and controllers and the robot because the host's Wi-Fi can't handle the traffic. The signal strength looks good, so hopefully that won't be something we have to deal with today. First-match jitters are bad enough without spotty connectivity.

An hour later, the Lobster is unpacked, all of the bits and pieces have been examined and tested, and we're ready for the first match. As with most competitions, this one works on the idea of alliances. There will be two teams—red and blue—and each team is made up of three schools. A random drawing paired us with a brand-new team from Waukesha and an award-winning team from Green Bay.

"I can't believe we got stuck with the Waukesha school," Mo mutters as we take advantage of the thirty-minute break before the first round of competition begins. "They look terrified." He nods at the team in question.

I glance at the team with their black logoed polo shirts and brand-new equipment. Their toolbox, if we could call it that, is half the size of ours, and by most measures, we have little more than the bare-minimum requirements. "If we're going to win, they're going to need all of our help."

One of the cool things about the competition is that the alliance structure really reinforces teamwork—we only succeed if everyone around us succeeds. It also means it's less likely on any level that there will be sabotage.

We approach their booth to check up on them. I let Mo do most of the talking. He's outgoing and likes people for the most part.

Their team captain is a girl named Molly who reminds me of Mitch. She's tall, blond-haired, blue-eyed, and seems to talk in monosyllables. She watches us suspiciously at first, but as soon as we start strategizing our challenge, she lets us take a look at her design.

Like us, they went with a pneumatic approach. Instead of arms to do the lifting, they created a simple vacuum. Simple, yes, but really smart. Use the vacuum to pick up the puck, take it to the stack, center above it, then release.

"It's got such a compact frame," I say, examining it a little closer. "Have you run into any problems with melting around the compressor?"

Molly nods. "At first. It was a challenge to get the spacing right. I mean, we knew the heat generated by the compressor would be a problem going in, given the materials and constraints of the challenge, but we tested a few different materials and locations until we found the right balance. The fan mechanism is small but seems to get the job done. We've run the experiment several times and haven't had any problems."

"Great. Can't wait to see it in action," Mo says, giving it another look.

"See you out there," I say.

"I feel a little better," Mo says. "They're newbies, but they know what they're doing."

"We should have gone with a vacuum. Ours is more complicated, more intricate, but it's not like there's extra points for complexity."

"You're the one who came up with the lobster design."

"Yeah, I know. And I think it'll get the job done. It's a nice reminder, you know."

"Sure," he agrees, but I don't think he gets what I'm saying. I'm not entirely sure *I* get what I'm trying to say.

The thing is, Maxie was always the one to keep us on track,

pushing the KISS principle. Somehow, without her involvement, we forgot about the "Keep It Simple, Stupid" approach.

Today, everything reminds me of Maxie. Or, more precisely, everything reminds me that she's not here with us. This is the first time in almost ten years that Mo and I have been part of a robotics competition without her. It feels . . . wrong.

A quick stop at the Green Bay team's booth makes me feel a little better about our design. They have as many components as we do, maybe more. We take a peek at a handful of other teams before returning to our area.

"Ready?" asks Mr. Rose, who took the truck to the parking garage while we started setup.

"Ready!" the team shouts.

"All right, then, let's do this. Gear up."

There are three arena areas—spaces marked off by chain-link fencing and filled with an assortment of obstacles. Hockey pucks are scattered along one side of the space, with ramps, blockades, and a gap with a timed bridge that will connect every forty-five seconds. The six schools making up the two teams will compete in a six-minute timed match.

The Green Bay team, the Waukesha team, and our team make up the blue side. A little blue flag is attached to our robot. We, along with the other two schools of the blue team, line our robots up along the edges of our arena.

I crack my knuckles to loosen my fingers. I double-check the connectivity and make sure my backup files are accessible. Next to me, Anna runs through the commands on the controller, testing the movement of the Lobster. Her face is set in a mask of concentration. Every time she adjusts the joystick, her mouth pulls tighter.

"Is the server overloaded or something?" she asks me.

I barely hear her over the noise of the crowd. "No, why?" I run the connectivity test again to double-check.

"I've got some kind of lag. There's a delay or something in the actions."

Percy, who's been examining the arena through the fence, spins to face her. "*What?* What's wrong?"

"Not sure," Anna mutters, running through another sequence of maneuvers. Her eyes are fixed on the Lobster.

"We don't have time for this!"

"Duh," she says.

"Teams, to your starting positions." The announcer's booming voice carries over the noise of the crowd.

Anna steers the Lobster to the starting position. Percy, Mo, and I analyze every inch it covers. Nothing is obviously wrong, so it might be Anna's imagination. Her nerves getting the better of her. I don't say that, obviously, and I'm not sure I believe it, but better the unlikely than the unknown.

I go back to my computer. The rest of the team huddles around Anna, everyone holding their breath as we wait for the starting buzzer. I swear, the volume in the convention center dims even as the blood pressure rises.

The starting buzzer erupts, and the surrounding volume triples, maybe quadruples, before the sound of the buzzer fades away.

I keep one eye trained on the Lobster, the other on my computer monitor.

The Lobster reaches its first hockey puck. The arm extends, pincers open, only to close bare millimeters before coming into contact with the puck.

"Damn it, Anna, what was that?" Percy stands on his tiptoes to watch the action in the arena. "If you can't do this, give the controller to Mitch."

"It's not my fault," she grinds out between teeth clenched in concentration. She adjusts her hold on the joystick, repositioning the robot. She goes for the puck again, and again, misses it by the smallest of margins.

The five other robots, including the Waukesha team's modified vacuum, successfully pick up their pucks, and traverse the obstacles. The Green Bay team has already collected three hockey pucks, and we haven't been able to pick up the first one.

Mitch looms behind Anna. "Can you adjust for the timing? Play into the delay?"

"I'm trying."

"I think there's something wrong with the solenoid valve, or the interface," Mo says, crouched low, eyes trained on the Lobster's mechanisms. "The grab release and the extension aren't in sync."

Percy and Mo start arguing about PSI levels and spike relays, and my stomach takes a dive. Dread fills me as I skim my code, looking for the solenoid trigger commands.

The solenoid valves are used to direct the air pressure from one port to the next, which is what makes the different pieces of the mechanism move. If the code that triggers the solenoid valves is not correct, it affects the breadth and scope of the robot's movements. Which means, if the solenoid valves are involved, either the valves are faulty, or my code is off.

Last week, sandwiched between English essays and calculus homework, I'd been finalizing the code for the command modifications, ones specifically tied to the solenoid valves. Then my stupid, out-of-date, piece-of-crap computer initiated another random system update. I thought I saved the correct version of the code, but what if I didn't? What if I saved, and then transferred to the team's computers, the wrong code?

I stare on in horror as Anna and the Lobster make another grab for a hockey puck, and yet again, miss.

"Shit shit shit," I mutter, fingers clacking over my keyboard, eyes scrolling through the code on the screen.

There it is. That one simple line. The one that earlier looked just a little bit off. The one I supposedly "fixed" last week.

"It's my fault." My voice is quiet, not nearly loud enough to break through Percy and Mo's argument, let alone the sheer volume of the competition around me.

The roar of the crowd starts to fade, then grow louder, then dimmer. It's like the rush and rest of an ocean tide—and everything around me lurches to a stop. To our right, the Waukesha team is collecting their seventh puck. The Green Bay team collects their ninth. And us? We can only stand here and watch as our robot keeps moving from one puck to another, futilely reaching forward, pincers out, but incapable of doing their main function.

Another minute ticks down, the stacks of hockey pucks grow for all of the other teams, while we have yet to cross the arena. I swear I can feel the other teams staring at us, standing here arguing among ourselves and watching as the Lobster essentially does the hokey pokey, putting its right arm in, right arm out, then spinning all about.

"The coding is wrong," I say with a little more force.

"What," Anna says, no inflection in her tone, so it doesn't really sound like a question. Her hands tighten on the controller.

"I can fix it." I hope. God, I hope I can fix it quickly.

I think back to the day I'd been working on the final tweaks. I can picture my calculus textbook. And my essay. I can even picture the bottom corner of *What to Expect When You're Expecting*.

Around us, the crowd starts to chant the countdown to the end of the round.

One by one, my teammates turn to me.

Percy's red face looks hot enough to combust.

Anna's narrow-eyed stare sends shivers down my spine.

Mitch glowers at me, and I half expect the weight of his glare to crush me where I stand.

Mo's face is twisted with pure confusion.

". . . Three . . . two . . . one!" The countdown to the conclusion of the longest six minutes of my life comes to an end. The buzzer sounds, and everyone in the room bursts into cheers. Everyone, that is, except my robotics club, and the rest of the blue team. All three schools win or lose together. No matter how well they did, it won't be enough to cover for the zero pucks we collected. It will take some kind of miracle for us to take home one of the first-place trophies. Sure, we have nine more rounds to go, and even if—no, not if, when—I fix my coding mistake, we'll need one of the other schools or teams to bomb. I calculate the numbers in my head . . . the best we can hope for at this point—again, barring some kind of miracle—would be third place.

The thing is, I'm pretty sure I'm all out of miracles.

Third place is nice, but it may not be enough to save the team.

I can't believe I made such a stupid mistake. I should have checked the code again after my computer finished whatever random program updates it decided to install. I've never screwed up this big before.

"What the hell happened?" Mo hisses at me as we make our way back to our assigned workstation.

I don't take the time to explain exactly what happened. "I saved the wrong version of the code."

"Can you fix it?" he asks. I'm sure he has more questions—like *how* and *why*—but in the end, it doesn't matter.

"Yeah."

"In time?"

That's a harder answer. "I think so."

Mo grabs my arm, halting my progress. Other people are forced to move around us, but I don't think Mo notices, or cares.

"Don't think, just do it."

Percy doesn't give me any time to get my laptop settled onto our table before grilling me.

"Who was supposed to double-check your work?"

It's a fair question. All roles are supposed to have backup, and every step of the process is supposed to be reviewed by someone else.

I shrug. "Mark's my backup, but he's still . . ." I let my words trail off. It's not fair to bring Mark into this. He's a decent programmer, but we all know he's not yet qualified to validate my work. Before that, well, before that, Maxie would have been the only one we'd trust to double-check my code.

"It doesn't matter now," Mr. Rose says, walking over. His expression tells me he saw our—my—complete failure. "Let's fix it and move on." He looks at me. "Do you know what needs to be adjusted?"

I nod. "I think so."

"Okay." He checks the display on his watch. "Next round is in fifteen minutes. See if you can get it working by then."

I bury myself into the code, ignoring everyone else around me. If I did it before, I can do it again.

A small, insidious voice in the back of my head whispers that if Maxie were still on the team, we wouldn't have made colossal fools of ourselves.

CHAPTER 12

I wave at Mo and his parents as they drive off. My head buzzes and my eyes hurt from squinting at code all day. The fifth-place trophy that will be added to our display at school isn't as satisfying as it should be. If we're going to save the team for next year, we need to do better than fifth place. It doesn't help that I think we'd have gotten at least second place if Maxie had been there. I shoulder the door open and stop.

"James again?" Roger asks. He's in the kitchen, so I can't see him, and even though he doesn't speak loudly, the words carry through our small house. The question could have been casual or mildly curious, but Roger's tone says otherwise.

Mom must notice the weariness in his voice too. "Yes," she says carefully. I hear the scrape of chair legs against the linoleum-covered floor and I picture Mom settling into one of the kitchen chairs.

"You've been talking to him a lot lately," Roger says.

"Well, yes," Mom says. "He's been helping Ben with the baby thing."

Baby thing? Is that what she calls this? The disappointment from the competition fades under the suffocating tension in the house.

"And that requires daily conversations?"

If there was an ounce of anger or aggression in his tone, I would step in, do something to break up the tension building between them. But he doesn't sound mad. I know I'm not always the best at deciphering the more subtle emotions, but he sounds so beaten down, I can't mistake it for anything else.

"We're working out the details—"

Roger snorts. "Wrong. *You're* working out the details. James is working out how to get you back."

My eyes widen. I let my backpack slip to the carpet at my feet, careful to make as little noise as possible. This feels like something I shouldn't be listening to, but I don't know how to avoid it without drawing attention to myself. Another part of me doesn't want to miss a word. I hold my breath as Mom makes a disbelieving noise in the back of her throat. "No, he's not."

"He made it a point to tell you he'd split with his wife."

"That's not . . . it doesn't mean anything. He was catching me up on his life."

"Right."

"What do you want from me, Roger? I need James. *Ben* needs James. We need a family lawyer working with us, and he's a damn good one. And, frankly, we can't afford to hire someone else. We can't afford to turn away free qualified legal representation. I'm not willing to lose that connection simply because it makes you uncomfortable. You're being unreasonable."

"I'm not asking you to cut ties with the man. I'm just tired of tripping over him."

The room grows silent. I count to twenty, waiting for some kind of sign that it's safe to head to my room. A second later, though, Roger speaks. "I'm worried. I'm worried about you. And I'm worried about what this situation is doing to our family."

Situation. It's a vague word. One that assumes all parties to the conversation are on the same page as to what the *situation* is. I don't think I'm on that page. What situation is he talking about? The baby or Mom's frequent conversations with James?

A weird hollow feeling settles into my stomach. Mom and Roger are fighting about me. Sure, technically they're fighting about James, but for once the subtext seems glaringly obvious to me.

I've always thought Mom's relationships end because she chooses men who need to be fixed, and when they are fully functioning again, they no longer need her. A kind of give-and-take thing that balances her need to nurture and fix and their need to be fixed. But what if that isn't it? What if it's been my fault all along? Not my dad, of course, but the others. What if I was too much? What if Mom had to spend so much time and energy on me that James and Paolo had gotten tired of it and decided to cut their losses? Is that what's happening now with Roger?

"I'm a mom first and foremost, Roger. I've made that clear from the very beginning. There are times when what Ben needs will be the priority."

"I know Ben has to be your priority. I've known from the start that you're a package deal. I don't resent that."

"That's what it sounds like."

"Damn it, Eliza. Look, I don't think it's unreasonable to ask that we make time to do things together, the three of us. And we need to do things as a couple, as you and me. Things that don't revolve around Ben's baby."

"The baby's a pretty big deal. I'm not sure what you expect me to do. Bury my head in the sand and pretend everything is okay?"

"That's not fair. I'm worried, Eliza. Things are changing. A lot. I hadn't planned on playing grandpa quite so soon in our marriage, but I'm not afraid of that. I am afraid of what this is going to do to you, though, and to him."

"We'll be fine. We'll get through this like we've gotten through everything else."

There's another long pause. This one seems to take all the oxygen out of the room. I hold my breath, though I'm not sure why.

"Together. You and Ben, right?"

Mom doesn't answer right away.

"Right. Is there even room for me in your *together*?"

Mom doesn't say anything and I can hear Roger's sigh from the hallway. "I get that it's been the two of you for a long time. But I'm here now. I love you and want to be part of your family. I hope one of these days Ben will let me get to know him better, and that we'll build a solid relationship. I know that will take time, and I'm going to keep trying. There's a lot going on, and the situation with the baby has to be a priority, but, Eliza, our marriage needs to be a priority too."

I hold my breath and listen as Roger's footsteps bring him toward the living room. Shit. I'm going to be caught eavesdropping. At the last second, I open the outside door and slam it shut again as Roger crosses the threshold.

"Hey," he says warmly, as if he hadn't just had a serious conversation with my mom. "How'd you guys do?"

"Oh, um . . ." I rack my brain, trying to switch gears from family drama to robotics. "Fifth place."

"That's fantastic." He hurries to me and claps me on the back. "Well done."

"Eh, it's not awful. Should have been better. I messed up thanks to my piece-of-crap, out-of-date computer. We figured it out, but not soon enough."

He shakes his head, still smiling like he's happy for our mediocre finish. "Don't be so hard on yourself. We should celebrate. Let's order pizza for dinner and you can tell us all about it."

I agree, because what else can I do?

CHAPTER 13

Gio is late.

I lurk below the flagpole at the side entrance of the school, feeling like a trespasser. Usually Gio is waiting for me at the curb, but with him MIA, I feel awkward and out of place. One more reason, if I need one, to dedicate some time to getting my license. Not that I can afford a car and everything that goes with driving, but this being stuck at the whim of others is a pain in the ass.

I check the display on my phone. There are no messages, but the clock ticks down another minute. It's 3:21 and Gio and I always meet at a quarter after.

A black car pulls up to the curb and I do a quick check to see if it's Gio. It's not. Gio drives a Toyota of some kind, and this car is . . . something else. Clearly my car knowledge needs some work.

Where is he?

I glance at my phone again. It's 3:23. When I look up, I catch a glimpse of forest-green wool—the same bulky sweater Maxie wore in calculus today. It's too warm outside for wool sweaters, but

Maxie doesn't seem to notice. Her face is pale and her curly hair is frizzier than usual, and her posture tells me she is 100 percent aware of my position thirty feet away from her. It's also obvious to anyone who knows her—and despite everything, I do still know her—that she's hoping I don't notice her.

Even though I'd promised Percy to talk to her weeks ago, she's done a good job avoiding me. And, to be honest, I didn't try too hard to connect. Mom warned me to not put any pressure on her, right? But maybe it's about time I reach out. I take a deep breath, letting the fall air fortify me, then walk toward her. Her shoulders stiffen, but she doesn't walk away. It's better than nothing.

"Hey," I say when I reach her. Not the most creative opening, but the awkwardness is probably unavoidable. Unavoidable, but totally our new normal. I haven't figured out how to put us back to the way we were.

"Hey," she says.

Silence.

When she moved to Milwaukee when we were eight, she'd walked straight up to Mo and me and announced that the girls Mrs. Spinelli had her sitting with were boring because they only talked about silly things. Since Mo and I had long decided the same, we nodded. Then she proceeded to tell us that the coding game Mo was showing me was okay, but the Python version was better than the Java version, and that her mom told her she could join the local Lego robotics league, and had we heard of it. All of this in one long sentence during which she'd barely taken a breath. We'd never been awkward, not even from the very beginning.

"This is awkward," I say.

Her whole body relaxes. "I know." She releases a gusty sigh. "It's ridiculous. We're being ridiculous."

I stand next to her, both of us facing ahead, not looking at each other. "Yeah," I agree. "We'll get over it eventually, right?"

She shrugs. "I hope so."

More silence.

"So," I say.

"So," she says.

"How's the social experiment going?" Okay, small talk. Not ideal but a good start, right?

She narrows her eyes at me. "Really, Ben?"

"Really what?" I ask. "Is it not going well? Are you still dissecting virginity as a social construct, or have you moved on to one of the other social constructs on your list, like gender, or sexuality?"

"I can't believe you." Her arms cross over her chest.

Clearly I'm missing something. "I'm just trying to show an interest in what you're working on since you haven't been going to robotics lately. I don't know why you sound so exasperated."

"You don't know why I'm exasperated? Seriously, Ben?"

"No. I mean, I get that I don't understand all of what you're looking for, but what you said about virginity made a lot of sense to me—" Oh, crap. I cringe and look toward my feet. "Oh, yeah. I get it now."

She snorts but doesn't say anything. Once again, awkward silence falls around us. I should leave her alone before I make things worse. But part of me missed hanging out with her, and the team does expect me to reach out to her.

So I try again. "We really could have used you last weekend."

She clears her throat. "Yeah. I heard. But fifth place is pretty good."

I snort. "It's barely a ranking. Definitely not good enough, not if we're going to save the team. I just don't get why you quit."

"It was going to happen eventually, so there was no need to put it off."

"But why?"

Her gaze darts to a huddle of soccer players several feet away. They seem intent on their conversation, so she finally meets my eyes. "Because I'm pregnant, Ben, and I'm going to be a little too busy to worry about the team. I'm going to have to worry about keeping up with my classes and making up my work when . . . *after*."

This doesn't make sense to me. "Why?"

Maxie sputters at me. "*Why?* Ben, I'm going to give birth. I'm going to be tired and fat, and that's before the delivery. It could take weeks—*weeks*—after delivery for me to be recovered enough to go to school, let alone worry about a *club*."

"Oh." That actually makes a lot of sense. "But why drop out now? The baby isn't due until"—I stop to do some quick mental math—"May."

A couple of the soccer players move away from the group. I keep my eye on them in case they get too close.

Maxie plants her hands on her hips and spins toward me, more like the Maxie I've known since fourth grade. "I don't have time, Ben. I've got pregnancy and childbirth classes to take—"

"I'm taking them too," I interject.

"—meetings and strategizing so that I don't fall behind in school, and interviews with prospective adoptive parents—"

"*What?*"

"—so, yeah, I don't have time for robotics anymore."

Soccer players forgotten, I grab her arm so she can't turn away from me. "No, seriously, Max. What interviews?"

She sighs, her face softening into what looks like pity. "Ben—"

I shake my head. My fingertips tingle and my head feels full of static, a rushing, pulsing white noise that makes it hard to focus. "But, Maxie—"

"My parents said—"

I force my mouth open. Close it. Lick my lips. Words. I need words. I clear my throat, pushing past the panic filling my brain. "It's my baby too, Maxie!"

A choked sound pulls my attention from Maxie. I look over my shoulder. Son of a bitch. My heart stops. My brain freezes. I'm so screwed. One hundred percent, all-in, screwed. Someone overhearing our conversation and coming to the right conclusion would be bad enough. But this is Peter Owens. He gapes at us, eyes taking in everything from my pleading posture to Maxie's frumpy sweater. Something I can only describe as glee brightens his face.

Peter and I, we're not friends, but he's not a dick. However, we've been in the same homeroom for six years, and I know there are two things Peter gets excited about: soccer and gossip. There are no secrets when it comes to him.

Asking him to keep his mouth shut on this is probably a futile wish, but I have to try. I'm hoping to have more time before anyone has to find out about Maxie, the baby, and me. "Peter—"

"But, dude, aren't you gay?"

"I—"

Maxie's face pales, and she seems to be looking at me to say something. She should know better. "I—"

Peter shakes his shaggy head, grinning like he's just personally scored the winning goal at the state soccer tournament. "Dude, way to go." He offers me a fist, like I'm supposed to do some fist bump. When I don't follow through, he shakes his head again, hitching his backpack into place before jogging off.

"*Excuse me?*" Maxie glares at the retreating figure. She shakes her head. "Neanderthal."

Before I can say anything in response—not that I have the words—a horn honks. "Shake a leg, Benji. We're gonna be late." Gio. I ignore him. I need to do something about this. About all of this. About the adoption. About Peter. If only my stupid brain-to-mouth functionality would engage.

Another honk.

And with that, my focus shatters and the hard-to-find words evaporate.

"Please, Maxie." I don't know exactly what I'm asking her for. Forgiveness for Peter's discovery? For a chance to talk, to plead my case for custody? A chance to beg her not to make any decisions yet?

She turns away from me, biting her lip.

The problem with knowing someone for years? She knows exactly what I am trying to say. And I know it won't make any difference.

I've been outed. So to speak. It's only a matter of time before the whole school hears, thanks to Peter's big mouth. *Why did it have to be Peter?*

I want Mom. No, I need her. I need her to help me figure out what to do next. I need her to help me convince Maxie not to go through with any stupid adoption plans. I need her to help me convince Peter to keep his mouth shut.

I race to the staff restroom when we arrive at Greco's. Instead of changing into my busser's uniform, I lock the stall and call Mom.

"Mom?" I hate the way my voice cracks when she answers.

"What's wrong, Benny? Are you okay?"

I skip over the Peter thing. I only have a couple of minutes before my shift starts, and I need to focus on the bigger issue at hand. "Maxie and the Jacobsons are going to be interviewing potential adoptive families."

She sighs. "We knew from the beginning that adoption was their plan."

"But we told them—"

"We did, but they're going to continue pursuing that option until anything is finalized."

"But why?"

"Ben, everything is still up to them. We will continue to push, but ultimately, it's Maxie's decision. You need to be prepared for that."

"What else do we need to do? How do we stop them?" My knuckles ache from the force of my grip on my phone.

"I'll call James," she says.

CHAPTER 14

Roger picks me up after work that night. "Where's Mom?" I ask as I drop my backpack into the back seat of his Escape.

His lips tighten before he says, "James stopped by. He had some info for her. And for you, I guess." His voice reminds me of the scene I eavesdropped on the other day.

I check the time on the dash. I know she said she would call him, but I didn't think she'd be able to arrange a meeting so soon. "At this time of night?" Nine thirty isn't exactly the middle of the night, but it's definitely late enough to assume company would be on their way out the door.

"Apparently."

"Why? Did something else happen?" My hands seize on the seat belt at the sudden thought. What if the late hours mean more bad news? Late-night in-person legal advice seems highly indicative of . . . something.

"Oh, no. Nothing like that!" Roger rushes to assure me. He reaches out, and for a second, I think he's going to pat my shoulder or something. But he pulls his hand back before he makes contact. He flexes his fingers on the steering wheel. "I'm sure it's a timing thing. Probably they couldn't figure out a different time to meet."

"Oh, okay." But if it isn't serious, why can't they talk on the phone or over email like they have been the last few weeks?

He sighs and drops the topic. Several weighty minutes later, we pull into the driveway. A shiny silver sedan is parked on the street in front of our house. It's fancier than we usually see in this neighborhood, so I guess James is still inside.

The sound of Mom's giggle and James's deeper chuckle greet us as I open the front door. I can't imagine what about this situation is so entertaining. Roger slides past me to head into the living room. His jaw tics, but he doesn't say anything.

The giggles stop. The squeak of the chair leg scraping along linoleum, then Mom peeks past the entrance to the kitchen. "Hey, Ben, how was work?"

Since I've been distracted by Maxie's news, I barely remember anything that's happened.

"Fine. I only broke two glasses," I say.

"I guess that's some improvement." Her statement feels more like a question.

"Why's James here?" I blurt out.

She deflates. "You should come into the kitchen."

Uh-oh. Kitchen means action plans. They've been plotting.

I drop my backpack against the wall, then turn into the room.

James stands up, coming around the table to greet me. "Oh, wow, Ben. Look at you. I can't believe how old you've gotten."

Did he expect me to be the same seven-year-old he saw last? That would be weird, especially since he's helping me get custody of a child of my own.

"Hey."

"Really, Ben, it's good to see you." He claps me on the back.

Nine years have added a little silver to his blond hair, but other than that he still looks as polished and put together as I remember him. Even though it's after nine thirty at night, he's wearing a slate gray suit and shiny, pointy shoes. A royal blue tie trails out from a pocket, and the top button of his pale blue shirt is left undone. The shirt color matches his eyes, almost perfectly. Is it a coincidence?

I don't think much is a coincidence when it comes to James.

"Yeah, you too." I pull out a chair and sit on the edge.

Mom takes her seat too. I know it's hers because there's a cup of tea next to a thick notebook full of her loopy handwriting. The seat next to hers—why next to her instead of across from her?—is clearly James's, with the slim laptop and stack of files.

I nod at the different stacks. "So, can we stop Maxie from putting the baby up for adoption?"

James settles onto his chair. "Well, as to that, it's something we're working on. Essentially, the law is not in our favor. I can file a couple of appeals if it comes down to it, but in this state, the mother of the child has complete autonomy regarding decisions around her pregnancy and the child's birth. Until paternity is established—and it would take a lot to convince a judge to mandate a paternity test prior to the baby's birth—it's Maxie's call. Even after the child is born, and even if paternity is established, there's no guarantee that a judge will give you custody."

"Because of my age?" I chew on my lip.

"Not entirely. Even adult men fighting for custody have an uphill battle if the mother doesn't agree. Once the baby is born, we can submit a letter of parentage—basically, a legal statement that you are claiming paternity of the baby. If Maxie disputes it, that's when we'll be able to request the courts order a genetic test to confirm. That's all pretty standard. It's after that when your age becomes a factor. If you were a legal adult, claiming and proving paternity through genetic testing would be enough to halt that adoption. But since you are a minor, Maxie and her family could get the courts involved. All they have to do is prove that you are not capable of legal parenthood. I'm not going to lie. It will be nearly impossible to prove that a sixteen-year-old boy is a better choice for a baby than an adult couple."

I force myself to take deep, even breaths, even though my lungs are seizing. "What does that mean?"

He leans back in his chair. "It all depends on the Jacobsons. They could tie us up in court appearances and appeals, investigations, and social services visits for a long time, with no guarantee that we'll see the result we want. The better option is to convince Maxie and the Jacobsons to come to terms on a custody arrangement."

Mom covers my hand. I don't notice until then that I'm clenching my fist hard enough to whiten my knuckles and make veins bulge in my wrist.

I close my eyes and count to five. When I'm done, I blink up at James. "So we have to wait until May and hope Maxie's parents see reason? I know you said that Maxie has all the say in this, but her parents are definitely the ones calling the shots."

"I'd agree," Mom says.

"Well, yes and no," he says.

I half wonder if wishy-washy answers are a lawyer thing. James hasn't said anything particularly definitive since we sat down at the table. It was all *yes and no* and *not entirely.* CYA, lawyer style.

"There are a lot of things you can be doing between now and then to help. If it goes to the courts, we need to have evidence that you will be able to raise a baby. You can put together a parenting plan and a financial plan. The parenting classes you're signed up for will be critical. Start thinking about how you intend to care for a baby while in school, and think about your post-graduation plans. Do you plan on continuing school?"

"Of course!" I nearly roll my eyes. University has always been the plan. "Mo and I are looking at MIT." Then, thinking about the tuition cost, "Maybe University of Michigan or even Northwestern. Those are closer, at least."

Mom and James share a look I can't decipher. It's not a happy look, that's for sure.

"Benny," Mom says gently, "you may have to lower your expectations a bit."

"You don't think I can get into those schools?" I've done my research, and I'm certain my grades qualify. And the robotics club will definitely help too.

The thin lines branching off from her eyes deepen, and she suddenly looks older, more weary than I'm used to. "It's not that. These schools are expensive, and challenging, and two months ago I'd have been cheering you on all the way to Massachusetts. But it will be incredibly difficult to raise a child, tackle an ambitious academic program, and live so far from home all at the same time."

"If you stay local," James says, his somber tone matching Mom's, "you have a support network—people to help you out. If you move away, you lose that. You're going to need a solid, *practical* plan to present to the courts."

My thoughts grind and churn like unaligned gears—jerky and slow, and a little painful. "Are you saying if I keep the baby I can't go to college?"

"No, not at all." Mom scoots her chair closer to me, then cups my face between her hands. "But *raising a child* is a twenty-four-seven job, Ben. It's a lot of work, and it's erratic, never-ending, and all-consuming. You may want to look at MSOE or part-time options that can give you more flexibility. And you'll need a job—probably full time with benefits—so a flexible school schedule is going to be important."

I'm paralyzed in my seat. It feels like my brains and my skin and my bones are melting into a noxious sludge, settling sickly in my belly. For a second, I think I'm going to puke, which, given the paralysis, would be a very bad thing.

Mom traces the edge of her thumb along my cheekbone. "Breathe, Ben."

I suck in some air. It helps a little bit with the nausea, so I suck in some more. After I've repeated the inhale/exhale exercise a few times, I focus back on Mom and James. "That's a lot to process. I'll . . . I'll have to think about it."

Mom searches my face, for what, I don't know. Finally, she nods. "Good. Now, the other thing we think you should do in the meantime is stay involved in the process with Maxie."

I scrunch my brow. "How so? You've already got me attending birthing classes with her in a couple of months. I've been doing some research on prenatal meal planning, and I have some ideas for her—"

James chuckles. "Do yourself a favor and keep your meal planning ideas to yourself."

"Goodness, Ben, the last thing a pregnant woman wants is some well-meaning man, especially someone your age, telling them what they should or should not eat. Let her doctor be the bearer of that particular message."

"But—"

"Trust me." She leans back in her chair, the heavy tension of a minute ago waning. "And, yes, the birthing classes will help. But you should also offer to go to any appointments she'll let you tag along on. Show you're interested in her and the baby's health. And—and this is a hard one, Ben—you should attend the interviews with the potential adoptive parents."

The words in my Modern American History text start to twist and dance on the page. The display on my alarm clock tells me it's creeping on to one in the morning. I still have eight pages to read and two essay questions to answer. And even though it's not due until next week, I really should get a head start on my analysis paper discussing literary feminism in "The Wife of Bath's Prologue."

The clock flashes and the display shifts from 12:54 to 12:55.

Might be exhaustion or stress. Or even the trauma of Maxie's announcement compounded by Peter's discovery. Either way, I can't seem to concentrate on the interwar period between the World Wars. Or maybe it's what Mom and James want me to do.

They can't really expect me to actively participate in the Jacobsons' plans to put the baby up for adoption. But, yeah, they really do.

Mom: "It will show the Jacobsons that you care about the future of the baby and are at least willing to consider that adoption might be the best approach."

James: "It will show the *courts* that you explored adoption as an option, and it will demonstrate a commitment to the process, which could prevent the Jacobsons from fighting your bid for custody. It could also show the courts that you're fully invested in your child's future, whatever happens."

Mom: "And things might change. You might change your mind. Wouldn't it be better to have a hand in the decision-making process?"

That. Mom and James can give me all the excuses in the world, but that last one is the real reason they're pushing this. They think there's a chance that I'll change my mind. Do they really think I'll be more okay with strangers raising the baby because I got to ask them a handful of inane questions?

James: "Ben, don't lose sight of the significant likelihood that the courts will not rule in your favor if it comes to adjudication. This way you have the opportunity to have your say in the final decision."

There it is. The final straw. Nothing else he or Mom could say would make me agree to their ridiculous plan. But if there's a chance that despite my best efforts and planning that someone will say the child cannot be with me, then yes, I want to make sure he or she has the best possible future.

Blinking dry eyes, I realize I haven't absorbed any of the last three paragraphs I've "read." I scrub the heels of my hands over my forehead, clearing away the distraction.

Eight more pages, then bed.

Everything else, including the Wife of Bath, Maxie, and Peter's revelation, will have to wait until tomorrow.

CHAPTER 15

We had a pop quiz in history class. I'm pretty sure I failed it.

The worst part is, my failure has nothing to do with not knowing the information and everything to do with my new infamy.

Eyes follow every step I take. Whispered conversations happen behind cupped hands. Not-whispered conversations happen in front of me. If I were a hashtag, I'd be trending right now: #babydaddy.

Damn Peter and his big mouth. I expected it, sure, but I don't think there would have been any way to truly prepare for how invasive everyone's curiosity would feel.

I find Mo at our regular table in the lunchroom after fourth period. I plop onto the bench across from him and can't quite meet his eyes. I don't need to ask if he's heard the rumors. The answer is obvious by the thin line of his mouth, and the curiously neutral expression on his face. I take my time digging through my lunch bag before pulling out my basic PB&J. I take my time separating the seal of the Ziploc sandwich bag. I take my time, knowing even as I do, that it won't put off the conversation I'm about to have. I look up from my sandwich to find Mo watching me, still without a definable expression. I take an unnecessarily large bite of peanut butter and strawberry jelly, which renders me mostly mute. At least for a minute.

"Are you really not going to talk about this?" His veggie wrap and dish of fresh fruit sit untouched in front of him.

I chew, but can't quite swallow past the sticky, clogging goop in my mouth.

Mo nudges his unopened bottle of unsweetened apple juice at me. I ignore it.

I need the time that struggling past the peanut butter is giving me. I've worried for weeks about how Mo would take the news. How he would take me lying to him. But during all that worry, I didn't come up with the words to lay my truth out for him.

He waits, and watches.

The food in my mouth takes on an unpleasant consistency, so I can't put it off any longer. I swallow, then sigh. "I guess I don't know what to say."

"First, you could say if it's true."

"It?" I ask.

Mo levels an angry glare on me. He can be intense sometimes. This is the first time this particular look has been aimed at me. He answers me anyway, even though we both know he doesn't have to. "Is Maxie pregnant?"

The single bite of sandwich I've taken churns in my stomach. "Yeah."

He waits.

I wait.

He narrows his eyes at me. "And you're the father?"

"Yeah." I fist my hands in my lap to hide their trembling.

"And?"

I groan, falling forward to bang my head against the table. I barely miss my partially eaten sandwich. "Just tell me what you want to know."

"Everything!"

I jerk upright. Kids at nearby tables gape at us. Holy shit. Mo yelled. At me. He never yells. Not like that.

He shakes his head, then lowers his voice. "I want to know everything. What the hell is going on? How long have you known? Why didn't you tell me about this? What are you guys doing about it?"

The answers he's looking for are playing hide-and-seek in my head. I know what they are, and I know they're there, but I can't get a single one of them to come out of my mouth. I lick my lips. I open my mouth. Nothing.

Mo sighs, then rubs his eyes. "Come on, Ben. Since when do you keep secrets from me?"

Words build and swell in my chest, they throb in my head, but still, nothing escapes my mouth.

My heart beats fast and hard behind my ribs, and I seriously think I'm going to hurl. My hands shake and chills make goose bumps prickle over my skin.

But still, no words.

Mo waits, jaw tense.

And still, no words.

Finally, he stands up, face twisting in a smile that lacks all warmth and humor. He shoves his lunch back into the insulated bag he brought. "You know what? Screw this. Screw you. I thought we were friends, but I guess that means something different to you."

I want to reach out, to stop him. To explain. But I can't force the words past my constricted throat.

He steps away from the table and, with a last angry look at me, stomps out of the cafeteria.

I feel every single eye in the room burning through my body. I itch and burn, and my skin crawls. The rippling sensation climbs from my toes to my calves, over my knees, past my thighs. Then it stabs me deep in my gut, and I really am going to throw up. I trip over the bench, losing precious time. I need to go. I need to run before I vomit in front of the whole school.

I make it only as far as the trash can near the entrance before tossing up the one bite of sandwich I ate, along with half my internal organs. My throat burns, and my eyes water. A second later, another spasm hits me, and I'm bent over the garbage again.

When the worst of the heaving calms, I suck in a breath. The entire cafeteria is silent.

A hand lands on my shoulder. I assume it's a teacher. But it's not a teacher who says, "Hey, Ben, you okay?" in a gentle voice. No, not a teacher. Gio.

Then another voice, harsher and shrill: "I didn't know dudes got morning sickness too."

I choke back a sob and tear free of Gio's touch.

Then I run.

Five minutes later, I sit huddled on the bathroom floor, back against the tiled wall, my face pressed into my knees. The tears have stopped, but my breathing is still choppy and rough.

Isn't he gay?

I didn't know dudes got morning sickness.

#babydaddy
How does that work?
I flinch at each remembered whisper and comment.

Someone knocks on the door. Nobody knocks on school bathroom doors. Somebody clearly knows I'm in here and is looking for me. If I stay quiet, maybe they'll go away.

"Ben? Are you okay?"

Shit, Gio. Again. Better than a teacher, I guess, but still humiliating. "Go away," I shout, but my voice lacks conviction. I try again. "I'm fine. Just . . . just leave me alone."

After a long moment, he says, "I'm coming in."

Since the door can't lock from the inside, there's nothing I can do to stop him. I give it one last attempt. "Really, I'm fine."

The door eases open, and Gio pokes his head around. He eyes my position halfway between a rust-stained sink and an occasionally malfunctioning hand dryer.

"The bathrooms in the science wing are definitely not as gross as the ones by the gym, but I can't help but think sitting on the floor is still a bad idea." He reaches into a stall and pulls out a handful of toilet paper. He examines the floor closely before sliding down next to me. The limited space means our shoulders brush and our elbows cross the invisible line of personal space between us.

I scooch a bit to the left, but don't get far before coming up against the sink.

He passes the handful of tissue to me. I stare at the wad of paper blankly for a second, before remembering the tears, snot, and probably traces of vomit dripping down my face. I scrub my cheeks and around my mouth, unable to look at Gio.

We sit there for a few minutes, silent. I like that Gio doesn't ask me if I'm okay again. I like that he doesn't ask for any explanations or offer any advice. He's just there. And it's nice. Comforting, even. Eventually my breathing and heart rate slow, and my brain comes back online.

I let out a long breath, and then run my fingers through my hair. Before the humiliation kicks in that Gio is seeing me at my worst — *again* — and before I can offer up any kind of apology, Gio jumps up, offers me a hand, and says, "I think we need to get out of here."

I squint at him. Maybe my brain is still scrambled from the lunchroom drama. "What?"

He rolls his eyes, but his smile is gentle. "Let's get out of here. We'll go for a drive, or get some fresh air."

"But lunch period is almost over."

"And?"

"What, skip school?"

He arches an eyebrow, his dimples deepening with his grin. "You ever ditch class, Benji?"

"Of course not!" I should be outraged at the idea, but I can't ignore the little rebellious thrill that runs through me. I can't. Can I? "Won't we get into trouble?"

He shrugs. "Maybe. But what could they do? Call your mom? It's not like you make a habit of skipping. And you're not failing any classes, right?"

I think briefly about the half-assed homework I've been turning in. Failing? No, but definitely not working to my usual standards.

"C'mon. You need to get out of here, and I don't think missing a couple of classes will hurt." He waggles his offered hand at me.

CHAPTER 16

We sneak out a side entrance facing the student parking lot. Because students can technically go off campus for lunch, no one would have a reason to stop us. But afternoon classes start in less than ten minutes, and with the extra scrutiny I'm glad to stay under the radar.

It takes me a while to figure out where Gio's taking me. We head toward the lake, following East Wisconsin Street, and it's not until I see the yellow structure on the horizon that I get an inkling. He pulls into the familiar parking lot of the Betty Brinn Museum.

"Really?" I ask, turning to him. It's the first word I've spoken since we left school. The silence hasn't been awkward or uncomfortable. In fact, his quiet support steadies me. But I can't let this pass. "The children's museum?"

"We're not going into the museum," he assures me. "Though, I remember you used to enjoy your time here."

"Yeah, when I was seven."

"We're never too old for Science City or Be a Maker space. But today, we're heading to the walking paths along the shore. I always find the *shush* of lapping water soothing. Something tells me you need that right now."

My shoulders tense at the reminder.

He reaches over and pats my knee. I still, the contact as steadying as the quiet was. "Don't overthink it."

He turns the key in the ignition, killing the engine. Pocketing the keys, he opens the door before looking at me. No demands, no prodding, but I pick up on the challenge and expectation anyway. Or maybe it's in my head. Either way, I slide out of the car and face him over the hood.

It's cold this close to the lake. December has come in with gray skies and biting winds, and here by the lake, the cold, moist air seeps through my skin and into my bones. I tug my coat's zipper up to my chin and tuck my hands deep into the pockets. We walk in silence as we make our way to the jogging paths along the lakeshore.

Being the middle of the day, the trails are mostly empty. There's an older man with an ancient bulldog shuffling ahead of us, but other than that, we have the place to ourselves.

"So, let's talk about what's going on," Gio says.

I duck my head. I tell myself it's to avoid the cold breeze. "I'd rather not."

"I get that."

I sigh, but my relief is short-lived.

"But, Ben, you've got to talk to someone. Things are clearly eating at you, and if you don't talk to someone . . ."

Damn it. Him and Mom, two freaking peas in a pod. "Why do people think that talking about things makes them better? I mean, it won't change anything. Talking to you or talking to my mom won't make Maxie less pregnant and won't change the score on my last calculus quiz."

"No," he agrees. "But it might make you feel better, or you might get a different perspective on things. Sometimes pushing the anger and fear out into the universe rather than internalizing it might make it easier for you to breathe."

Doesn't that sound mystical and new-agey or some shit. "Pushing my anger into the universe?"

"Why not? It definitely won't hurt anything."

I grunt. I'm not sure that's a selling point.

We walk for a few more minutes. Every now and then Gio bends down to pick up a loose rock.

"Mo's really mad at me." The words come out, almost without my permission.

"Why?"

I like that Gio doesn't automatically try to reassure me.

"I didn't tell him about the baby."

Gio makes a noncommittal sound in the back of his throat. He doesn't look at me, which is oddly helpful.

"I mean, I guess I get it. I pretty much tell him everything. This is the first time I've kept anything from him."

Gio scoops up another rock, adding it to the collection in his pocket.

My words, which at first come out slowly, almost hesitantly, start to tumble out. "I thought he'd be on my side. I mean, we've been friends forever. He should support me, not attack me. Everyone at school is talking about me. Everyone. About the gay kid that got some girl pregnant. They examine me like I'm some kind of new alien technology and they're trying to figure out how I work. They don't talk *to* me. They don't say anything directly to *me*. They talk about me *in front of me*, like I'm some kind of inanimate object that can't understand spoken language."

My footsteps keep pace with my words until I'm nearly speed-walking. Gio matches me step for step.

"I'm not a fucking science experiment!"

I stumble to a halt, nearly tripping over my feet as my shout echoes around us. Gio catches my arm, steadying me.

"Doesn't that feel better?"

I don't know if it does. I'm a little light-headed, more than a little shaky, and a lot nauseated. Like the crash after an adrenaline rush.

The winter air stings my cheeks. I swipe the back of my hand across my face, shocked by the wetness. Great. More tears. I turn to face the lake. I need a moment to pull myself together.

Gio holds a rock toward me. "Here."

I blink down at the rock that is roughly the size of a chicken nugget in his hand. "Huh?"

He presses the rock to my palm then wraps my fingers around it. Nodding to the lake, he says, "Throw it."

My brain struggles to make sense of his order.

He blows out an amused breath. Grabbing another stone from his bulging pocket, he holds it up, then hurls it into the murky water. "Throw it."

"But why?"

He shakes his head. "It'll make you feel better. I promise."

I squint at him, trying to decide if he's making fun of me.

He cups both of his hands around my hand holding the rock. "Seriously, Ben. It's a safe way to unload the aggression and anxiety. Gets endorphins going and doesn't hurt anyone. Whenever my emotions get going and frustration or anger builds and I don't have anyone to vent to, I find something to throw. In the winter it's usually snowballs. I'll stand outside and throw snowballs at a brick wall. Something my dad taught me. Usually makes me feel better. We don't have any snow yet, but small rocks and a big lake will let you do the same thing."

I bite my lip and look around us. The old man and his dog are gone, and I don't see anyone else.

"Fine."

I set my shoulders and brace my feet. I adjust my grip on the stone. With a quick glance at Gio, I pull my hand back and throw the rock.

It lands in the lapping water with a *plop*. Ripples spread from the point where the rock penetrated the water. I hold my breath as they expand several feet before dissipating.

Gio hands me another rock.

I draw in a breath and throw the stone. Another *plop* as it hits the water. A sensation, like a bubble popping behind my ribs. As soon as the ripples clear, I empty my lungs.

Before I have a chance to think about it, I grab the next rock Gio offers, and launch it as hard as I can. I grunt at the effort. Another *plop* and the release of tension in my chest. Tears stream down my face even as I reach for the next stone. Each rock represents something different.

C+ on a calculus quiz. *Plop.* Ripple. Exhale.

The Jacobsons' disdain. *Plop.* Ripple. Exhale.

Dude, aren't you gay? Plop. Ripple. Exhale.

Mo's anger. *Plop.* Ripple. Exhale.

Baby. Baby. Baby. *Plop, plop, plop.*

I don't know how long we stand there, Gio handing me rocks, and me throwing them, but I'm sobbing by the time his pocket is empty, and my shoulder aches. But the impotent frustration and anxiety have dissipated with the last dying ripple on the water.

I drop to the ground, trying to catch my breath. Gio kneels

next to me. He hands me a paper napkin with the Greco's logo embossed on it. I squint at it before wiping my tear-stained cheeks.

"I seem to collect them somehow. I always manage to have one or two in my pockets at any given time," he says. "Feel better?"

"I guess I see the benefit of rock throwing." I blow my nose into the napkin. "My ass is getting cold. I need to get off the ground."

Gio laughs. He grabs my arm, hauling me to my feet. "There's a bench over there." He points down the path.

I should be embarrassed, right? Gio has now seen me lose it twice in one afternoon. He's watched me mop my teary and snotty face twice. The thing is, I'm not embarrassed. Maybe if it seemed like Gio judged me for it I would be, but it doesn't. He doesn't appear fazed by any of this in the least. Of course, that's probably because he still sees me as a brother he needs to look out for. Ugh. Probably a little brother. The part of me that's harbored a secret crush on him for the last few years dies a little.

The bench is nearly as cold as the ground was, but Gio sits close enough that the heat from his right leg warms my left.

"Can I ask a question? You can tell me if it's none of my business."

Answers are the least he deserves for getting me out of there. "Sure."

"How did it happen?"

Heat blazes up my neck and to my cheeks.

He holds up a hand. "I don't mean it like that. I know where babies come from. But you and Maxie. And, well, you *are* gay, right? Not bisexual or pan or whatever?"

"Yes, I'm gay. But I guess I wanted to make sure?" It comes out like a question. "Strangely, that's something I don't understand. I wanted to make sure, to get proof, but now it seems like everyone knew and didn't question it. It's not like I made an announcement."

Gio's lips quirk. "All it took was one person who knew. People talk."

"Still. But it's like everyone knew before I said anything. Or, I guess, they weren't surprised."

Before I can dwell too much on that—like is gaydar a real thing? Is there something about me that screams queer to the other students?—Gio says, "And you thought sleeping with Maxie was the best way to make sure?"

I lick my lips and explain about Truth or Dare, and the experiment.

As my explanation winds down, I finally look up from my lap to gauge his reaction. His narrowed eyes and the severe line of his dark brows show his concern. "What?" I ask.

"I can't figure out why you'd do that without a condom." His tone is the same as it was when he lectured me about my comments about Mom the day I filled out the paperwork at Greco's. The judgment absent after my breakdown is fully in place now. "I figured you'd be too smart to do something that . . . reckless."

"Of course we used a condom." I'm a little insulted he thinks I'd do something that stupid. Or, stupider than sleeping with Maxie as some kind of proof. I guess skipping the rubber isn't a far stretch from having done it in the first place. It's not like I honestly thought there was a chance I was straight. But in the end I'd also ruled out bi or pan, so there's that. "But it broke," I admit.

"Ah." He grimaces. "I guess that would do it."

After a long pause, I say, "We got it from one of the guys at camp. He didn't mention that he'd had it in his wallet for two years 'just in case.'" I roll my eyes. "You'd think science geeks would be smarter."

"I think I get why you did what you did. I can see how you'd find it logical. But what about Maxie?"

"What about her?"

"Why did she offer to sleep with you?"

"She said she was taking ownership of her sexuality."

Gio cocks his head, looking a bit like a skeptical puppy. "What does that mean?"

"She has this theory about sex and virginity—basically that virginity is a social construct, and as a result, it puts unrealistic pressure and expectation on teenagers, especially girls. It started when she fell down this rabbit hole on TikTok and kind of grew from there. She started pulling together data and stories and theories. It was a true sociological experiment. She wanted her own firsthand empirical knowledge. She told me that she wanted to get it—sex—over with, and as one of her best friends, she could trust me."

The skeptical puppy look is still in full force. "And you believed her?"

"Of course. Maxie wouldn't lie to me."

Gio scrubs his hands over his face. "Sometimes I worry about you."

"So you think she lied?"

"Not lied, exactly, Ben. But she probably didn't tell you the whole truth."

I cross my arms over my chest.

"Did you consider that maybe she has a crush on you? That maybe she was hoping you'd change your mind or something?"

My arms drop. "Don't be ridiculous. We've been friends forever. There's no way she'd see me that way. I'm too"—my gesture incorporates my body, from red hair to scuffed running shoes—"me."

He shakes his head. "You actually believe that, don't you? You honestly don't think someone could be interested in you."

"Why would they? I'm a mess. I'm the epitome of a scrawny

geek, I don't relate to most people well, and now I'm that gay kid who got some girl pregnant."

Gio reaches over and grabs my hand. His skin is cool, but the contact warms me. His dark eyes meet mine with an intensity I can't translate. Usually eye contact like this makes me uncomfortable, but I can't make myself look away. It doesn't feel awkward, it feels important. "You should give yourself more credit. Maybe give others more credit too."

I scoff, but what I really want to do is cling to his hand. I don't want to make more of the touch than there is to it. Gio's just being supportive. Both he and his father have always been quick to hug, or pat someone on the back, or touch. Little touches, to guide, to comfort, to kid. Until I started spending more time with him, I'd almost forgotten what it's like. Most people in my life aren't so comfortable with casual touches. I know it doesn't mean more than that, but it's hard to remember when he's touching my hand and gazing into my eyes. It's not personal, but it *feels* personal.

"I mean it, Benji. Sure, you may not be the most social person, but you're smart, and driven, and focused."

"Those are great qualities for a project, but not so much for making friends. They certainly won't make someone fall for me."

"Anyone who doesn't see those for the traits that they are doesn't deserve you. They make you who you are, and you're pretty awesome. Your awkwardness is adorable, and you're cuter than you seem to think. There are people who like that combination."

I really want to believe him, and not for Maxie's sake. I want *him* to believe it. I want *him* to think I'm adorable, that I'm cute. I pull my hand free to cross my arms over my chest again, and my knee starts to bounce. "I still think you're wrong, but I don't see that it matters. Everything will get back to normal after the baby is born."

"Ben . . ." He sighs and shakes his head.

"What? Okay, I don't mean *normal* normal, but like not as much, I don't know, uncertainty. Or whatever."

"Never mind that. How is Maxie doing with everything?" he asks.

I shrug. "She seems okay. Mostly. She won't let me come to the doctor visits with her, and she gets mad when I ask about her blood pressure and sodium intake."

Gio chokes. "Jesus, Ben, tell me you don't actually ask her that."

"Of course I do. One of the books I read says that high blood pressure is a warning sign of potential birthing complications."

He shakes his head. "I admit I don't know much about girls, especially pregnant ones, but I'm surprised she didn't kick you in the balls for that."

"But—"

"That's not what I meant, in any case. I don't mean physically, I mean in her head. How's she feeling about everything?"

"She hasn't said."

"She hasn't said or you haven't asked?" Suspicion drenches his voice.

"I didn't ask. But she'd tell me how things are going if she thought I needed to know, right?"

Gio closes his eyes and slouches on the bench until his head rests on the back. "You're hopeless, Benji."

"Don't call me Benji," I say automatically. "What do you mean, hopeless?"

"Who does she talk to when she needs to vent?"

I think about it for a second. "Mo and me, usually."

"But now that things are weird between you two? Do you think she's been talking to Mo?"

"No," I say slowly, "Mo didn't know anything about any of this until today."

"How about her family?"

"Well, her mom goes with her to all of her appointments."

"But is she supportive? Is she someone Maxie can talk with about things?"

Six months ago, I would have said yes. But lately they seem to have some kind of invisible force field between them when I see them together. "Not really, I don't think so."

"She's probably freaking out. All the crap you're getting at school today, she's getting too. Maybe even worse."

His words hit me like a fist to the gut. "What are they saying?"

"She's a pregnant sixteen-year-old, what do you think they're saying? It's the same shit they say whenever any high school girl gets pregnant."

I narrow my eyes at him. "Like what?"

"That she's a slut. That she's been sleeping with all the guys on the robotics team. And that sex with her is what turned you gay."

"*What?* Who's saying that?"

"The same people who are spreading shit about you."

I surge to my feet. "Why do people suck so much?"

"My point is," Gio says, grabbing my arm and tugging me back to the bench, "all the emotions you're feeling, she's probably feeling too. But you have a mother who supports you, and forces you to talk about stuff. You've got people on your side. It doesn't sound like she's got any of that."

"I hadn't thought about that."

"Have you two talked?"

Something in his voice tells me I need to think about my answer before speaking, that his definition of *talked* might be different than mine. He means *talk* the way my mom does. Not the exchange of words, but the exchange of feelings and understanding.

"Not really, no. Not since she brought the adoption papers to me."

"So you don't know what she's thinking? How she's feeling about the baby?"

I shake my head.

"Ben?" He lays his hand on my shoulder and waits for me to meet his gaze. "Have you—has anyone—asked Maxie what she wants to do with the baby?"

"Well, she's been talking about the adoption stuff. She had the paperwork and her parents have set up some interviews and stuff."

"That sounds like what her parents want. But did anyone ask her what *she* wants to do?"

My mind goes blank. "I . . . I don't know. Maybe not?"

He groans and bangs the bench seat with a fist. "Shit, Ben. You need to talk to her about what she wants. That should have been the first thing you asked her."

"But she wants to put the baby up for adoption." *Doesn't she?*

"Did she tell you that, or did you assume?"

"Well, she's the one who gave me the parental rights termination so the baby could be adopted. Why'd she do that if she didn't want to?"

"Probably because her parents didn't ask her either."

"Huh."

"Hopeless," Gio sighs. "You're hopeless."

CHAPTER 17

We spend another hour on the lakeshore, with a quick stop at a convenience store for a restroom and snack break. When it's late enough that we have to head to work, we load up into Gio's car. He cranks up the heat. My toes and fingers are mostly numb, though I don't realize it until the warm air begins pumping out of the vents.

"We're going to get into so much trouble tomorrow," I say. Now that the panic from earlier is gone, the consequences of my afternoon of freedom come crashing back.

"It'll be fine."

"Maybe. I'm going to have to face everybody at school tomorrow. Knowing that they know, and they saw me freak out. It's going to suck so bad."

"I'm a little surprised you're worried about that, to be honest."

"What do you mean?"

He lifts his shoulders slightly. "Only that you don't usually seem to care too much about what people think of you. Not the way most of us do."

I should maybe be offended. That doesn't sound like a good thing. "I care."

"No, I guess I mean that you don't seem to be influenced by it the way some people are. I've always admired that about you if I'm being honest. You were into robots and science stuff like that as a kid, but didn't let peer pressure or anything stop you from focusing on it. I know kids in middle school weren't always the nicest about that."

"Well, no, but middle schoolers are assholes."

Gio laughs. "True. But sometimes it seems easier to give in to what others expect than to just do your own thing no matter what."

"You don't do that."

This time his laugh edges on bitter. "Of course I do. I might be struggling with parental pressure, not peer pressure, but I'm still giving in."

"Your dad—"

He shakes his head. "Not Dad."

"But—"

"It's not a big deal," he says, pulling out of the parking lot. "Just remember, others may not see you the same way you see yourself. And sometimes they're the ones who are right."

I let it go because he clearly wants to drop the subject. But it makes me think Mom's theory on his relationship with his mother might be right. "Sure."

While he drives us to Greco's, I check my phone. I keep it turned off during school, and with the way we snuck out at lunch, I haven't thought to turn it back on. The number of notifications surprises me. There are missed calls from Mom, messages from Percy, a series of texts from Mo.

My fingers tremble as I debate whether to read the messages.

The missed call and voice mails from Mom probably need to be addressed first. I hit the voice mail icon, then press my phone to my ear.

The first message: *"Hey, Benny. I got a call from the school about you ditching class. What's going on?"*

The second message: *"Seriously, Ben. You need to call me. I'm not mad, but I am worried. Call me, please."*

The third and final message: *"I've been assured you're not dead in a ditch somewhere. I covered for you at school, but we will be talking about this tonight. Love you, kiddo."*

Who assured her? And why would she cover for me?

"Problem?" Gio asks, momentarily taking his eyes from the road.

"I don't know." I squint at the phone, trying to make sense of Mom's messages. "Mom apparently knows I skipped class, but she somehow made it okay at the school."

His cheek twitches, a dead giveaway.

"What do you know?" I ask.

He taps his thumb on the steering wheel.

"Gio."

"I may have texted her when you went to the bathroom earlier."

"Why did you do that? What did you say?" I straighten in my seat.

"I told her that things were rough at school and you needed to get away for a while."

"But—"

"You feel better now, right?"

"Well, sure, but you didn't have any right—"

"Would you rather get detention for skipping? Don't you have enough to do after school without throwing in an extra hour with Mr. Stewart?"

Honestly, an hour with nothing to do but focus on homework sounds pretty great about now. But with my current schedule, I'd have to shuffle work or robotics or something to make the time. I bite my lip. Just because I understand doesn't mean I appreciate him blabbing. I shrug irritably and look back at my phone.

I skim Percy's message—something about silicone tubing versus rubber—before getting up the nerve to open Mo's messages.

The first message: *Where are you? Did you really ditch school?*

The second message: *We should talk.*

The third message: *First you lie to me, now you ignore me? What the hell man?*

The fourth, and final message: *You know what, as soon as you pull your head out of your ass you can call me.*

I shove my phone into my coat pocket, then immediately pull it back out. I power it down, then jam it back into my pocket. "Why is everyone so determined to talk about shit? Why can't we just leave things alone?"

"I'm pretty sure your mom will have many answers to that."

I grunt. "No doubt." I lean against the headrest, closing my eyes for a second. When I'm sure I've got a lockdown on my whining, I roll my head against the rest to look at Gio.

"Why are you doing this?"

"Doing what?"

As if he doesn't know. "Why are you here with me now? Why would you cut class to walk with me along the lake? Why do you care what happens?"

"We were family once, Benji. I'd like to think we're friends now."

Friends? I guess that doesn't sound so bad, but after today it doesn't feel quite right. We ride the rest of the way in silence, but I swear I can feel Gio's eyes on me. When I look his way, he's focused on the road ahead, but I can't shake the weight of his attention. He pulls into the parking lot, puts the car into Park, but doesn't kill the engine.

"Can I ask you another none-of-my-business question?"

"Ask away, though I think by this point you already know every-thing about me."

He bites his lip, hesitating.

I look at the time display on his dash. "We should probably get going. What's your question?"

"You slept with Maxie to find out, or to prove, I guess, that you're gay."

My cheeks burn, but I nod. It helps that I've already explained this a few times. "Right."

"Did you try the same thing with a guy?"

I suddenly understand the phrase *swallowing your tongue*, as it feels like I'm trying to do exactly that. I gurgle and gargle, but even-tually I make legitimate words form. "Um, no. I mean, I've never—"

"Don't you think you should? You know, for proof."

"You think I should have sex with some boy?" My voices edges toward a screech.

"No! I mean, that's not what I—" He stops, his face relaxing. He unhooks his seat belt and shifts to face me. "Have you kissed a guy, Ben? Maybe you're asexual or . . . or something."

The blazing heat in my face dims, but something else lurches in my stomach. It's odd, kind of queasy but not exactly uncom-fortable, and leaves me a little breathless. "Uh, no. I've never . . . not yet. But I'm not asexual. At least I don't think so." I slam my mouth closed. Gio does not need to know about the guys I think about. Especially since he's the main character in most of my less-appropriate thoughts.

"But you've never tested it?" He reaches over, hesitates, and searches my face for something I can't possibly guess at. After a solid three seconds, he lets his fingers brush along my jaw.

I swallow so hard my throat clicks, and all the moisture in my mouth evaporates. I can't form any words, so I shake my head.

"Don't you think you should?" He leans nearer, and I focus on his eyes. Each distinct eyelash, the golden skin, the nearly invisible hint of veins in his lids. He's so close. I feel the puff of his breath against my chin.

This can't be happening to me.

He traces his thumb along my cheekbone. "Ben?" he asks softly, reminding me he's asked a question. Though how I'm supposed to think right now, I have no idea.

I nod. Acknowledgment. An answer. Permission.

The dimples on his face deepen, then his lips touch mine before retreating. I gasp, eyes falling shut. I can't believe this is happening. Gio. Kissing me. His mouth settles on mine again, lips moving against mine, before he pulls back.

I force myself to breathe, even as I try to untangle the crazy ball of sparking wires in my brain. What is this? Sure, I've thought about Gio and me kissing. I usually consider it a dream like winning a Nobel Prize or inventing something that would revolutionize something significant. Big dreams. Highly improbable, if not impossible, dreams. But I'm not dreaming the remembered feel of our lips pressed together.

His cheeks are flushed, and he bites his lip. "Was that okay? I probably shouldn't have—"

"It was"—great, amazing, perfect—"fine."

His face tightens and he lowers his eyes. "Right. That . . . that's good then. It's important to have all the data, right?"

My heart stops the wild, irregular beat it has taken up. In fact, it feels like it's stopped beating altogether. What I'd hoped was my first real kiss—I'm not sure the perfunctory, tentative kisses I'd explored with Maxie last summer count—has been another freaking experiment.

For a second it looks like he might say something, but instead

Gio kills the ignition and reaches for his door, then stills, staring out the windshield.

It takes my scrambled brain a minute to catch up. When I notice what caught Gio's attention, I gasp.

"Maxie?" My gut tightens like I maybe got caught doing something wrong.

Maxie stares back at us from where she leans against the back wall of Greco's. She's hunched into herself, hands buried in her pockets, shoulders practically at her ears. The look on her face is hard to read. It reminds me of my mom's neutral expression, the one she uses to keep her thoughts and feelings to herself. I can't tell if she's upset or simply cold.

What's she doing here?

I don't realize I said that out loud until Gio answers. "No idea. Let's head in. I'll let Monica know you'll be ready in a minute."

We exit the car and head to the back entrance of Greco's. "Hey, Maxie," Gio says when we reach her. He pulls the door open. "It's cold out here. Why don't you come in to talk?"

"I'll only be a second," she says.

"Suit yourself," Gio says. He looks at me. "Don't take too long. Monica will only accept so much before writing you up." After a last long look at me, he slips through the door and leaves me alone with Maxie.

"What are you doing here?" I ask.

"I needed to talk to you and you weren't at school."

An icy wind blows through, ruffling Maxie's curls. She's not even wearing a scarf or hat. I fiddle with the zipper pull on my coat, suddenly very aware of the chill. "It's cold out here. We should go in."

She shakes her head. "It's fine. I'll be quick."

"Where's your hat? Or scarf?"

She cocks her head and crosses her arms. "Where are yours?"

Fair point. But, "You're pregnant."

She narrows her eyes. Yeah, I probably don't need to go there.

"What's going on, Max?"

"Why weren't you at school?"

"You came all the way out here to ask me why I wasn't at school? Why didn't you call me? Or text? Or DM?"

"My parents are monitoring my phone."

"They're what?" The anger surging through me reminds me of that night our families met at Greco's. "That's a bunch of bullshit."

"Yeah, well, I apparently have to earn their trust back. Phone checks, curfews, and regular check-ins are part of it. I'm already pregnant, I'm not sure what other kind of trouble they expect me to get into. I can't wait for this to be over."

There's something about the bitterness in her voice that puts me on edge. What does she mean by *over*? "Maxie?"

"Oh, not that," she said. "I'm not doing anything drastic. I'm just tired. Tired of the stress. Tired of my parents' expectations. Tired of the speculation."

I flinch. Speculation.

Her voice gentles. "Is that why you left today? Because of what everyone is saying?"

"Yeah. It was . . . a lot." Remembering what Gio said, I ask, "How are you? Anyone giving you a hard time?"

She looks away. "Eh, a few. But screw 'em."

"There's been enough discussion of my sex life, thanks."

For a second her expression blanks, then she bursts into laughter. "I can't believe you said that."

Honestly, I can't believe I said it either. "It's been a strange day," I finally say.

She arches a brow. "Including kissing Gio Greco?"

That is probably the strangest part of the whole day. "It didn't mean anything."

"How can it not mean anything? You've had a thing for him since seventh grade. And now you're kissing?"

"He . . . it isn't like that." I don't want to get into the whole "data" discussion with Maxie. She's probably still pretty raw over our last "experiment."

"Uh-huh, sure." Her lips tilt in what I've come to recognize as amused exasperation. For a minute it feels like old times, like the distance between us has been reduced.

"Seriously, Maxie, how bad are things at school for you?"

"It doesn't matter. What can I do about it? Short of dropping out of school—which I refuse to do—or transferring—which my parents refuse to allow—I'm stuck. I'll get through it, and in a year and a half, I'll go to college and put this whole thing behind me."

She says it so matter-of-fact. She's certain. Obviously, she's made up her mind. But with the conversation with Gio still fresh in my mind, I wonder if she believes what she says, or if it's some kind of front. But I don't know how to ask, so I let it go.

"I'm sure it will get better," I say. It's one of those things that people say when they don't know what else to say. I end up saying things like that a lot.

"Sure," she says, shoving her hands into her pockets. Her breaths are visible in the air, emphasizing the rapidly dropping temperature.

"If you won't go inside, we should talk about whatever brought you all the way to Bay View."

"Right." She rocks on her feet, clears her throat, and starts again. "The first interview with adoptive couples is next weekend. Saturday morning."

It feels like the temperature drops another twenty degrees. That's the only explanation for the sudden freezing of my blood.

"Your mom, or maybe your lawyer, put some pressure on my parents, so they won't keep you out. This way you can meet them, ask them questions, whatever."

"Oh. Yeah, okay. That would be . . . that would be good."

"Saturday at ten. In case you need to, you know, get time off work."

I nod. "Work. Right."

"Ben?"

"I'll check the schedule," I say. I've known it was coming, but to have real plans in real time makes the whole thing, well, real. I don't want to meet with the people Maxie's parents want to give my baby to. I don't want anyone to think I agree or approve or accept that adoption is going to happen. Only James's warnings that the odds are against me and his and Mom's assurances that taking an active role in the process will help my cause keep me from yelling in frustration. It's not Maxie's fault, and I know it, but right now she's a convenient target.

"Have you even talked with your parents about letting me have the baby? It's not their choice," I say. "It's yours."

She stares at her feet. "You wouldn't understand."

"If you don't explain it to me, how can I possibly understand?" I ball my fists. "Everyone talks like I don't know what I'm getting into, but then they only tell me about half of what they mean. How can I do everything I need to do, understand everything I need to make the best choices, when I'm only given part of the information?"

"Well, maybe if you didn't keep talking about the baby like it's an object. Keeping it. Having it. It's not a possession, Ben, it's a baby. Someone you'd have to take care of, to nurture, to raise."

"Are you saying that because I don't use the right words, you won't talk to your parents about it?"

"No, Ben." She sighs, tangling her fingers into her curly hair and yanking. "Why is this so important to you? Ben, I don't get why you're pushing this. Why would you let this disrupt your life, your plans, when you don't need to?"

Crossing my arms over my chest, I give her the same words she gave me. "You wouldn't understand."

She chews her bottom lip the way she does when she's working through something. After a minute of internal debate, she says, "I've got an ultrasound coming up after Christmas. You can come if you want."

"Yes!" This could be one more way to prove to everyone I'm serious about this.

A knock comes from the other side of the restaurant's door. It opens slowly until Monica's head peeks around the jamb. "Your shift's starting soon, Ben. Everything okay?"

"Yeah, sure," I say. I turn to Maxie. "Can you send me the details about Saturday? And"—my gaze bounces to Monica—"the other thing?"

"Sure," she says.

I watch to make sure she reaches her car okay. As soon as her engine rumbles to life and her headlights flash on, I slip inside Greco's. Monica holds the door open for me, saying something about the party room reservations and needing to split my time between the main dining room and the side room. I barely hear her, my thoughts are so loud.

Though I've been doing a lot better lately, tonight I manage to break five dishes.

CHAPTER 18

Mom's waiting for me when Gio drops me off at home that night.

She's lounging on the sofa, an obnoxious orange afghan covering her lap. I asked her once why she would buy such an outrageous thing, and she replied that it was a gift. Then I asked why she kept it—it really was a terrible color—and she said one doesn't throw away gifts. Personally, I'd toss the garish monstrosity in the trash and feel no guilt. Probably. Maybe.

She sets a hardcover book on the table and folds her hands in her lap.

"Did you have a good day?" she asks, and there's no sign I can decipher that she means it sarcastically or facetiously.

I shrug. "I've had better."

She sits up and pats the cushion next to her. I hook my coat on the knob of the closet door and head over. I settle on the edge of the couch. Her earlier warning about talking about things flashes in my mind. "What happened? Walk me through it," she says.

"I've got a lot of homework," I hedge.

"You don't even have your backpack," she says. Which, now that I think of it, is going to be a problem. I didn't think of that when I escaped the school this afternoon. Not only will I be behind in my classes, I'll fall farther behind on my assignments. I can't even remember what is due tomorrow. Is there another reading assignment for English? Or a test in calculus? I don't even know.

"Yeah, but—"

She stops my protest with a hand on my knee. "Skipping school, Ben? You need to tell me what you were thinking."

What was I thinking? That's the question. I wasn't thinking. I'd been *feeling*. Feeling too much about too many different things. The snide comments, the rumors. An angry Mo. The thrill of ditching class. The kiss. Maxie. I'd run the gamut from mild anxiety to flat-out panic attack.

I shrug.

Mom sighs. "Damn it, Ben, if you shrug at me one more time, I'm going to ground you. This is serious. I need you to take this seriously. *You* need you to take this seriously. This isn't like you. I need to know what kind of headspace you are in."

"Gio said he told you."

She tucks the edges of the terrible blanket more tightly across her hips. "Gio told me you needed to get out, that people at school were talking and you were overwhelmed."

"Right. Well, that's what happened." It was bad enough experiencing the day, I definitely don't want to relive any of it.

"Ben." She doesn't say anything else. She doesn't need to. Her tone of voice tells me everything.

I push myself deeper into the couch, the act making me feel somehow smaller and safer. "People at school found out about Maxie. And people are assholes. It's a rough combination." I share some of the things people said, and even with the distance of several hours, I feel each word like a needle jabbing my skin. At least I don't freeze the way I did with Mo.

Damn it. Mo. My stomach lurches. I pull the ugly afghan onto my lap, pulling at the soft yarn. I clear my throat. "Then Mo got pissed, and I had a panic attack or something. Puked in the lunchroom in front of practically the whole school. That's when Gio decided we needed to get out."

Mom covers my fiddling fingers with her hand. "Ben," she says.

Again, no other words are necessary. My name said with the sticky syrup of empathy and maternal understanding gets straight to the point. After this afternoon's waterworks, I wouldn't have thought I had any more tears in me, but Mom's hand, her gentle voice, and the weight in her tone are too much for me. Tears gather at my lids and my sinuses prickle. A gentle tug is all it takes. A sob gets caught in my throat and I fling myself into my mom's arms.

"Mo is so mad at me, Mom." I bury my face into her shoulder.

She holds me tightly, her delicate arms surprisingly strong. Her grip and her soothing murmurs loosen the grief in my chest. I sniffle and scrub my hands across my cheeks, even as I pull away from her.

She hands me a tissue from the box on the coffee table. I take a second to make sure I've regained control of myself.

"Tell me about Mo," she says. "Why was he upset?"

I squint at her. "Because of the baby."

"But why," she repeats, emphasizing the word the way she does when I don't get what she's trying to say. "Why is he upset about the baby? Is he anti-children?"

Of course Mo isn't anti-children. At least not that I know. It's one of Mom's little tricks, one I don't think I've ever analyzed too closely until recently. She says something a touch ridiculous.

It breaks the tension a bit, while at the same time giving me an idea of what she's looking for.

"I don't know why," I say. "Not exactly."

"Is he mad about the pregnancy? Or is it something else?"

"No," I say slowly. "I mean, I don't think he's in favor of it."

"Nobody's in favor of teen pregnancies," Mom agrees.

"Right," I say. "Well, things are harder in the robotics club now that Maxie dropped the team."

Mom shakes her head. "Oh, Ben. Do you really think Mo is upset because of the impact to the robotics club?"

I replay the lunchtime conversation. Did he say anything about the team? "No, he seemed angrier about me keeping things from him."

"You didn't tell him?" Mom asks.

"No." Without emotion choking me and the stress of being under the public microscope, his anger makes a lot of sense.

"So he first heard about everything when the rumors started at school?"

"Yeah."

Mom grimaces.

I flinch. Yeah, that definitely isn't the way I'd wanted Mo to find out about the baby.

"Why didn't you tell him, Ben? He's your best friend."

That's the question. "At first I didn't know what Maxie wanted." I pause, trying to wrangle my spinning thoughts. "After a while, the excuses I'd given him seemed too much like lies and I didn't know how to backtrack. I didn't want him to be mad at me." Which sounds stupid now. He's more pissed now than he'd have been before.

"There's more to it, isn't there?"

Mom's always read me well.

"I guess . . . I guess I didn't want him to judge me, to think less of me. Mostly I don't care so much about what other people think of me, but with Mo and, well, with Maxie too, they matter. Things with Maxie are weird and awkward and now I'm worried that we won't ever get back to where we were. I didn't want that for Mo too."

Mom reaches over and cups my cheek. She angles my head to meet her gaze. Her sad expression twists my stomach. "The thing is, Ben, things with Maxie are different now and you probably won't get back to where you were. She's a different person now. But Ben, you're a different person too. Your relationships with others—Maxie or Mo or anyone else—aren't ever going to be the same as they were. Lies, even lies of omission, erode trust, and break apart relationships."

"What can I do?"

She's quiet for a moment, then she squeezes my shoulder. "Talk to him, Benny. Try to explain, and give him time if he needs it. He just learned something pretty major about his two best friends. It's going to be a lot for him to process."

A door opens at the back of the house and floorboards creak. Mom and I look up to see Roger walking to the kitchen. He must have been back in their room. He and Mom used to watch TV in the living room together, but lately he's been spending more time on his tablet in their room.

"Oh, hey," he says, noticing Mom and me huddled together on the couch. "Good night at work?" he asks me.

Since my face is probably red and my eyes bloodshot, I suspect the answer is obvious. "It was all right," I say.

His eyes dart to Mom, then he nods toward the kitchen. "Grabbing a snack. Anyone want something?"

My stomach growls before I can say no. I was too worried to eat anything during my break, so the idea of a snack before heading to bed sounds like a good idea. The fact that it also lets me leave the uncomfortable discussion with Mom is just a bonus.

I push myself off the couch and follow Roger into the kitchen.

"There's a letter for you, by the way." Roger points to a thick, magazine-sized envelope on the counter under the wall-mounted landline phone that hasn't been in service for at least two years. I leave Roger to the snack-making and detour to the counter. The last time someone gave me a thick envelope, it contained paperwork renouncing my rights as a parent. Is this some kind of new legal document? But no, if it's something like that, Mom would have told me, not left it lying on the counter.

One look at the silver clockwork duck logo in the corner tells me it's not legal paperwork.

"No way. No freaking way!" My hands shake as I snatch up the packet.

Roger looks up from his position at the open fridge door. "What is it?"

"The Jacques de Vaucanson Summer Academy." I need a letter opener. *Do we even have a letter opener?* I yank open the flatware drawer and pull out a butter knife. I slip the edge of the knife under the flap and carefully open the envelope. I ease a glossy brochure and a few sheets of fancy paper out. This has to be a good sign. They wouldn't have sent all of this if it was a *no*, right?

The words covering the top sheet of paper dance and wiggle. I blink a few times, trying to bring them into focus.

Dear Mr. Morrison,
The Jacques de Vaucanson Summer Academy
is pleased to offer you a spot in the summer
engineering and robotics practicum. Enclosed you
will find . . .

"Yes!" I shout, shaking the offer letter triumphantly. "Yes, yes, yes!"

"What is it?" Roger asks again.

I shove the paper at him. "Check it out!"

Mom hurries in, worry dragging her brows together. "Ben, why are you so excited?"

"This is fantastic. I don't know exactly what this means, but it sounds great." Roger claps me on the back, passing the letter to Mom. "Congratulations, Ben."

Mom is the only one who doesn't seem excited.

Roger picks up on this the same time I do. His smile dims.

Mom must not get how big of a deal this is. "Mom, thousands of kids apply for this program. Thousands. They only take like fifty. This is huge. There are actual recruiters as part of this program. College recruiters. Major colleges. And scholarships."

"Ben," she says softly.

I cross my arms over my torso, hoping to contain the swishing sensation in my gut and the tightness in my chest. "What am I missing?"

Roger's hand lands on the back of my neck, heavy and steady. Instead of jerking away from the touch like I normally would, I let it ground me.

"It's a summer camp, right?" Mom says.

"Yeah. It starts the first week of July and runs through August. Six weeks."

"And it's expensive, right?"

"Kind of. I mean, yeah, it's pricey, but it's worth it. It's in Boston, but attendees almost always end up with amazing grants and scholarships. And I've got some money saved from Greco's."

"Ben."

No. No no no. She isn't telling me I can't go. She can't.

"You said I could go. When we filled out the application online, you said we'd make it work if I got in."

"That was before," she says. "Things are different now. You're going to be a father of an infant. You won't have the time, the money, or the energy to attend summer camp."

"It's not a camp, it's a practicum. This is a huge opportunity." My brain refuses to connect the dots. I know—I *know*—on some level that Mom is right, but I can't see past the opportunity. Her words, her logic, are white noise in the background. All I know is that she's changing the trajectory of my future. The Jacques de Vaucanson Summer Academy isn't just the first step in securing my future—it's the proof that my future is meant to be. And now Mom is telling me I can't go?

"Ben—"

"Stop!" I gather the envelope, the brochure, and the offer letter to my chest. "Stop saying my name like that. Stop—" I struggle for the words. I'm so angry, so unbelievably angry. I don't want to be reasonable, or logical, or practical. The pressure builds inside me, threatening to overwhelm me.

I tear free from Roger's grip and storm to my room.

I slam my door behind me. The impact jars the framed photograph of my father loose and it falls from the wall, crashing into Sonic's enclosure. Sonic squeaks and scurries to hide behind his plastic wheel. I toss the academy information onto my dresser and reach for the frame. The glass front is cracked and at least a couple of pieces are missing.

It wasn't just the glass either. The entire subject of the picture is gone too. Of course that's the picture I break. I toss the photo—broken frame and all—on top of the dresser next to the brochure. The things I'm missing out on, together in one convenient place. Perfect.

Damn it. I look at the four-foot enclosure, the paper shreds, and Sonic's little cowering body. The only place the missing glass shards could have gone are into his bedding. As much as I want to say screw it and go to bed, it's not safe for Sonic if I leave the glass in there. The last thing I want to do is dig through soiled paper shreds. The odor coming from the cage tells me I'm probably overdue for changing the bedding.

I stand there, fists clenched, breathing ragged, trying to decide what to do. I wish for a second that I were back at the lakeshore with Gio, throwing rocks into the water. The thought of Gio and the process of venting stress physically is enough to clear some of the fog. This isn't a complicated problem. There are only three options, but I try to quiet my brain enough to make a decision.

I suck in a breath, then hold it. Option one: leave the enclosure as is. Leave the glass, leave the bedding alone, leave Sonic alone, and deal with everything tomorrow after I've calmed down. I exhale. Option one isn't a real option, obviously.

I suck in another breath, then hold it. Option two: grab a pair of latex gloves from the cleaning supplies and sift through the bedding until the glass pieces have been located. Kind of gross, kind of tedious, but depending on how soon the glass is found, would potentially be relatively quick. I exhale.

I suck in a third breath, then hold it. Option three: change out the bedding altogether. This would ensure that not only is the bedding safe for Sonic, it also gets a much-needed, overdue refresh. However, while the process to clean the enclosure isn't extensive, it requires a number of steps and processes that I'm not sure I want to deal with right now. It would also mean going to the garage to get the supplies and possibly interacting with Mom or Roger.

I exhale on a growl. My mind clears enough to know option

three is the most logical and practical, but the whole thing pisses me off.

I reach into the enclosure and lift Sonic out. I haven't played with him in a while, I realize. Handling and socializing are important for hedgehogs. It isn't fair to him that I've been neglecting him. "I'm sorry, buddy," I say, cradling him to my chest. "I'm sorry I scared you, and I'm sorry I neglected you. I'll take better care of you, I promise."

I cuddle him for a minute before depositing him on my bed. I have an enclosure to clean, even though I want to do almost anything else. But it's the right thing to do—the best of unwelcome choices—and I can hear my mom's voice in my head, reminding me that sometimes doing the necessary thing, even when you'd rather do anything else, is the right thing to do.

I spare a quick look at the brochure on my dresser. *Sometimes doing the necessary thing, even when you'd rather do anything else, is the right thing to do.* Damn it.

CHAPTER 19

It's been two whole days and I still haven't talked to Mo. In class, he pretends like I don't exist. In robotics, he spends his time with Jay and Mark, the new guys on the team. If we have to speak, it's short, to the point, and completely on task. Yesterday, I tried to pull him aside, but he turned his back on me and walked in the opposite direction from his locker. Mo's always been logical and now he's not acting logical. I don't know what to do with that.

The acceptance letter from the Jacques de Vaucanson Summer Academy sits on my dresser, registration incomplete, mocking me.

I haven't quite come to terms with not being able to go. I want to talk it through with someone, specifically someone who will understand what this opportunity means. Someone who will understand how painful not going is. No, not *someone*. I want to talk to Mo.

I can't count the number of times I've reached for my phone, pulled up his contact information, then remembered he's pissed at me.

Things are quiet at Greco's this afternoon. Monica has me rolling flatware into napkins at a back table while we wait for the dinner rush. It's a mindless task, which is good and bad. On the plus side, I can't break any plates or eggplants with this project. On the down side, the monotony gives me way too much time to think. And I have a lot to think about.

I've got a nice rhythm going—grab the silverware, roll, wrap, tuck, place in the bin—which frees my mind to wander. Rather than letting my mind dwell on the situation with Mo, I decide to tackle Saturday's meeting with the prospective adoptive parents. Mom wants me to make a list of traits that I'd look for if I were to agree to an adoption. What makes a good parent? What would make me comfortable agreeing to someone adopting the baby? I think it's a waste of time, but I promised Mom I'd put in "good faith effort." Along with that, I'm making a list of warning signs. Things I'm going to look for that I can use to show why I'm a better choice as parent than the prospective adopters. I'm calling these my "Okay, Maybe" and "No Way" lists. No surprise, the "No Way" list is way longer than the "Okay, Maybe" list.

When I run out of pressed napkins, I take the bin of wrapped flatware to the bussing station, where they will be ready to grab when we reset the tables throughout the night.

I turn into the alcove and nearly drop the bin when Monica rounds the wall. It's a close call, but I manage to maintain my grip with nothing more than the dull clank of shifting napkin-wrapped cutlery.

"Oh, hey you," Monica says. She moves out of my way, letting me drop the heavy tub onto the counter. "I was going to come find you. If things stay this quiet, I may have to send you home early."

"Oh, okay."

"I promise, Ben, it doesn't happen very often."

"It's not a big deal." I need the money, sure, but a couple extra hours for homework sounds like the best news I've had all day. My science book might distract me enough to keep me from drowning in a swirling tidepool of anxiety. Goodness knows wrapping silverware didn't cut it.

"Thanks for being flexible," Monica says. "Do you need to call for a ride? I need Gio to stay at the front tonight."

At my nod, she says, "Why don't you go make that call now?" She checks her watch. "We'll cut you loose at six thirty. Sound good?"

One of the servers rushes over, pulling Monica aside. I head to the back of the restaurant where my backpack is hanging from an iron coat hook near the time clock. A quick call to Mom confirms that she'll pick me up at six thirty. After I disconnect the call, I shove my phone into the front pocket of my bag, but when I go to hang it back on the coat hook, the top gapes open, dropping two textbooks, my scientific calculator, and my lucky pencil to the ground.

"Why am I always picking stuff off the floor?" I grumble to myself as I squat to retrieve my belongings.

The back entrance to the restaurant bursts open, startling me so I fall back on my ass with a *hmph*.

A pretty blond lady rushes past, not acknowledging me sprawled out in front of her. In fact, I don't think she even saw me. She doesn't hesitate, intent on her trajectory to the office. When she turns to swing the office door shut behind her, I see the tears leaking from her red-rimmed eyes.

Uh-oh, this can't be good.

A few seconds later, Monica appears from the dining room,

brow scrunched and mouth turned down in a concerned frown. "Lisa?"

If I remember correctly, Lisa is Monica's wife. I've seen her a couple of times in passing, but I've never gotten a good look at her. Not enough to recognize her in the crying blond woman from a second's glance.

Whatever's going on is none of my business. I tell myself this even as my ears try to home in on their conversation. It's like once the kernel of curiosity is planted, common sense is a lot harder to pay attention to. As quietly as I can, I gather my dropped books and settle them into the backpack. I tug the tab of the zipper as gently as I can so it makes as little noise as possible.

The door didn't latch behind Monica when she entered the office so there is a six-inch gap—just enough to let most of the conversation through.

"Why, Mo? Why do they keep rejecting us?" The blonde's— Lisa's—voice is ragged, and her breath catches in obvious pain. "I don't know if I can keep doing this. The constant ups and downs of hope and disappointment. It's too much."

"I know, babe, I know." Monica's tone is softer, trying to calm and soothe, but there's a tightness, a tension, I'm not used to hearing from her.

"What's wrong with us?"

I don't know Lisa, obviously, but the pain in her words hits me straight in the chest. It's so powerful, so piercing, even I can feel it.

"There's nothing wrong with us. Nothing at all. We'll keep trying. There are other agencies—"

"But we've tried so many already!"

Deep sigh. "We'll keep trying. There are other options too. International—"

"International is too expensive. We've talked about that. We'd never be able to make it work."

"We'll make it work," Monica says. "We'll find a way. I know it sucks right now, but eventually it will happen, and all the waiting will be worth it. You'll see."

"I just don't understand why we're not enough." Lisa is quieter now, the words slightly muffled.

"Sure you do. Same-sex, mixed-race couple in a red state? We knew there'd be hurdles."

"I thought I was prepared for hurdles, Monica, but not the stonewalling, or the heartbreak."

I definitely don't belong here, but now I'm stuck. To escape, I either have to leave the restaurant through the very loud back entrance or walk past the partially open office door on my way back to the dining room. Either option will likely draw attention to me. The last thing Monica or her wife needs right now is some random guy eavesdropping on their hugely personal conversation.

There's soft murmuring I can't quite discern, before I hear Monica again, closer to the open door. "Let me tell Gio he's got the floor, and then we'll go home. We'll pick up a couple pints of ice cream and a bottle of wine."

"You shouldn't take the time off," Lisa says, but it doesn't really sound like she means it.

"It's fine. We're slow tonight and Gio can handle it. I think we need a night together, just you and me, right now."

I freeze as her shadow crosses the threshold seconds before she does. I spin to face my backpack, futzing with the zipper in an attempt to look occupied, and not like I just listened in on something I have no business hearing.

Monica pauses. "Were you able to get ahold of your mom?" she asks. Is she suspicious? Is she angry? I can't tell, so I play it off.

"Yeah. Six thirty." I turn away from her and hustle back to the dining room. There's a bin of olive oil bottles that need to be filled with my name on it.

I try not to think about what I've overheard. It's not like I don't have enough of my own crap on my plate right now without worrying about some drama in anyone else's life. But the bleak expression I caught on Monica's face is still there the next day. I admit I don't know her well, but over the last couple of months, I've only seen the outgoing, dynamic woman I met on my first day. This sadder, sedate version takes some getting used to.

There's a lull at about four o'clock, probably the last one we'll see before the dinner rush hits, so Monica sends me and Gio on break.

Gio grins and waves me to an empty table in the back. He snags a pitcher of water on his way before settling into the maroon-upholstered booth. The minute his butt hits the seat, he loosens the button at the throat of his pressed maroon dress shirt. It doesn't matter if he's on break for a few minutes or done for the day. If he's playing host or any other role that requires the button-down shirt, as soon as he's away from his post, he loosens the shirt.

He pours ice water into two glasses on the table, pushing one to me. "I'm starving. Brad's bringing over some garlic bread for us."

"Oh, I shouldn't—"

"Of course you should. The Packers are playing on Monday, which means they're not playing tonight. We're going to be swamped. Eat up now while you have a chance."

We only have fifteen minutes for a break. I'm super conscious of the time, because I'm already the guy who breaks all the dishes.

I don't also want to be the guy who takes long breaks. If the bread arrives soon, I should have time before getting back to work. Besides, Paolo's garlic bread is amazing, and my mouth is already watering at the thought.

"You've been pretty quiet the last week or so," Gio says, lounging back, arms stretched over the back of the booth's seat.

I shrug. "Just really busy," I say, toying with the water glass in front of me.

"And that's it?" Suddenly his casual pose doesn't seem to match the intensity in his eyes.

"Uh, yeah. You know, with school, and the robotics club, and the baby, I've got a lot going on," I say, probably a bit more defensive than his comment actually calls for.

"And it has nothing to do with the kiss?"

I choke, just like that. Not even eating or drinking anything, I manage to sputter and cough and make a huge spectacle of myself. "Excuse me?"

Gio pushes the glass of water in my direction.

His dimple flashes and I'm tempted to punch him. But first I have to learn to breathe, and maybe flee to a foreign country for a decade. Then I'll punch him.

"You can't say something like that," I wheeze after taking a gulp of water.

"How else was I supposed to bring it up? The couple of times I've tried to bring it up more . . . subtly, you're either completely oblivious or in total avoidance mode."

I honestly don't remember him bringing it up, subtly or otherwise. I've replayed that moment, his lips on mine, over and over again. I'd have noticed if he'd said something. Right? Or have I been so caught up in everything else that I was, as he puts it, oblivious?

"I don't know about that," I say, "but there's nothing to talk about. It's fine. Everything's fine."

"The thing is," Gio continues as if I hadn't spoken, "I think I gave you the wrong idea."

No, no, he was perfectly clear. That had been about data, an experiment. "No, I got it. I get it. You don't need to worry that I'll try to make it something it wasn't."

"That's not—"

"Seriously. It was good information. Or evidence. Proof, I mean."

Gio reaches over and places his finger over my lips. "I like you, Ben. You're quirky, and smart, and funny. I wanted to kiss you. Not for science, not for data, for me. It's been nice hanging out, and that day felt . . . important . . . and I wanted to kiss you."

My surroundings blur, colors fade, swirling and dripping around me, like watercolors on wet paper. It's a dream, right? Some weird out-of-body experience, where I'm imagining things. Because this can't be real. This can't be happening.

Because I want this, have wanted it, so much and for so long. But now it's too late. Too much has happened.

Gray shadows bleed into the abstract watercolor scenery around me.

"Don't," I say, pushing his hand away from my face. "It's not fair to do this. Not now." The words are hard, but I manage to force them out.

"If not now, then when, Ben?"

I shake my head. "There's too much going on right now. I'm being pulled in too many directions. I don't have time for this. I don't have time for you."

His expression shutters, and he pulls back a bit. "I see."

"It's not you—" I begin.

He folds his arms on the table in front of him. A small movement, maybe, but the barrier it creates is impenetrable. "Right."

"Don't be like that," I plead.

"I'm not being like anything. I gave it a shot, you shot me down. It is what it is."

This reminds me of Mo, the way he acted when he found out about Maxie. I drop my fisted hands into my lap. "Can we . . . can we still be friends?" I sound pathetic, but I can't help it. "I just . . . I can't lose you too. I've lost everyone else. I . . . I don't know what I'd do if you back off too."

He sighs and rubs his hands over his face. "Yes, Ben. We are still friends. I'll always be your friend. I promise."

I've never understood the idea of bittersweet as an emotion before. Like, how can something be painful and comforting at the same time? But that's exactly what this moment is. Bittersweet. Because, while I hate—absolutely *hate*—that Gio is one more sacrifice I have to make, the fact that he's promising to be my friend forever fills me with sunshine and cotton candy. I can't tell Gio any of that, so I say, "Good."

CHAPTER 20

I tug at the suddenly choking collar of my winter coat as I walk up to the Jacobsons' front porch. It's a Saturday morning, sure, but instead of my typical jeans and T-shirt, I'm wearing the khaki pants and polo shirt I wear whenever Mom drags me and Roger to any of her work functions. It's not as formal as the button-down and tie I had to wear to Greco's the night of our dinner with the Jacobsons, but it's close. I can't even blame Mom for strong-arming me into the nicer clothes. No, I made this decision all on my own. I want to prove I'm a mature, responsible person, after all.

Wiping my sweaty hands on my pants, I reach up to ring the doorbell. Before the last half of the chime sounds through the house, a silver sedan pulls into the driveway. My hands tremble as I realize who this must be.

I can see the couple through their windshield. Unlike Mom's or Roger's vehicle, this car is shiny and clean. December in Wisconsin means roads are covered in salt and sand. No one's vehicle escapes a layer of sediment. Except these guys, somehow. I know immediately, illogically maybe, that I don't like them. Anyone so focused on preserving an immaculate car can't be trusted with a baby. Babies are messy, right? Right.

The couple who exits the car are as polished and perfect as their vehicle. He's wearing a black peacoat that looks brand new along with leather gloves that probably cost more than the coat. Her maroon coat is no less fancy. They're older than I've been expecting. Maybe about Mom's age. His hair is cut military-short, with some silver glinting along his temples. Her blond hair is cut into a sharply angled bob that doesn't seem to move in the icy December breeze. Each observation is another strike against the couple. They look like they should be posing for a magazine geared toward urban executives, not talking to pregnant teenagers about adopting their baby.

"Don't stand there, Benjamin. Get inside and out of the way."

I jerk my head back to the doorway. Mr. Jacobson glowers at me from the other side of the screen door. I cringe internally when I see he's wearing khaki pants and a dark-blue polo shirt. Perfect. I'm twinning with the man.

He swings the door open and gestures me through. "Shoes off," he reminds me.

This is not the first time I've been in his house. I've been aware of the No Shoes on the Carpet rule for years.

I toe off my tennis shoes and hang my coat on the rack next to the door.

"Jim, Janice. I'm glad you found us," Mr. Jacobson says heartily, his tone a complete 180 from how he greeted me. "Come on in. It's freezing out here." He stands back to let them through. I hang back, not quite sure where this conversation will be held. Dining room? Den?

I can't help but notice that Mr. Jacobson doesn't make Jim

and Janice take off their shoes. And, seriously, Jim and Janice? Alliterative names are the worst. They probably have a whole list of J names for their future children. Ugh. Alliterative names isn't on my "No Way" list for potential adoptive parents, but it should be. I make a mental amendment to my list.

"We're really excited to talk with Maxie," Janice says. "We can't tell you how much we appreciate you arranging this visit. I can't imagine this whole thing has been very pleasant for you."

"It's unfortunate, to be sure. But if we can make something good come from the situation, that will help. A silver lining, as it were."

"Sometimes these things work out for the best. One of the reasons we're pursuing private adoption is so that we can meet the birth mother. There are so many unknowns, otherwise. You have no idea what kind of genetics there are, what kind of medical history. This is ideal. Not only do we get to make sure the birth mother is healthy, knowing she comes from such a good family eases our mind."

"What do you mean by 'good family'?" I ask.

All three adults swing their heads to me.

Mr. Jacobson glares at me.

Jim looks confused.

Janice says, "I didn't know you had a son."

"I don't," Mr. Jacobson says curtly. He doesn't offer any other explanation.

"I—"

"That's enough, Benjamin. You're here as a courtesy only. Do not interfere."

I grumble under my breath, but head toward the dining room, where I find Maxie sitting on one side of the table. The frumpy beige sweater she has on is one of her favorites, with long sleeves that drape over the back of her hands, nearly to her knuckles. She folds her fingers down over the bottom part of the sleeve, and while the sweater's hood is not up, she has it arranged in such a way that it covers her neck almost like a scarf. It's like she's trying to cover as much of her skin as possible.

She bites her lip when I come in. I start to walk to the seat next to her, but her mom, who's been arranging coffee cups on the counter, clears her throat and nods to a chair on the exact opposite side. Maxie gives a little shrug, and I change course and slide into the indicated seat. A few seconds later, Mr. Jacobson, Jim, and Janice file in.

Another round of chatter as Mrs. Jacobson greets the couple. It becomes increasingly clear that the four of them already know each other. This is confirmed when Maxie's mom turns to Maxie to say, "Maxie, I'm sure you remember the Reynoldses from church."

Maxie nods. "Hi," she says softly, standing up to shake the couple's hands. She has to release her grip on her sweater sleeve to do so. I don't know why I notice that little detail, but it's like she's removed part of her shield. Her hands tremble as she goes from Jim to Janice before taking her seat again. As soon as her butt hits the chair, the sleeves are tucked around her closed fists again.

I guess when I thought about how this would go, I expected the potential parents to be asked the questions, not to be the askers. As soon as everyone is seated, with coffee for Jim and Janice (Maxie's mom didn't offer me a drink), the couple starts asking Maxie questions, like she's the one being interviewed.

They ask about her health.

They ask about how the pregnancy is going.

They ask about her academic achievements.

Mr. Jacobson chimes in every now and then to clarify a point or two, but on the whole Maxie is left to field the queries herself.

Maxie answers each of their questions but doesn't ask any of her own.

Then Jim and Janice direct their questions to Maxie's parents. They want the family medical history, relatives' professional achievements, and a bunch of other things that don't make any sense to me at all. And while the whole Ancestry.com thing is interesting from a purely academic perspective, I don't understand what's going on.

After Mr. Jacobson finishes extolling the virtues of some great-uncle, I've had enough.

"Why should you get to adopt the baby?"

Four adult faces turn my way. Jim and Janice look really confused, so I think they must have completely forgotten about me.

"Excuse me?" Jim asks.

Mr. Jacobson starts to say something, but I don't give him a chance. "Why should you get to adopt the baby? What makes you a better choice than someone else?"

Mr. Jacobson opens his mouth, but before he can say anything, Jim says, "We can provide a comfortable life for a child. We are financially stable, and we can afford the best schools, the best opportunities." He makes it sound like the most obvious answer. I don't know what the right answer would have been, but that definitely is not it.

I roll my eyes. "Not good enough."

Jim turns to Maxie's parents. "I don't understand. Who is this boy, Dave, and why is he here?"

Mr. Jacobson presses his lips together, and his face tightens.

Again I interrupt before he has a chance to speak. "I'm the

baby's father. I might not know what it takes to be a good parent, to be the right choice, but I do know that money's not it."

In unison, Jim and Janice rear back, then swing their heads from me to Mr. Jacobson, and back again. Maxie's mom shakes her head and closes her eyes. She looks like she's saying grace or something. Maxie watches the whole proceeding with wide eyes.

"I didn't think he was still in the picture," Jim says to Mr. Jacobson, talking over my head as if I were a toddler or a pet, someone unable to comprehend or speak for themselves.

"Well, I am," I say. "And this is a waste of time."

Maxie's mom narrows her eyes at me, and I can practically hear her hissing at me to be quiet.

I'm *this* close to snapping at her, telling her to *bring it* or something equally useless. I am not a dog or a baby. I bite my tongue, but barely. I need to be part of this process, if only to make sure the worst-case scenario is avoided. Doesn't stop me from hoping she can see my response in my expression. I let my eyes give her all the snark and clapback I won't say.

Mr. Jacobson plows through the tension between his wife and me. He's not oblivious, not really, but he's not going to draw attention to it. "Well, we should probably move on to the nuts and bolts of it all. Then we'll iron out the final details with the private adoption lawyer, of course, but I thought a face-to-face would be a good idea."

This is probably what he sounds like talking at one of his departmental meetings—outlining the agenda, laying out expectations, calculating. All nuts and bolts and dollars and cents. Normally I like that kind of straightforward approach. Things get muddled and messy when we go off on too many tangents. But this feels like a situation that shouldn't be quite so cold-blooded.

"Absolutely," Jim says. "As we discussed over the phone, we're looking for a closed adoption, and we'll cover all of the upcoming medical expenses and legal fees."

His words are two devastating punches to my torso. *Closed adoption.* Of all the adoption options, that was my biggest fear. In a closed adoption, the birth parents' information is sealed. According to one of the articles I read, most of the time the biological father's information is omitted entirely. I've held on to a slight hope that if the worst happens, and the baby is put up for adoption, there's at least a distant possibility of the child looking for me at some point. But a closed adoption . . . That's a blow straight to my heart.

The money's a hit to my gut. I believe what I said earlier, that money does not make someone suitable to be a parent, let alone the parent of my baby, but the J-Team can afford to pay for everything—the medical expenses, the legal fees, all of that. I can't. Heck, I can't even afford to buy Mom a present for Christmas. All my money is going straight to the bank to buy all the stuff the baby will need. And to be able to put a dent in all the costs associated with the baby *after* the birth. And the money I'd set aside on the off chance I'd get accepted into the Vaucanson Summer Academy? It's as good as spent.

Do Mom and James have a plan for this? If I keep the baby, will I have to pay for things like Maxie's medical expenses? The court costs? The weight on my chest makes it hard for me to take a full breath. The shallow puffs I can manage aren't enough.

"This will all be contingent on the results of Maxie's next checkup," Jim is saying. The adults in the room are oblivious to my panic attack.

Maxie notices. As Jim, Janice, and the Jacobsons—damn, it's an alliterative match made in heaven—continue to discuss the finer points of the offered agreement, Maxie watches me, brows furrowed in concern. She mouths the words *Are you okay?* That little thing, that small sign, is enough to unseize my lungs. I can't keep my brain from cycling through the worries and variables, but at least I can breathe.

The discussion pauses a few minutes later. Janice asks to use the washroom and Maxie's mom shows her the way.

This is my chance. "Maxie, I have a question about our calculus homework. Did you bring your book home?"

Her face twists in confusion. "Yeah, but—"

"Let's go look, quick." I jump up from my seat and head toward the stairs leading to her room. "We'll be right back," I say over my shoulder, noticing the wary expression on Mr. Jacobson's face.

Maxie follows me, but slowly. I understand why she might be a bit turned around. Between the two of us, I'm better at calculus. It would be really weird for me to need her help on an assignment in that subject. I should have used a different example—history or something that's not one of my strengths—but I need her out of the room, so I grabbed the first thing I could think of.

I shut the door behind her when we reach her bedroom.

"What are you doing?" she asks.

"You need to stop this," I tell her, pacing in front of the window that faces the Jacobsons' backyard. The backyard where we spent countless days playing together, building models together, hanging out. I've spent nearly as much time there as I have at Mo's or my own backyard.

Maxie's room reminds me so much of her. The bed is made, a practical, unpatterned royal-purple spread covering it. The art and pictures on her wall reflect her interests in all things space and astronomy, with a framed Princess Leia poster claiming a woman's place is in the resistance.

She plops onto the end of her bed, knocking a stuffed BB-8 onto the floor. "Stop what?"

I wave my hand, encompassing her room, the house, and likely the entire city of Milwaukee. "This. This. This whole adoption thing. Especially these two. This couple would be a terrible choice."

She props her elbows on her knees and looks up at me. Her expression is one I know—one that says I'm being ridiculous or dramatic. Usually she uses it when I'm too invested in the accuracy of anything scientific on television, especially in sci-fi. "There's nothing wrong with them."

"They have alliterative names."

"That's the stupidest thing I've ever heard you say."

I stalk from the door to her computer desk on the other side of her room, then I turn and stalk back. Finally, on the third pass, the words that have been trying to break out do. I spin to face her. "Why won't you help me with this? Why won't you tell your parents what you want?"

Her eyes narrow, and she barks out a laugh even I can tell is not the least bit amused. She surges to her feet. "What do you mean, what I want? No one—not one single person—has asked me what I want. Everyone has plans and expectations for me. For this baby." Her hand strays to her stomach. "No one cares about my plans, my needs." Her voice rises with every word, her cheeks flushing and hands fisting.

This is like what Gio said. Maybe instead of making assumptions, someone should find out where she stands in all of this.

"What do you want?"

She stomps closer to me, eyes a little wild. "What do I want? You want to know what I want?"

Honestly, she's scaring me a little, so I don't think I really do want to know. "Um, yeah?"

"What I want, Ben, is to not be pregnant. What I want is to get my life back."

She doesn't mean . . . I swallow hard, thinking about the implications. My eyes stray to her belly again. She's more than four months along now, so too late for her to do anything drastic, right?

She must be able to read my expression. She rolls her eyes and plants her hands on her hips. "Don't be stupid, Ben. I'm not going to do anything. You asked what I want, not what I'm going to do. Big difference. Really, really, really big difference."

"Then what—"

"I know going back in time and undoing our little experiment in August is out of the question, obviously. But outside of that, do you know what I want, Ben? What I really want? I want to no longer be the rope in this twisted tug-of-war between you and my parents. None of you care what this is doing to me. I'm not given any say in any of this."

"That's the thing, though," I say, reaching for her arm. She pulls it away before I make contact. "You *do* have a say. You, more than anyone else, have all the say. You can say you don't want J and J adopting the baby. You can let me take custody without fighting it in court. I need you to speak up."

"And what do you think happens to me in that scenario?" She crosses her arms over her torso and rounds her shoulders defensively.

"What do you mean? You go back to your life. You finish school, you go on to college, do all the things you planned on doing."

"And you and me?" she asks.

"What about me and you?" I truly don't understand her

question. I can tell she's frustrated with me, and I'm getting frustrated too. She knows I don't speak in subtext and innuendo. I need plain words.

"Jesus, Ben. You don't get it, do you?"

"Clearly not."

"Say I have the baby, and you get custody."

"Okay."

"We go to school together. We're going to have classes together. I'm going to see you almost every day."

"Right."

"And you're going to have the baby. You're going to raise the baby, take them to appointments, change their diapers, rock them to sleep at night. Right?"

"Of course," I say. That's part of it, isn't it?

Tears start to well up in her eyes, finally slipping past her lashes to trail down her cheeks. She swipes her hand across her face, angrily wiping the moisture away. "I'm going to see you every day. I'm going to be reminded *every day* about what I've given up. Don't you think it's hard to know I'm carrying a baby, and knowing that I can't keep them? I *can't* keep them, Ben. I'm in no position to be a mom. This baby, our baby, *my* baby, deserves more than I can give them. But if you keep them, I will be faced with that choice every single day. And every single day, when I see you, I'll be reminded, once again, of what I've lost. There's no going back to normal for me. I hope to God I'll be able to move forward. I hope I can create a new path or future for me, but my life has been torn apart by this."

She's sobbing now. I don't know what to do, what to say. "You'll be able to—" I begin.

"No, I won't be able to. I can't think. I'm tired all the time. My grades are slipping. I've had to pull out of my clubs. I'll be off for weeks after the birth. I'll be lucky if I don't end up having to take summer school to make up for the classes I'll miss."

I reach forward tentatively, pulling her into a hug. I'm afraid she'll push me away, still mad that I haven't gotten it, haven't understood what she is going through. Instead, she clings to me, and buries her head in my shoulder.

"And I'm pretty sure pregnancy brain is a real thing—I keep forgetting things I thought I knew. I'm exhausted, but I can't sleep. I have to pee like fifteen times a day." Her breath hitches on a sob. "And my pants don't fit anymore, damn it."

I pull back to look at her.

She looks at me, eyes wide. Then she bursts into a snotty-sounding laugh.

After a minute of near-hysterical giggling, she steps back, mopping her face with the sleeve of her sweater. "So no, Ben, it's not as easy as me making a decision to support you. The decision is bigger than that. I need to decide what is best for the baby, what is best for me, and to be honest, what is best for you too."

I leave her in her room, her words hanging over us. I don't know what to say. I don't know how to feel. I'm not used to not knowing the answer to a problem. I'm used to things being black-and-white, to calculations that only have one answer. Science and engineering have a lot of room for creativity, but in the end, there is a quantifiable way to show whether something did what it was supposed to do. There are proofs and investigations. And if something doesn't work, you refigure, recalibrate, and try again.

But nothing the last few months has been black-and-white. There is no check-off sheet, no scientific method to tell me what to try next.

When I reach the hallway outside the kitchen, I pause.

"Is the boy going to be a problem?" Jim is asking. Presumably he's speaking to Mr. Jacobson.

"Of course not. He's here as a courtesy only, in the hopes he'll leave well enough alone once he realizes things are resolved for the best."

That rankles.

"His mother and their lawyer have been putting some pressure on. Enough that he's being included in the process more than he should. But it's easier to accommodate it rather than fight them on it. It won't change anything. The law's on our side here. I don't know why his mother is enabling him in this. I guess she believes he'll come to his senses once he realizes everything he'll have to give up to be a father. It's the only reason she was able to convince us to let him participate in as much as he has been. More data, more truth. He'll eventually get scared away and will drop the whole thing."

I lean against the wall, my knees suddenly unable to hold my weight. Is that really what Mom thinks? Is that why she's being so supportive in everything? She thinks I'll drop everything as soon as I see all that's at stake?

"It's easier and cheaper for everyone to let him pretend now. It'll save us a bigger fight later. So no, Jim, he's nothing to worry about."

Mom doesn't have faith in me. Maxie thinks that what I want isn't what's best for me. I can fight a lot of things, but I don't know how to combat that.

Too mentally exhausted to deal with all of this at the moment, I walk out of the Jacobsons' house without a word.

Before I even realize I'm doing it, my phone is in my hand. I pull up a familiar contact and send a message. *Will throwing snowballs at a wall have the same effect as throwing rocks into the lake?*

As soon as I hit Send, I regret the question. It was too easy, almost automatic. That's not the kind of relationship Gio and I have. A couple months ago, I'd have messaged Mo without over-thinking it, but Gio? Our entire text history centers around our work schedule. Usually an update if one or the other of us is running a few minutes behind. Nothing personal. Nothing intimate.

Maybe I should tell him I meant the message for someone else? Right. Like anyone else would have a clue about the significance of throwing rocks into a lake.

Three dots flash, indicating Gio is typing. I hold my breath.

GIO
Rough day?

> **ME**
> Yeah. Sorry, I shouldn't have bothered you with it.

GIO
It's cool. You wanna talk?

> **ME**
> No. I'm fine.

GIO
I don't believe you.

I start to type out anther reply—another assurance that I'm totally fine and I have places to be—but before I hit the first letter, my phone buzzes, Gio's name flashing across the screen. I close my eyes before taking a deep breath and answering the call.

"I'm fine," I tell him.

"You're not. Otherwise you wouldn't have texted me about throwing rocks."

"I just . . . Look, it's just been a weird day. It's not fair to unload on you."

"Sure it is. That's what friends are for, right?"

My breath hitches in my throat. "Are we friends?" Why do I want his answer to be no? *Because friends don't kiss each other.* Which is a ridiculous thing to think. After all, Maxie is my friend and we've done so much more than kiss.

"Aren't we?" Gio's voice is softer, deeper, than I'm used to.

"Yeah." My body relaxes and I start the six-block hike back to my house. "Yeah, we are."

"As your friend, then, I want you to tell me what's wrong."

"Nothing," I say. Then, "Everything. I don't know. There's a lot going on in my head and I don't know what to do about any of it."

"Anything in particular?" There's a muted click and the sound quality around him changes, like he's shut a door to bar against random ambient noises.

"Nothing I want to talk about." The cold makes my nose run. What I wouldn't give for one of Gio's stash of napkins.

He waits me out. Damn it, how does he know me this well?

"It's my mom," I say.

"What about her?" Again, no judgment.

"I thought she supported me, supported what I'm doing, but she doesn't. She told the Jacobsons to let me participate in the process, that it would appease me or something. She told them not to worry, that I'd see everything I'm giving up and change my mind. She's never told me that, but she's told them."

"Where'd you hear that?" he asks.

"I overheard Maxie's dad talking to the bozo who wants to adopt the baby."

"Is it possible that he lied? Or that your mom lied to him?"

That stops me. I try to open up the logical side of my brain. The emotional part has been in control too long. "It seems unlikely.

Mom doesn't lie. She says she values honesty and transparency too much."

"Normally, sure, but this situation isn't particularly normal, is it?"

"What would she gain from lying to him?"

"You're being included in baby things, aren't you?"

I shrug, not that he can see it. "I guess."

Tired of the conversation—of the emotions swirling unproductively in my brain—I change the subject.

"You're picking me up on Monday, right?"

Monday is the first day of winter break, and with Mom and Roger working, I've had to find a way to get to Greco's for my shifts. Gio volunteered, which is a good thing since I still haven't signed up to take my driving test. It's on my never-ending to-do list, along with about a million other things. And, in the meantime, it's a good excuse to spend time with Gio. That doesn't factor into my procrastination, of course. Not at all.

"Absolutely. See you at two."

We spend the rest of the ten-minute walk to my house going over our work schedule. It's not until I disconnect the phone at my front porch that I realize the burning and twisting in my gut has subsided and the tension has eased from my shoulders.

CHAPTER 21

My plan is to sleep in. It's Christmas, after all. If there's any day of the year I can turn off the alarm, it should be Christmas. Mom and Roger have other plans.

"Up, up, up!" Mom hollers, beating on my door like it's a set of bongo drums.

"No!" I shout, covering my head with my pillow to drown out the sounds. Of course, that means I can't breathe. But at least I'll be able to sleep.

"Not a chance, kiddo. It's Christmas and we have things to do and places to go."

"Huh?" I lift the edge of the pillow, because oxygen really is a necessity, and because Mom isn't making sense. The only place we are planning to go is to visit my aunt Shannon tomorrow. Christmas is just for us. It's always been that way.

"Hop to it!" she shouts.

My lids droop and my pillow is suddenly the coziest, warmest, most comfortable place in the world. Nothing could compete with that. Not Christmas. Not a handful of presents. Not the ham dinner Mom will cook. Sleep and quiet and a day with no responsibilities is all I want.

I must fall asleep, because the next thing I know, someone is pounding on my door again. This time it's Roger. "C'mon, Ben. I don't think your mom's kidding. Jump in the shower quick. Breakfast will be ready in a few minutes."

I groan but shove aside the comforter. I push myself up to stumble bleary-eyed to the bathroom to follow Roger's instructions about the shower. The warm water helps clear the fog in my brain, but not enough that I can figure out why Mom insists I get up.

"Seriously, Mom, why the wake-up call?" I grumble, sliding into a seat at the kitchen table. Someone—probably Mom—has pulled out all the stops on the table. First, the red table runner that she only manages to pull out every other year or so stretches across the surface, and place settings are arranged around the table, including green napkins with wreath-shaped napkin rings, the good dishes, and matching silverware. There are *five* place settings. I look around the kitchen. Mom is at the stove, stirring a frying pan full of fried potatoes. Roger's at the fridge, pulling out a jug of orange juice. Mom. Roger. Me. That's three people.

"What's going on? Why are there five plates for the three of us? That math doesn't work."

Mom moves the skillet to a back burner.

"Russel and Miriam are joining us for breakfast."

This is probably some kind of weird dream. Some kind of weird, benign but odd, stress-induced dream. That is the only explanation I can think of for Roger's parents to be on their way over. "Russel and Miriam, who live in Arizona, are joining us for breakfast? That seems like a long way to go for scrambled eggs and hash browns."

"First," Mom says, reaching into a low cabinet next to the stove, "it's a ham-and-cheese quiche, with hash browns, cut fruit, and toast. Speaking of, Ben, why don't you get the toast going."

I stand and look for the bread to toast. "And second?" I ask. I haven't completely ruled out the dream idea, so rather than fight it, I figure I'll see how it plays out. Either I'm not dreaming and Mom and Roger have completely left me out of the loop on our holiday plans, or Sonic is about to burst into the room like a full-size mascot at a varsity football game.

"Second, they are in town for Christmas. Actually, they're in town for the day. They flew in last night to spend Christmas with Miriam's sister in Chicago. They'll spend the morning with us, and then drive down to Chicago for the big family dinner."

Roger sets the jug of juice on the table, then heads to the cupboard and pulls out some glasses. Five glasses.

"This isn't some boring dream, is it?"

Roger chuckles. "I hope your dreams are more exciting than breakfast."

"I did say it was boring, didn't I?"

The toaster pops, so I swap out the toast with more bread. Grabbing a knife, I proceed to slather butter on the toast before it cools too much. Which convinces me this can't be a dream, no matter how dull. Even at my most boring, I wouldn't dream about toast, right?

"Your family is having a big dinner this afternoon? Are you going to head down to Chicago with your parents?"

Roger looks surprised by my question. "No," he says. "I'll be staying with you guys."

"Why?" It's not that I don't want Roger to spend the day with us, but if his family is all getting together less than a two-hour drive away, I can't figure out why he'd hang out here.

Mom stills and we both wait for his answer.

Finally, Roger says, "It's our first Christmas as a family. We should spend it together."

Mom blinks at him, a broad smile blooming across her face. She closes the distance between herself and Roger, then reaches up to cup his face. "I love you," she says.

"Me too," he says softly before leaning down to kiss her.

It's weird and awkward and disturbing. I never want to see my mom being all mushy and kissy. Gross. But it's also kind of sweet.

Roger's phone dings, breaking up the moment. His eyes widen, and Mom bites her lip as he retrieves the device from his pocket. "They're here," Roger says after a quick glance at the screen. Mom looks at me, her eyes bright, before she clears her throat. "Well, let's go say hi."

I follow Mom and Roger to the front door. Something is going on, but I can't pinpoint what it might be. Mom and Roger are holding entire conversations without talking, and an air of expectation swells in the room.

Roger pulls the door open, and we squeeze in behind the screen door. Mom and Roger shuffle around a little, and I somehow end up between them. A small gray car pulls into the driveway and a larger SUV lines up along the curb in front of the yard. "Who else is with them?"

Miriam hops out of the SUV and waves. "Merry Christmas," she calls. She pulls open the hatchback of her car and hauls out a box full of wrapped packages. Roger tugs on a pair of tennis shoes and hustles across the snow-covered lawn to help her.

Mom stands at the threshold, propping the door open with her hip. "Merry Christmas!"

In the driveway, the driver's side door of the gray car opens, and Russel climbs out. He's as tall and thin as Roger, and it's obvious what Roger will look like in thirty years. He smiles widely before ducking his head back into the car. He emerges a couple seconds later with a ginormous red bow. The ribbon forming the bow has to be at least eight inches wide, and it takes both his arms to hold the many loops.

"Ho ho ho!" Russel booms before planting the red bow on the roof.

"What the hell?" I breathe.

Roger grabs the box of gifts from his mother, and the three Fergusons converge at the intersection of the driveway and walkway leading to the house. They stop at the concrete step, lining up shoulder to shoulder. Russel hands a small, silver-foil-wrapped box to my mom. Mom in turn passes the box to me.

What is even happening right now? The box is about the size of one of those fancy gift card holders you can buy at Walgreens. The kind I would never spend money on, because five dollars for a box when an envelope will do is ridiculous. "What is it?" I ask, turning the box over in my hand.

"Open it up," Roger suggests. Mom moves aside so he can drop the larger container of gifts behind her in the house. No one follows him into the living room. Instead, as soon as he sets down the presents, he comes back outside. Here we are, the five of us, standing around outside in December. Mom and I aren't even wearing shoes.

I look from one expectant face to the next, trying to read their expressions. I'm met with four brilliant smiles. "I'm so confused," I admit. If anything, their grins widen.

I peel away the sliver of tape at one end of the box. I don't think anyone breathes while I carefully remove the wrapping.

"Seriously, kid? You're killing me," Roger says.

I don't know how to explain that their weird anticipation is kind of freaking me out. My hesitancy in opening the gift is 100 percent me trying to make this whole thing make sense. As soon as I remove the paper, Mom grabs the scraps, and I lift the top of the tiny box.

I blink at the contents. It's a car key, complete with automatic locks and an alarm button on the fob.

"What?"

Mom reaches over and grabs the key, pressing one of the little buttons. The gray car in the driveway chirps cheerfully.

"Merry Christmas, Benny," Mom says, handing the key back to me.

The frigid morning air stings my widened eyes. A car? For me? "Are you freaking kidding me?" My voice cracks, and I stare at each of the adults surrounding me. "What did you . . . how did you . . . I mean, why? I don't even have my license yet."

"You're going to need a car, Ben. We need to schedule a time for you to take the test and get your license. This way you'll be able to drive yourself to school and to work, whatever you need." Mom slings her arm around me.

"But . . ." I look from Russel and Miriam, who are beaming at me, to Roger.

"My parents picked it up last night. We wanted it to be a surprise."

"Mission accomplished," I mutter. Realizing I probably sound ungrateful, I adjust my tone. "This is a huge surprise. I don't know what to say. I guess, thank you?" It would sound better if that last hadn't come off as a question, but neither of the Fergusons seem upset.

"You're welcome, sweetie," Miriam says. "I love surprises, and we're happy to be a part of it."

"Hey, let's go check her out," Roger says. "Grab some shoes and your jacket."

"Don't be too long," Mom says. "Breakfast will get cold."

"Just a quick check," Roger assures her. "We'll take it for a spin after we eat."

Mom escorts Russel and Miriam inside. I grab my coat and slip my feet into my shoes. Roger's practically bouncing on his toes while he waits. I've never seen anyone so excited about a present for someone else.

The car, it turns out, is a Honda Civic. It's seven years old and has eighty thousand miles on it. "It's nothing fancy," Roger tells me as he ushers me into the driver's seat, "but it's a great first car."

I settle in, and at his urging, I insert the key and start the ignition. It engages with a purr.

"I can't believe you did this," I say, breaking into Roger's monologue about the safety features of my new car. "I can't believe you got your parents involved."

He ruffles my hair, a gesture I'm sure should piss me off, but doesn't. I still can't wrap my head around the enormity of this gift. They bought me a car. An actual, honest-to-goodness car. And somehow roped his parents—people I've only seen that one time at Mom's wedding—into aiding them.

Roger's face gentles. "You need to be able to get around yourself," he says. "And once the baby is here, it'll be even more important. Besides, every sixteen-year-old should have a car. It's nothing fancy, but like I said, it's an ideal first car."

I swallow around a lump in my throat, then nod. "You're right. It'll be good to have something. It's . . . it's really nice. Thank you."

He squeezes my shoulder. "You're welcome. Merry Christmas."

I don't have much to contribute during breakfast. Mom and Miriam seem to carry the conversation between them. Roger and Russel participate, and everyone acts all jolly and festive. I try to remember when a holiday meal ever felt so . . . normal. Miriam talks about an art show she has coming up, something to do with watercolors, and Russel vents about his golf scores and some guy named George who keeps beating him during their Wednesday-morning games. Mom and Miriam compare notes on winter in Arizona versus winter in Wisconsin. It's all so tediously normal.

So why do I feel like it's the most abnormal meal I've ever been part of? Except for maybe the night at Greco's with the Jacobsons. But we didn't eat then, so maybe it doesn't count as a meal?

I push a bit of egg around my plate.

A car. They got me a freaking car for Christmas.

It's not the car that I struggle to deal with. Yeah, it's huge, but that's not what has my stomach in knots and my brain whirling. It's the planning it required. The collaboration. Getting the Fergusons involved to keep it a surprise? They added extra time to their trip so they could pick up the car before heading to Chicago to spend the rest of the holiday with their family.

"Ben?"

I look up at Mom. She must have been talking to me, because she's looking at me like she expects an answer.

"Huh?" I set my fork down and face her.

"Miriam asked you a question."

I blink, then turn my attention to Miriam. "Sorry. Can you repeat it? My mind wandered." That's a polite way to say it. Better than mentioning that I'm still freaking out about the implications of a significant present.

Her smile is full of understanding and sweetness. I'm not sure she has another setting. "I was just saying that I'm impressed with what you are doing. It's a lot of work, and it shows a great deal of integrity that you're stepping up."

Impossible as it sounds, it takes a ridiculously long time for her words to sink in. Then it hits me. The baby. She's talking about the baby. I clear my throat, then reach for my nearly empty glass of juice. "Oh," I say after I use the last drops of liquid to moisten my suddenly dry mouth, "thanks."

She pauses for a second—maybe waiting for me to say something else, something more meaningful. When I don't, she says, "Well, like I said, it's impressive. Roger tells me you've been working hard and will be taking classes. It's so important, and I don't think enough people take advantage of the training programs available. No one seems to realize how much work is required to raise a child. Good for you."

"Thanks," I say again. Mom kicks me under the table. Clearly, monosyllabic answers won't do. "I'm starting the parenting classes in January. I think they'll be useful. The birthing classes will be, obviously, geared more toward Maxie."

"Are you planning on attending the birth?" Russel asks.

I sure as hell hope not. "Maybe. Mrs. Jacobson, Maxie's mom, will probably be there. I don't know what they'll need me for."

"I remember Roger's birth," Russel says. "Most amazing experience of my life. Trust me, seeing the moment your child enters the world is unforgettable. Until that moment, I had no idea I could feel so much for someone so new." Russel grabs Roger's hand and squeezes.

Roger rolls his eyes, but I can tell he's pleased. There's a connection there, one forged more than thirty years ago. Will I have something like that with the baby? I try to imagine my life in thirty years. What will the baby look like? I try to picture it. Will I have a son or a daughter? Will they have Maxie's wild curls or my red hair? Brown eyes or blue? No matter how hard I think about it, I can't visualize what the baby will look like. Until now, the baby has been a concept, not a person.

The rhythm of my heartbeats speeds up, pressure like a strap across my chest, pulling tighter and tighter, squeezing the breath out of me. But seeing that connection between Roger and Russel, seeing the way they are there for each other, even when they live thousands of miles apart, does something to me. *I want that.*

"Well, I'm excited for you. I'm way too young to be a great-grandma, but these things rarely come out as planned. I've already started some illustrations for the nursery. Do you have any colors or themes?"

"Not yet," I say weakly, mind still reeling from the realization that the baby is going to grow up into a *person*, and I'll be responsible for an entire human.

Mom takes pity on me and turns the conversation onto something mundane.

After breakfast is cleared up and the dishes rinsed, we gather in the living room to open presents. Usually I get Mom something small, but she and Roger gave me strict instructions to deposit my money in the bank and not buy them anything. And after the car, I don't expect many gifts. I figure I'll get at least one shirt—it's a tradition Mom has had for as long as I can remember—and maybe a gift card to somewhere.

The first box I'm handed comes out of the packages the Fergusons brought with them. It's roughly the size of a shirt box, but when I grab it from them it's got some heft to it. Definitely not a shirt. The little hand-painted tag—likely Miriam's work—says it's from Russel and Miriam. "You didn't need to get me anything," I say.

"Of course we did," Russel says. "It's Christmas."

Mom sets down the necklace Roger gave her so she can watch me open this gift. She doesn't have the same expectant look as she did with the car, so I assume she doesn't know what this one is.

I tear the layer of holiday paper off the box and my hands

still. I really hope they are reusing the box and the contents don't match the external graphics. Otherwise . . . wow. "Is this really a computer?" I ask, forcing my gaze away from the box on my lap to look at the Fergusons.

Mom covers her mouth with her hand. "Oh, Miriam, Russel, that's much too generous."

"Nonsense." Russel flicks his hands as if the notion is inconsequential.

"Why would you do this?" I choke out, looking at the laptop.

Russel claps me on the back. "You're family now, Ben. Roger mentioned that your computer was a bit out of date, and that you were going to do big things and needed something with a bit more oomph. I've got connections, so was able to get a great deal on a good machine."

"But we're not family. Not really. We're stepfamily, if anything."

"*Step* is just a word," Miriam says. "Family is more than blood."

I've had to deal with a lot of family stuff lately, but I don't know how to deal with this. Why? Why would they do this? They're treating me like I'm one of them, like I belong, and it's too much to process. My lungs seize and I gasp for breath. I surge off the couch and shove the laptop at Mom. "I can't—" I try to say, but the rest of the words don't come out. "I . . . I . . . Merry Christmas."

I rush past the Fergusons and Roger and Mom, trying not to see their expressions. I can't deal with their disapproval or disappointment or whatever they're feeling right now.

I slam the bedroom door behind me and launch myself into my bed, pulling the covers over my head.

All the while I'm trying to catch my breath and regain some composure, Miriam's words echo through my head.

Step *is just a word.*

Family is more than blood.

CHAPTER 22

"Son of a bitch," I hiss, dropping the plate I've just picked up. I don't even have time to worry about breaking yet another plate. I'm too busy staring at the blood pouring from the palm of my hand.

Deep red liquid pools around the broken shards of the plate, seeping around the remnants of a customer's steak, covering the gristle and bone in a macabre scene that makes me gag. The steak knife I picked up at the wrong angle is smeared with red.

"Ben?" Monica's voice echoes hollowly from somewhere behind me. Only then does the pain of the slice hit me.

I suck in the breath the stinging in my palm stole from me.

Everything around me expands and contracts, covered in a wavy haze like some kind of heat mirage. I can't look away from my hand. I've never been good about blood, but I've never seen this much of my own blood in one place. Logically I know there can't be as much of the viscous substance as it seems, but that doesn't stop the nausea and light-headedness from grabbing hold of me.

I sway on my feet.

"Ben!"

Monica's voice centers me a bit, but it's not until she grabs my arm and presses a napkin against my palm that I snap to full awareness. "I think I'm gonna puke," I say weakly.

She doesn't ask any questions, which I'm grateful for. It takes everything I have to keep from passing out in the middle of the Greco's dining room. Instead, she shoves me into a chair, pushes my head forward until my ears line up with my knees and all I can see are the boring nonslip black shoes I have to wear when working.

I feel her pull the napkin away from my hand, but don't look up. No, much better to stare at my shoes.

"I don't think it needs stitches," she says. "It's not very deep, just deep enough and long enough to be messy. Let's get you into the office, get it cleaned up and take another look." Her voice is the perfect combination of no-nonsense and sympathetic to clear my head. She's handling the situation the same way Mom would.

She squeezes my shoulder. "Think you can sit up?"

Slowly, I pull myself up, gauging the likelihood of actually passing out. When there's no sign of light-headedness or additional nausea, I let out a deep breath. I open my eyes but avoid looking at my hand.

"Well done. Are you up for a walk to the office?"

I do a quick systems check. "Yeah."

She folds my fingers over the napkin until I'm holding it in place. "Keep up the pressure. Easy does it." She guides me up and out of my seat. "Gio," she calls over my head, "can you clean up the table? Blood-safety cleanup."

"Shit, Ben, are you okay?"

"Yeah. I mean, I think so." I glance at the bloodstained napkin in my fist. "I'm a little afraid to look."

"It'll be fine," Monica soothes. "We'll clean it out, slap some gauze on it, and tape you up."

Gio stands close enough I can feel the heat from his body. "You sure he doesn't need stitches?"

"I don't think so, but we'll take a closer look. Right now, I need you to handle cleanup." Her voice firms.

Gio nods, and with a last look at me, heads to the closet in the back that houses the bloodborne-pathogen cleaning kit.

Monica leads me to the manager's office. The last time I spent any time in this room was when we had to fill out the paperwork after the eggplant debacle. I suspect there will be another accident report to fill out after this.

The desk chair squeaks when I sit in it, and somehow I end up rolling back half a foot before I stop the momentum with my feet. Monica reaches into a cupboard above the computer and drags out a hefty-sized first-aid kit. She dons a pair of gloves then proceeds to set out everything she will need. She's focused but keeps up a gentle banter that immediately calms me. Even when she uses antiseptic wipes to clean the slice in my palm and I cringe back, her voice distracts me from the sting.

She's telling me a story about the time she stole her brother's skateboard when she was eight, convinced she'd be the next Tony Hawk. She gasps in fake outrage when I have to ask her who Tony Hawk is.

"I can't even with you kids these days. Look him up on YouTube. You'll be amazed. He was the shit back in the day. Unfortunately for me, I did not have the same skills, so when I tried to do a kick-flip, I did not flip, I tripped, and scraped the heck out of my arm.

I had pieces of gravel stuck in my skin, and I was convinced they were embedded in bone. Right here," she says, pointing to a small divot an inch below her elbow.

By the time she's finished her story, my hand has been cleaned, the bleeding mostly stopped, and it has been wrapped in gauze. "Call your mom to pick you up. I think you'll be fine wrapped up, but make sure she takes a look in case she does want you to get stitches."

"I'm on my way," Mom says after I've explained what happened. "Twenty minutes."

While we wait, Monica finishes the accident report. I've only been there a couple of months and this is the second accident report she's had to fill out. "I'm beginning to suspect I'm not cut out for food service," I tell her.

"Nah," she says, waving the thought off. "You're new yet, and accidents happen. Though you may be setting a record for broken dishes."

"Ugh." I slump into the seat.

She ruffles my hair. "I'm kidding, Ben. Seriously, these things happen."

A few minutes go by. She's doing something with credit card receipts as I listen to the muted sounds from the kitchen. Her mom vibe is strong, and maybe that's why I'm so tempted to unload everything on her. She's also like a neutral party, and maybe that's what I need right now.

"Hey, Monica?"

She looks up from her receipts, her expression open and patient.

"You know what's going on with me, right?"

She inclines her head, saying slowly, "I've heard some of it, yeah."

"Have you ever, I don't know, worked so hard for something, something big, something not entirely in your control?"

Clearing her throat, Monica shifts in her seat. "Yes, Ben. I think that's something everyone faces at one point or another."

"How do you know if what you're doing is the right thing to do?"

"Wow, you don't ask the easy questions, do you?" She huffs out a deep breath, crossing a leg over her opposite knee. "I don't know if you ever know, not a hundred percent, if you're doing the right thing. There's always doubt and worry."

I run my thumb over the gauze on my injured hand, cataloging the texture change from waffled cotton to smooth tape. "How do you keep yourself going? How do you get past the doubt and worry?"

She takes a minute to think about her answer, which I appreciate. It tells me that she's not going to throw some clichéd platitude at me. "For me—and I can only speak to my own situation, you understand—for me I go back to the why of it all. Why do I want it? Why is it important? Is it important to just me, or to others as well? Am I doing it for the right reasons? Is the cost—the emotional and mental cost—worth it? Are the things I have to sacrifice worth it?"

"And that keeps you going?"

"Sometimes," she says. "If my answers continue to support the goal, so to speak. Here's the thing, Ben. Sometimes I think the more you want something, the harder you fight for it, the more doubt can take root. With every stumbling block, with every rejection, it's easy to question if it's worth it. And sometimes, in the end, it may not be worth it. Sometimes our goals change. Or we realize that working for it causes too much pain or hurts too many people."

I slump. "I'm not sure that helps. Why do things have to be so wishy-washy? Why are there so many variables?"

Monica smiles at me, but it's sympathetic. "Sadly, that's part of being human." She pauses, biting her lip, then asks, "Are you worried that you're not doing the right thing?"

It's my turn to bite my lip. "Sort of. But not exactly. I'm going to have a kid, right? But what if I'm bad at it? I'm trying to learn everything I need to know. I'm taking the classes, reading the books. I understand the basics of childhood development, and, at least academically, I've got a grasp of first aid."

Monica reaches over to squeeze my shoulder. "Look, Ben, being a good parent is more than academics. It's also about being present, being supportive. It's wanting what's best for the child and doing everything you can to make it happen. Sure, you can learn a lot of the practical aspects of parenthood, but a lot of it comes from the heart." She taps my chest lightly.

"You remind me of my mom." I don't mean to say that, but the words escape before I can rein them in. "You're going to be an awesome mom."

Her smile falters. "Thank you for that, Ben. One of these days I hope I'll be able to prove it."

There's a rap at the door, then someone cracks it open. Gio peeks in. "Ben, your mom's here."

Monica and I stand. I'm not sure where the urge comes from, but before I leave to see my mom, I wrap my arms around Monica. "Thanks for everything."

CHAPTER 23

The minute hand on the clock in the robotics room clicks over to the next mark. It's 3:27. When I checked the clock what feels like ten minutes ago, it was 3:25. How can only two minutes have passed?

Maxie's ultrasound is at four thirty, and the time is crawling. Doesn't help that Percy is droning on and on about the steps we need to take to prevent another situation like we had at sectionals. "Fifth place isn't going to cut it," he's saying, pounding his fist onto the table in front of him.

We're two weeks into January. It's been nearly two months. You'd think it happened yesterday the way Percy talks. Eventually they'll have to move on. Instead of moving on, however, the others murmur their agreement.

I will absolutely never live down that one mistake.

I look at the clock. Seriously? Still 3:27? Is the clock broken? I slip my phone out of my pocket and look at the display. It also says 3:27.

Mo clears his throat.

I jerk my head up. Is he actually going to talk to me? The last several weeks have been weird, not hanging out with Mo. I've thought about a dozen ways to approach him to figure out a way out of our current situation, but whenever I'm faced with Mo, I can't find the words.

But no, he's not trying to talk to me. He's getting my attention because somebody else wants to talk to me. In fact, everyone in the room is looking at me expectantly.

I clear my throat. "Ah, sorry. I missed that."

Percy shakes his head, reminding me so much of my mom when she's exasperated with me that I picture him with her long red hair. I almost laugh but manage to hold it back. No one in this group looks ready to be amused. "I said," Percy says, "I need you to work with Jay to make sure he's got a grasp of the coding we need for the regional meet. We need to make sure all the prechecks and safeguards are in place to avoid mistakes."

I flinch. I hate the reminder of my failure almost as much as I hate the doubt the team now has in my abilities. "Sure. I can do that." I look at Jay. "I've got something tonight, and I work tomorrow. Maybe Thursday?" Except, no, Thursday is the first of the parenting classes. "Sunday?" I offer.

Percy isn't the only one glaring at me now. "Sunday? That's practically a week away."

"It's five days," I say.

He narrows his eyes at me. Equal odds he's going to hiss at me or throw a punch. "Not the point," he grits out. "We can't afford to wait *five days*. We need this piece locked up so we can cement our plan."

"Sorry," I say. I'm not sorry, though, so I don't know why I'm apologizing. I have enough to worry about, and enough responsibility piled onto my plate that I don't have time to worry about his feelings. "My schedule is packed. It's Sunday or never."

Jay speaks up. "I can do Sunday, as long as it's after church."

Before Percy can argue some more, I agree. "Great. How about three o'clock?" Three would be perfect for me. It'll give me enough time to at least start on my homework.

I chance a quick look at the clock on the wall. It's 3:35. At least we're making progress.

I have to meet Gio at the entrance at four. I don't even know how it happened. One minute Maxie texts me the time of the ultrasound appointment, the next Mom tells me she can't drive me because of a staff meeting she has to attend. I even asked Roger if he would drive me to the clinic. He agreed before immediately backing out. He gave some kind of excuse about mandatory overtime at work. He also reminded me—gently—that I have a car I can use, as soon as I make the time to take my driver's test.

Yeah, I'll get on it. Eventually.

I then tried to convince Mom one of those ride-share apps would be perfectly safe.

Somehow, instead of downloading the Uber app, Mom convinced me to ask Gio.

Riding together to Greco's over the last few weeks, we've managed to avoid any discussion of a personal nature. Even the extra hours we've worked at the restaurant during the holiday break were sort of "business as usual." He hasn't said anything about our conversation, the one where he admitted he'd *wanted* to kiss me, and I've been as diligent in avoiding the topic. To be honest, I've been a little preoccupied, what with interviewing adoptive parents and learning of Mom's betrayal, strangely emotional Christmas revelations, and the upcoming ultrasound. I haven't had much time to dwell on, analyze, or dissect the moment in the car or the discussion later.

The Mom's betrayal thing is another issue I haven't had time to do anything about.

I don't know if it's procrastination or protection, but I'd much rather ignore it all for a while. I have bigger fish to fry, so to speak. Besides, talking to Mom would mean facing the fact that she doesn't really support what I'm doing. So, yeah, better to pretend everything is normal.

Except having the boy who kissed me, the boy I have feelings for, drive me to an ultrasound appointment with the girl I had sex with five months ago is decidedly *not* normal.

Mo clears his throat again.

I look up, and the whole team is staring at me. Again. Damn it. "Sorry."

"Whatever. Just get your head in the game one of these days. There's too much on the line, and you're messing it up for all of us."

My phone beeps, letting me know it's time to grab my stuff and head to the front. Thank God.

I stand up, grabbing my backpack from where it sits at my feet.

Mitch and Anna cock their heads in unison. Percy sighs.

"Um . . ." I look around. Even the new guys seem ticked. "Sorry. I've got an appointment."

Mr. Rose pushes his glasses up his forehead. "Ben, why don't you swing by during your lunch period tomorrow?" His dark brown eyes pin me in place and dread seeps into my guts.

Shit. That can't be good. Mr. Rose is usually pretty chill. He lets us do our thing and almost never steps in on person-to-person issues. But whenever he does, it usually leaves us feeling guilty that we've disappointed him. So him stepping in now is definitely a bad sign.

"Sure," I say. I add it to my mental list of things I have to do tomorrow. I also add it to the ever-growing list of things to worry about. Unlike the others, at least this one will fall off the list in less than twenty-four hours.

"So, you ready for this?" Gio asks as I hop into the passenger seat of his car.

"Yeah, I guess. I've been doing some research. The twenty-week ultrasound focuses on fetal development. The purpose is to make sure the baby is progressing as it should. It's noninvasive, and technology—"

"Dude, I meant are you ready to see your baby for the first time?"

"Oh." I think about it for a second. *Am* I ready? "I mean, I won't actually be meeting the baby. I'll be seeing an image derived from ultrasound."

"Okay, Ben. We'll go with that." Gio turns his attention back to the traffic, but there's a slight smile on his face.

The clinic is in a strip mall, which feels wrong. Something as important as this shouldn't be two doors down from a hair salon, and four doors from Dunkin' Donuts. I assumed—wrongly—that the ultrasound equipment would be in a hospital. Nope.

"I'll wait for you out here," Gio says when we pull into the parking lot.

"You're not coming in?"

He snorts. "Not a chance. You're on your own for this one." He pulls out his phone, then flicks his fingers at me, urging me to go.

I do a quick scan of the parking lot and see the Jacobsons' Acura.

Okay. I've got this. I tug the hem of my coat and straighten the stocking cap on my head before exiting the car and stepping out into the January air. I hustle to the entrance.

Maxie's obstetrician's office looks like any other doctor's office I've been in. Lots of beige and pastel colors, a somber silence weighing heavy in the air. The pictures on the wall are serene landscapes, and large potted plants decorate the corners. Maxie and her mother sit on the far end of the waiting room, Mrs. Jacobson reading a *Good Housekeeping* magazine and Maxie doing something on her phone. They're the only two people in the room who don't seem to notice me right away. There are three other women sitting in the room, and another two women are parked behind the reception desk. Seven women . . . and me.

Nope, I don't stand out at all.

"Can I help you?" the older of the two ladies at the reception desk asks.

"I'm with them," I say, nodding at Maxie and her mom.

"Of course," the lady says, but stares after me as I cross the room like she's never seen a boy before.

Mrs. Jacobson studiously ignores me when I take the chair next to Maxie.

The wait seems to take forever.

I'm too keyed up to wait patiently. Five minutes after I sit down, I stand up. I dig through the discarded stack of magazines on a low table in front of us. Five minutes after that, I've sorted through the magazines, alphabetized them by title, and arranged issues by date. Five minutes later, I'm back in my seat, knee bouncing furiously as I watch yet another clock move slower than a depressed sloth.

I lean over to Maxie. "How much longer?" I whisper.

She angles her eyes at me but doesn't turn away from her phone. She's got some kind of word game going. She shrugs.

Mrs. Jacobson sniffs, turning a page in her magazine.

I spend most of the wait time watching Maxie. Her whole

expression—her whole demeanor—is closed off. If I didn't know better, I'd think she doesn't want to be here. She's closed in on herself, her arms and legs tucked tight to her body, her head angled down.

Finally, when my phone screen displays 4:55—a full twenty-five minutes after the appointment time—Maxie is called in. We haven't made it past the front desk before the nurse who called on Maxie stops us.

"Will you be joining us?" she asks me.

I don't care for her tone, but I try not to let it get my back up. "Yes," I say simply.

The nurse turns to Maxie. "Do you consent to his presence in the room with you?"

Maxie doesn't hesitate, thankfully. "Yes."

The nurse studies Maxie for a long moment. She looks at Mrs. Jacobson as though waiting for her to step in. When no one objects, we're led into a hallway behind the main desk and escorted into a small room with an exam table, a cart holding what I assume is the ultrasound machine, and a couple of chairs.

Mrs. Jacobson takes a seat while Maxie settles onto the exam table. I stand away from the table, not quite sure what to do with myself.

The sonographer, a small woman about Roger's age wearing peach-colored scrubs, explains to Maxie what she can expect.

"I'll put some gel on your belly first. Then I'll use a transducer"—she holds out some kind of handheld device—"to get the ultrasound images. This uses high-frequency sound waves to create images of what is happening inside your body. Hopefully the baby will cooperate so we can get what we need. Are you ready?"

Maxie nods. A moment later, she lifts her shirt, exposing the mound of her pregnant belly.

"Holy shit." My eyes widen at the sight. How have her baggy sweaters hidden that?

Mrs. Jacobson hisses at me, something about my language, but I barely register it.

When was the last time I really looked at Maxie? I see her nearly every day at school, but have I really looked? The image in my head is of a slightly rounder, slightly softer version of the Maxie I've known. That Maxie isn't obviously pregnant. But this Maxie, with her pale skin stretched over what is clearly a baby bump, is undeniably pregnant. "You're really pregnant," I tell her.

"Benjamin!" Mrs. Jacobson snaps.

Maxie reaches down as though to tug her shirt back into place.

Replaying my words, I curse myself. "Sorry. I didn't mean it like that. I hadn't noticed . . ." I let my words trail off. I'm making things worse.

The sonographer glances around the room at us. "Are we good to begin?"

She waits until Mrs. Jacobson gives the go-ahead. The sonographer shifts the waistband of Maxie's leggings down a bit, tucking some kind of towel under the lower curve of her belly. Maxie sucks in a breath as the sonographer slathers some gel over her skin. "The images will show on the screen over there," the sonographer says, pointing to a monitor on the wall. "Before we start, I need to ask if you want to know the sex."

"Yes," I say.

"No," Maxie says.

"What?" I ask. "Why not?"

She looks away. "We can talk about it later. But I absolutely do not want to know the sex."

The look Mrs. Jacobson sends me keeps my mouth shut.

Maxie lies there through the procedure, not looking at the

monitor. She changes position whenever the sonographer asks her to, but other than that she doesn't engage in the process at all. She's detached, distant.

Me, on the other hand, I'm completely fascinated.

Almost immediately when the sonographer presses the wand to Maxie's belly, I hear a whooshing sound and images flicker onto the screen. At first it looks like white shadows pulsing here and there against the black backdrop of the monitor. I squint at the screen, trying to make anything out.

The sonographer moves the wand, and suddenly there's an image I recognize. It's a profile view of what is clearly a fetus. There's a head, a nose, lips, a chin. The curve of a back.

"Oh my God," I whisper. "It's a baby." I step closer to the monitor to get a better look.

The sonographer continues through whatever checklist she has to get through. She examines the brain, pointing out the cerebellum when I ask. She even shows me what looks like a bubble but is in fact the eye developing. That little fluttering speck is the beating heart. "This is the coolest thing ever," I say. "All this with the use of sound waves. So freaking cool."

Now I have questions. Lots and lots of questions. What is she looking at? What is she looking for? What does that show? Is that normal?

The sonographer is patient with me, even though she doesn't answer most of my questions. She'll tell me what something is, but not whether it's normal or healthy. She'll explain what she's looking for, but not what she's finding.

"The doctor will go over this with the mother," she says.

All of the nonanswers make me nervous. Does this mean there's something wrong and she doesn't want to be the one to tell us? Are there signs of birth defects?

"Shut up, Ben!" Maxie snaps.

Everyone in the room freezes, even the sonographer.

Somehow I've forgotten she was in the room. I've been so focused on the images on the screen and the answers—and nonanswers—from the sonographer, that I completely tuned out Maxie's presence.

"Do you need a minute?" the sonographer asks. "We're about done here, but if you need to stretch or use the restroom, we can do that."

"No," Maxie says. "I want to get this over with." She turns her head and meets my eyes. "I know your science brain is fully engaged now, but I can't deal with this. I want to pretend I'm not here right now. The more I know, the more I see, the more real it is. I can't afford to get attached, Ben. So you either need to back off and stop asking questions or go home."

The crack in her voice and the tension in her face convince me more than her words. I nod.

The rest of the appointment proceeds under an almost suffocating silence. It gives me too much time to think. Too much time to reflect.

For the first time since Maxie told me about the pregnancy, I'm scared. Not about what people will think of me, or what Mom wants me to do, or about the changes I have to make. No, I'm not scared about how this affects me.

No, I'm afraid for the baby. I'm scared that I won't be enough. I'm scared that I'll mess something up and the baby—*my baby*—will be hurt by it.

This baby is not a theory or a concept anymore. It's a baby, a tiny human baby, with a heartbeat and toes and veins. This might be the realest thing to happen to me, and I don't know what the hell to think about any of it.

CHAPTER 24

When I get back to his car in the lot, Gio is watching some kind of video on his phone. He doesn't notice me until I knock on the window to get his attention. He hits the locks and I drop into the passenger seat.

"How'd it go?"

I shake my head. I'm not ready to talk about it yet. "What were you watching?"

He looks at the phone he's dropped into a cup holder. "Oh, nothing really. Some cooking videos."

"Yeah? What kind?"

He clears his throat. *"The Great British Baking Show."*

I can't hold back my snort of laughter. "You're not serious."

He crosses his arms over his chest. "What wrong with the show?"

I blink at him. "Um, nothing, I guess. But a baking show?"

"I like baking." He says this like he's daring me to laugh again.

"Since when?" I can't think of a single time in as long as I've known him that he's baked anything.

"The last couple of years I've really started getting into it. It's this great combination of science and creativity."

"Yeah?"

"For sure. So many baked things have to have specific ingredients in specific proportions. Miss a step, the whole thing is ruined. Take bread."

"Bread," I repeat dumbly.

"You've got to activate the yeast, which requires certain ingredients and certain temperatures, and the dough has to rise, which requires specific proofing times. You have to knead the dough to build up the gluten. If you don't knead it enough, the gluten doesn't form and your dough lacks strength and will fall apart when baked. Knead it too much, and the bread or whatever is too tough. It's all science. Then you have the flavors and additional elements. For everything you add or change, you have to know what the impact will be."

"It is like science," I say, a little awed. Not about the science of baking. No, it's Gio. I don't think I've ever heard him so excited about anything. "What's your favorite thing to bake?"

"Bread, really. But I've been playing around with some Italian cookie ideas for the restaurant."

"That is so cool. Can I try something when you bake next? I don't know anything about baking, but I can't wait to try a cookie or some bread that you've made."

"Maybe," Gio says, reaching for his seat belt. "I'm not going to have a lot of time to bake. Baseball starts soon, and my mom wants me to look for a summer internship, or at least a job 'in my field.'" He hooks his fingers into quotation marks around this last.

"Your field? You haven't graduated yet. What could your field possibly be?"

"I'll be heading to UW for journalism in the fall. It's a great program, but super competitive. Mom thinks I should get some practical experience before classes start."

His voice has completely changed. When he spoke of the science of baking, he was enthusiastic and excited. When he mentioned journalism, his tone dropped, and he could have been talking about going to the dentist for a cleaning. "Can't you go to school for baking?"

"I looked at a couple of culinary programs, ones with good pastry courses, but my mom flipped her lid when I brought it up."

"But Paolo would approve, right?"

Gio grunts, putting his car into gear. "Which is one more reason for my mom to freak out. She acts like my dad is trying to force me into the family business. Mom used the words *over my dead body*."

"What's her deal with the restaurant? It's not like your dad's some kind of deadbeat."

"She blames the restaurant for their divorce. It's a lot of work, a lot of long hours, and such a small margin between success and failure."

"I don't get it. She's afraid you'll have to work too much?"

"Not at all. It's more that she feels like Dad chose it over her, and now she won't let me choose him over her. And anything having to do with the restaurant, cooking, or food in general is, in her mind, me choosing him."

"Doesn't she care what you want?"

His hands tighten on the steering wheel. "It's not that she doesn't care what I want, it's more that she doesn't trust me to know what I want."

"But you're doing what she wants, aren't you? Journalism at UW?"

"Don't you start," he warns.

"I'm not starting anything. I want to understand. Why are you doing what she wants if it's not what you want? Shouldn't you be able to choose?"

"It's not like I hate the idea of journalism. I think I'd be good at it, and there's a lot of options for me. I figure I give it a try, finish my degree, and then see how it feels. If it doesn't work, I can always go to culinary school at that point."

Personally, it feels like a lot of wasted time and money, but it's not my life. "Okay."

He reads something in my voice. "Look, you don't know what it's like. Sometimes I feel like I'm caught in some kind of tug-of-war battle between what I want and what my parents expect. It's easier to go along with things, at least for now."

I want to no longer be the rope in this twisted tug-of-war between you and my parents.

"Maxie said something like that. That she's getting pulled between what I want and what her parents want."

"I'm not surprised. Did you finally talk to her about this?"

"A few weeks ago. You were right. She said no one asked her what she wants, that we're all making decisions for her."

"What do you think?"

I slump down in the seat. "Yeah, we kind of are. I want the baby, her parents want the baby to be adopted."

"And what does Maxie want?"

"She wants none of this to have happened. She wants it over with. But it's too late for either of those options."

"How'd it go today?" He repeats his question from earlier. This time I don't look for a way to distract him.

"It's so freaking cool. I saw the baby's heart, and their little feet, and their cerebellum. Amazing what they can do with sound waves. They could have told us the gender, but Maxie said no."

"Did you want to know?"

I swallow hard. "Yeah, kind of. I mean, it would have been cool. I could have started coordinating things. But she didn't want to know. I guess knowing the gender makes it too real for her."

"I can see that," Gio says. "Especially if she's trying to stay detached. It's got to be hard for her."

"Yeah." I don't say anything for a minute. I sit and watch the amber lights of the streetlamps in the midnight blue of the winter twilight. "It's a little terrifying," I admit.

"Knowing the gender?" Gio asks.

"No. Not really. But the whole ultrasound thing. It was cool, right? Super interesting. But totally scary too."

"How so?"

"Well, you know what they're checking? There's the baby measurements and stuff, to make sure they're developing right. But they're also looking for things like defects, conditions, abnormalities. Things like spina bifida and Down syndrome. I had this moment, right, when I had to think about that. What if. What if there is something wrong with the baby? Like, raising a child is tough enough, but how would I deal with something more?"

"That's . . . a lot." Gio looks away from the road long enough to meet my eyes.

"What if I'm not ready?" I whisper.

His face tightens, but he doesn't say anything.

"The thing is, I can't talk to anyone about this. Anyone else," I correct, since clearly I'm willing to talk to Gio for some reason. "If anyone even suspects I have doubts, even momentary, well-justified doubts, I'll lose everything. I know no one understands why I'm doing this. Or why I'm not backing down. They don't know why this is so important to me. Mom says she supports me, and will help me. But does she support me? This whole time she's been helping me, she's also been expecting me to give up. She's waiting for me to break."

I don't even realize we've pulled over until Gio puts the car into Park in a grocery store lot.

"Haven't you talked to your mom about what you heard Maxie's dad say yet?" Gio watches me with surprise that I think might actually be disapproval.

I cross my arms over my chest. "Not yet. I keep meaning to, but then I get so mad, and I'm afraid of what I'll say. I've never not been able to talk to her about things, but I can't talk to her about this."

"About what she told Maxie's parents? Or about your fears?"

"Both. If I tell her about the fears, it'll prove to her that I'm not ready. And if she thinks I'm not ready, she'll stop supporting me."

"My therapist says—"

I swing my head toward him. "Your therapist? You see a therapist?"

"I did. After my parents' divorce and again after our parents' divorce. That's not the point, though."

Man, how I want to ask questions. But, yeah, it isn't the point right now.

"The point is," he continues, "a parent isn't a mind reader. They will do the best with the information they have, attempt to make the right decisions and hope for the right outcomes, but that means that sometimes, especially when it's important, you have to be able to tell them the truth. Tell them, and trust that they will react the way you need them to."

"And how's that working for you, journalism major?"

"Just because I don't follow the advice, doesn't mean it's not good advice." He rolls his eyes, lips twisting into a wry smile. "But let's break it down. What do you want from your mom? No, let me say it differently. What do you *need* from your mom?"

What do I need? "I want her to support me. I want her to accept that this is important to me and that I'm not going to give it up, simply because I have to change some plans."

"What do you think she needs in order to give you what you need?"

"Are you quoting your therapist now?" Deflection, yeah, but looking for the answers to his questions makes me queasy.

He rolls his eyes. "Just go with it. I think it'll help. What do you think she needs?"

I close my eyes and tip my head back against the headrest. What would Mom need?

I want her to accept that this is important to me. But have I ever told her why it's important to me? I swallow back the nausea creeping through me, because the answer is *no*. No, I've never told her the real reason this is important to me. I've given her reasons, but not *the* reason.

Emotions suck.

"If I tell her the truth, it will hurt her feelings," I say quietly.

"But if you don't tell her the truth, she won't understand. And that hurts you."

"Yeah, well, it is what it is."

"But it doesn't have to be."

I don't say anything to that. Instead, I fold my arms in front of my chest and stare out the window.

Gio sighs, putting the car back into Drive. "Just think about it. You both deserve more than what you're giving."

CHAPTER 25

"Knock knock," I say, tapping on the doorframe to Mr. Rose's classroom at the beginning of the lunch period.

He looks up from the catalog on his desk and peers at me over the top of his reading glasses. "Oh, good morning, Ben. Glad you remembered."

I spent most of last night and all of this morning worried about today's meeting with Mr. Rose. I was so keyed up, in fact, I managed to not talk to Mom, even after the conversation I had with Gio. Though, Gio would probably tell me I'm using the meeting with the robotics team advisor as a convenient excuse. Whatever.

I shift my backpack on my shoulder and make my way into the room. He gestures to a stool at one of the workbenches and stands to join me.

I mentally prepare myself for the lecture I'm about to get. I'm ready for anything from my attitude with Percy to my commitment to the team. He might even have something to say about the last batch of coding I did, since it was not at all up to my normal standard. I'm not ready for what he says.

"How are you doing, Ben?"

My knee, which started bouncing as soon as I sat down, stills. "Fine?" My answer is more of a question than a statement because I'm not 100 percent certain I heard him right. Don't get me wrong. I like Mr. Rose, and he is one of those teachers you know actually likes his job and his students, but he's never been one to ask what could be considered personal questions.

He pushes his glasses up to his forehead, and his dark eyes nail me to my spot. "Things have been difficult for you lately."

"Oh, no—" I'm not sure why I object to what he's saying. Maybe because I've been trying so hard to keep all my balls in the air, or ducks in a row, or whatever stupid cliché means I'm doing what I'm supposed to without missing anything. But the knowledge that I haven't been able to hide my personal . . . challenges from him, someone I want so much to be proud of me, embarrasses me.

"I'm not asking for details," Mr. Rose says. "You don't have to share your personal business. But I want you to know that if you need a break from the team—"

"No!" How could he ask that? I absolutely, positively, without a doubt do not want a break from the team. It's my future. All my dreams for the future are based on robotics and engineering. "That's the last thing I'd want to do."

He watches me without speaking for so long I start to squirm on my stool. Finally, I break. "I know my time's been a bit divided lately, but I can make more. I'll work with Jay like Percy wants. I'm sorry I let you down—"

"Ben," he says, stopping my words. "You haven't let anyone down. But I am concerned."

"I'm fine—"

"Ben, you're exhausted. You're pale and have dark circles under your eyes big enough to park a bus in."

"I had a paper due—" I begin.

He sighs, pinching the bridge of his nose. "Ben, look at your shirt."

My shirt? What's wrong with my shirt? I look blankly down at the faded gray fabric.

"It's inside out," Mr. Rose says.

"Oh." I finger the seam that should not be facing outward. "Whoops."

"Ben?"

"Yeah?"

"It's also backwards."

I slap the collar, the rough texture of the tag scraping my palm. Heat sears up my neck. "It was a long night. I'll be fine."

He presses his lips together, and I think he's going to push the issue. He doesn't. Instead he says, "Do you know who George Vaughn is?"

The name rings a bell, but my tired brain can't quite remember why.

Catching my uncertainty, Mr. Rose says, "He's a friend of mine."

"Okay."

"We went to college together," he says.

"That's cool," I say. Why in the world are we talking about one of his old friends?

"He's also the director of the Vaucanson Academy?"

My breath catches. "No way. Really?" That's why I know his name. I've read his bio on the Vaucanson website and found some articles about him.

As much as I respect Mr. Rose, I had no idea he's friends with someone at Vaucanson. Like, Mr. Rose is a high school teacher and Vaughn is a nationally—if not internationally—renowned engineer and inventor.

"Really? That's so cool."

"I think so. But the reason I'm bringing him up is you."

"Me?" I squeak. My stomach lurches and my knee renews its bouncing.

Mr. Rose folds his hands together in front of him on the black-painted surface of the workbench. "Why didn't you mention you'd been accepted into the Jacques de Vaucanson Summer Academy? It's a huge accomplishment. I'd have thought you'd want to celebrate."

I cringe. "Yeah, well, I don't think I'll be going."

Mr. Rose jumps up. "What? Why? This is huge. You can't miss out on this opportunity. If it's a matter of the cost, there are things we can work on. Fundraising, grants. Heck, we could open a GoFundMe. This program practically guarantees scholarships to a prestigious university."

"I know. But my mom says—"

"I can talk to her. Explain what an important opportunity this is for you, for your future. She may not understand."

His words sting. It's not like I don't know what I'd be losing out on by not accepting the place at the summer academy. "I think she understands, but with the whole Maxie thing, she thinks my priorities have shifted."

"Maxie thing?"

He doesn't know? "The baby," I offer.

"Maxie's pregnant? And you have new priorities?"

I nod.

He settles back onto his stool, eyes wide in sudden understanding. "Different priorities, indeed."

How could Mr. Rose not have heard about me, Maxie, and the baby? As far as I can tell, *everyone* knows about the gay kid who got a girl pregnant.

"So that's why she quit the team."

I nod again.

"And you're going to . . ."

Again, I nod. It's not like he's expecting me to answer. His unseeing eyes are fixed on some point over my head. I'm pretty sure he's waiting for everything to sink in.

"I see," he says half a minute later, focusing on me again. "Maxie's pregnant, you're the father, and now you're skipping a once-in-a-lifetime chance to attend the Jacques de Vaucanson Summer Academy."

"Right."

"What the hell, man!"

Mr. Rose and I swing to face the classroom doorway. A seriously irate Mo charges into the room, fists clenched. "Are you out of your damn mind?"

"Mohammed," Mr. Rose warns.

"No, you don't get it," Mo says in a tone of voice he really shouldn't use in front of a teacher. He points to me. "He's been working toward this for the last two years. This is supposed to be his stepping-stone to getting into MIT or one of the other big schools. And he's throwing it away? It's bullshit."

"I don't disagree," Mr. Rose says.

"I can't believe he'd— Wait, what?" Mo squints at Mr. Rose. "You don't disagree?"

My heart sinks.

"No. But it's not my business, nor my place to judge." Mr. Rose gives Mo a long look. "Neither is it yours."

"It is my place, because he's my best friend. If I don't call him on his bullshit, who will?"

My heart leaps. Mo still thinks of me as his best friend? I hadn't let myself hope for that.

"Or at least I thought he was," Mo says.

And my heart sinks again. It's getting quite the workout, what with all the leaping and sinking.

"You two should head to class. The bell's going to ring soon." Mr. Rose shifts his attention back to me. "If you need to talk, you can come find me. Hold off on turning down the spot at Vaucanson. Things might change and you won't want to burn any bridges. I can talk to George if it comes down to it."

On some level I guess I appreciate that Mr. Rose wants to help, but I can't ignore the fact that now there's one more adult who thinks I'm going to change my mind, or who thinks I'm making the wrong choice. I wish people would understand. This isn't something I'm taking lightly. I'm going into this whole parenthood thing with my eyes wide open.

Mo and I leave the classroom and head toward the language arts wing for our shared English class. It's almost like old times. Except instead of planning our next experiment, bitching about his mom's refusal to allow sugar in the house, or dissecting the most binge-worthy sci-fi television series, Mo is glaring at me.

Finally, he stops trying to glare me to death. He spins so he's in front of me, facing me. "Why are you ruining your life? You're giving everything up for this . . . Why?"

Like the day in the lunchroom, I have trouble making the words come out. I know he won't let me get away with not answering. "I don't know if I can explain," I say. "It's not that I don't want to," I add when he looks like he's going to turn away.

"I need you to try, because right now all I see is you giving up everything you've ever wanted. Neither you nor Maxie will tell me anything, and I'm stuck without either of my best friends and I don't know why. Maxie's hiding from everyone and you're spending all your time with Gio, and I'm left all alone. I need to know what's so important that you're sacrificing your future and . . . and me."

His voice cracks on that last part and I feel like shit. I've experienced my share of embarrassment and anxiety over the last few months, but this is the first time I've actually felt shame. I did this. This whole time I've been acting like Mo deserted me, but all along it was me.

The bell rings, a last reminder that class is about to start, but I don't have time for that. I need to make this right with Mo. Or, if not right, better. Which means I have to open up. I tilt my head toward the bathroom. I can't think of anywhere else we can have some privacy.

He raises his eyebrows at me. Yeah, skipping class isn't something we do. At least, I hadn't done it until Gio took me to the lake. I bite my lip, leaving it up to him. A second later, he hustles to the boys' bathroom.

With the door closed behind us, I try to wrestle my circling thoughts into some kind of order. Mo keeps his eyes trained on me, not giving me an out. Not now that we're this far.

"You don't know what it's like to be without a father. To watch all the kids and all the dads every day, knowing you don't have that."

Mo shakes his head.

"Right, because your dad is awesome. And he's *present*. He goes to all your events, helps you with homework, even coached your kiddie soccer team. He supports you every step of the way. I didn't have that."

His thick brows draw close over his eyes. "But you had your mom. She did all of those things."

"No, I know my mom is awesome. She's always been there, sure, but it's different."

"I don't get it. How's it any different?"

The words try to scramble in my brain again, but I pluck out a couple of examples. "Who taught you to shave?"

He glides his fingers over the barely there fuzz at the corner of his lips. "My dad."

"Right. Mom had to watch a YouTube video to make sure she explained it right. Apparently shaving your legs is different."

"Okay," he says, still sounding confused.

"And who talked to you about wet dreams, and sex, and masturbation?"

His eyes widen and his face blazes fuchsia. "Your *mom* talked to you about that?" He looks scandalized.

"Who else?" It involved more YouTube videos and a series of articles. And don't get me started with the resources she gave me after coming out.

He shakes his head. "I guess I get what you're saying, but I don't see why this means you need to have a baby. There are a lot of single parents out there. Moms and dads. *You* will be one of them. What if the baby's a girl? All those examples with your mom will be true for you too."

"It's not the same. My mom will be there, so the baby will have a positive female role model too."

"It's not about male or female role models. That can't be it. There are so many more dynamics. Same-sex couples, single parents, foster families with happy, well-adjusted kids."

"You don't get it. You can't."

"Damn it, I'm trying here. I'm trying to understand. But you're not acting rational. You're always rational, so I don't know what to do with any of this. Your mom is amazing and is everything a parent should be. Even your different stepdads were pretty great. I can't figure out what you're trying to make up for."

"They didn't want me, Mo. All the men, the dads, they all left and didn't come back. My child will know they are wanted and that their dad won't leave them."

CHAPTER 26

The school at night is nothing like the school during the day. It's actually freaking me out. My footsteps echo weirdly on the tile, mirroring my heartbeat. It shouldn't be this strange. I mean, I walk these halls almost every day. There, to my right, the corridor leading to the science wing is a dimly lit cavern, the red emergency exit sign flickering at odd intervals, causing my imagination to run wild. I've been at the school over weekends and even in the summer, so the lack of people and activity really shouldn't bother me. But something about the school at night . . . Of course, it might not be the nighttime atmosphere that's the issue. It might be what's waiting for me around the next corner.

Birthing classes.

My stomach drops at the reminder. I've already completed the four-week Parenting Skills class Mom dug up for me. And it doesn't end there. My mom's been dumping pamphlets for classes about early childhood development, children's health and development, and even fiscal planning. I think she printed everything she found on the American Pregnancy Association's website. I don't know why she's convinced I need to attend this particular class. I totally understand why I need the parenting classes. I get it. I do. But the birthing class? It's not like Maxie's going to let me be at the birth. But it's one of Mom's rules, so I'm here.

I hitch my backpack more comfortably on my shoulders. The weight of it—of what's inside it, to be more specific—reassures me. Less reassuring is the total silence coming from the darkened hallway. I check the digital clock display above the top edge of lockers. It's 6:54. Class is scheduled to begin at seven o'clock. Where are the students? The instructor? I've deliberately planned my arrival to cut it close without any chance of being late. No way am I the first person here.

I pull the registration confirmation I printed from my pocket. I've memorized the room number—108—but the double-check calms my nerves. Room 108 is the same room where I spent a semester studying health and development as a freshman. Appropriate, I guess. Yep, here it is in black-and-white. Room 108.

I search the hallway, looking for some sign of Maxie. Or, hell, anyone else. But there's nothing. No one.

A flash of hot pink on the door stops me.

PREGNANCY AND CHILDBIRTH EDUCATION—MOVED TO THE DANCE STUDIO!!! SEE YOU THERE!!! :)

Yes, the sign has *six* exclamation marks and a smiley face. Not a good sign for things to come.

I check the time again. It's 6:56. I curse under my breath. The dance studio is off the gym, which is on the complete other side of the school. If I run, I *might* be able to get there on time. And since I hate being late, I run.

Three and a half minutes later, the rubber soles of my shoes squeaking on polished tile, I wrench open the dance studio's door.

Panting and sweating, I try to catch my breath, only to realize eleven people are staring at me in shock.

Damn it.

"Oh, ah, hi." I wave somewhat weakly.

Eight people wave back from where they are situated on blue gym mats and beanbags.

A woman I assume is the instructor sweeps over, a long blond braid swinging behind her. She's wearing some kind of flowy, flowery shirt over gray leggings, with flat sandals on her feet. She doesn't look like any kind of teacher or nurse I've ever met. She reminds me of a combination of my mom and the lady who sells healing crystals at the farmers' market on Saturday mornings.

"Good evening," she says. "I think you must be in the wrong room. This is a pregnancy and birthing class."

"Um, yeah, I know. I'm registered."

She blinks at me, face blank for a moment, before taking my hand between both of hers. She draws me to the front of the room. "Welcome! Welcome! I'm glad you found us. We were about to start introductions. Since you're here, you can go first!"

It probably doesn't need to be said, but public speaking is not a strength of mine. In fact, my speech class freshman year was the closest I've ever come to getting a C. Hot, sweaty, out of breath, and out of place? This is a disaster waiting to happen.

"Ah, I'm Ben. Benjamin. Benjamin Morrison, but you can call me Ben. Or Benny. Or even Benji. Okay, maybe not Benji. Ben. Ben is fine." *Someone please shut me up.*

I look at the couples arranged in front of me. Everyone is paired off, mostly in man/woman combos, but there is one set of two women, and then there is Maxie and her mother. All but Maxie and Mrs. Jacobson wave at me. In fact, they both look like they wish I'd leave the way I came in—in a rush. Mrs. Jacobson's face is pinched, and she doesn't make eye contact with me. Maxie's face is pale and she's biting her lip. The other couples watch me in open curiosity. Not that I can blame them. What sixteen-year-old kid voluntarily attends a birthing class solo?

"Hello, Ben," the instructor says. It doesn't sound like she's trying to be polite so much as she is trying to figure out what to say next. "And what brings you to this class tonight?"

"What do you mean?"

She clears her throat. "Well, there are parenting classes students can take for credit, or to be certified as a childcare-giver. But generally, the pregnancy and birthing classes are taken only by expectant parents."

"Oh. Um, I'm an expectant parent."

"You are?" The instructor clears her throat. "Right. Of course. And the child's mother? Will she be attending?"

This seems more like an interrogation than an introduction. "She's there." I point at Maxie, whose face and neck have turned a bright fuchsia. Mrs. Jacobson's, too, for that matter.

The instructor's face clears. "Oh, yes, of course. Why don't you have a seat over there? There are some more beanbag chairs along the wall."

While I wrestle a red beanbag chair into place, the rest of the room introduce themselves. Everyone, including the two women, are married couples. Everyone except Maxie, her mom, and me. Once the last of the couples give their names, the instructor claps her hands.

"Welcome, everyone, and thank you. My name is Willow Wolzniak, but everyone calls me Willie. I've been a childbirth educator for the last ten years, I'm a certified doula, and I also teach community and court-mandated parenting classes. I recognize some of your names, so I suspect I'll be seeing you in an upcoming parenting class as well."

I shift in my seat, trying to get comfortable. The fake leather rubbing against the gym mat makes a rude flatulent sound echo through the room.

Everyone turns to stare at me.

Heat blooms from my chest, to my neck, to my face.

Maxie angles her head toward me. "Seriously?"

"It . . . it . . ." I sputter for a second, then notice the way her lips tilt up a bit at their edges. She's more relaxed than she was a moment ago. Great. If childish humor eases some of the tension between us, I'll deal with the embarrassment. "Whatever," I mutter.

Willie hands out a syllabus for the class. It's on the same violently pink paper as her sign was. Before I can read through the outline of the next four weeks' lesson plans, the lights dim and a screen descends from the ceiling. "We'll start today with some birthing basics. We'll watch two live births—one bed birth and a water birth. This will show you some of the options when it comes time to welcome your little sweetheart into the world. It will also give you context for some of the lessons and discussions we'll have over the next few weeks."

I reach for my backpack to grab a notebook and pencil. It looks like the books on birth, expecting parents, and prenatal care that I picked up at the library won't be needed tonight.

"Oh my God, Ben. Are you taking notes?" Maxie whispers to me.

I glance up from the clean page in my notebook. "Of course." I look around the room and realize no one else has taken out paper and pens.

She shakes her head. "Put that away."

"But—"

"You're embarrassing me," she hisses.

Mrs. Jacobson is very deliberately not looking at us, but her shoulders stiffen at our continued conversation.

"Fine." I shove my stuff back into the bag and settle in to watch the videos. I have a good memory for details, but notes are a great way to record information that I may need to reference later. Maybe Willie will send me the link to the videos in case I need to follow up on something?

Ninety seconds later, I've forgotten all about any notes I may have needed to take. In fact, I'm pretty sure my brain has stopped functioning altogether.

Naked. The lady in the video is naked. Her face is flushed. The taut mound of her belly is lurching in ways that can't possibly be normal. Her bare breasts jiggle with every panting breath.

I look around the room, but no one else seems to be concerned. Clearly my brain is not ready for the reality that is giving birth.

A narrator begins to speak over the events playing out on screen. The woman's belly lurches sickeningly. I have no idea what the narrator is saying now. Breasts bounce and sway. I can't seem to focus on anything else.

I turn to Maxie. "Why is she naked?" Because, seriously, *Why is she naked?*

"*Shh!*"

"I mean, is it necessary to be naked? Can't she have a gown, or a blanket or something?"

"*Be quiet, Ben!* Just watch the video, okay?"

So I watch, growing more and more horrified by the second.

The lady on the screen is grunting and squeezing the hand of the guy with her. He's encouraging her to breathe in a particular pattern. The narrator is nattering on, something about dilation and contractions and timing. His words are my mental lifeline. If I can focus on them, I might be able to make sense of . . . all of this.

The camera pans lower, zooming in.

Why why why?

The women in the room lean forward as though engrossed.

The men in the room lean back as if grossed out.

Things are stretching and expanding and I really, really don't want to see it. I can't force my eyes away from the screen.

White sparkles and dark clouds dance across my vision and my head starts to whirl. I suck in a breath, trying to bring the all-important oxygen into my system. Inhale. Exhale. Repeat. Anything so I don't pass out. My heart beats too fast, but that's a lost cause.

"Jesus, Ben, get a grip," Maxie hisses at me.

Why would anyone want to do that?

Ten minutes later, the baby has been born, the umbilical cord has been cut, and the baby taken to be cleaned up. I figure I'm safe now. They will turn off the screen and I will never have to see anything so traumatizing again in my life. Ever.

But no. No, that's not how it works. Then there's the placenta.

Why why why does Mom think this is a good idea?

"How was it?" Mom asks with a cheerfulness I will never forgive her for.

Horrifying. Terrifying. Weirdly fascinating. Embarrassing.

"It was . . . interesting," I say as my insides wriggle queasily at the memories.

"Did you have any questions you wanted to ask about what was covered?"

My brain flashes to images from the videos, images that will haunt me forever. Images I don't want to think about in context of my mother. "Good God, no!"

"There are things I'm sure you have questions about—"

"Nope, no questions." I quickly turn on the radio and crank up the volume.

The human race should have died out eons ago.

CHAPTER 27

This time when I walk up the sidewalk to the Jacobsons' house, I have a better idea of what to expect. *What to expect, ha!* My brain automatically fills in the rest of the book's title. I've read and reread so much of that book that the spine is cracked and several pages are dog-eared. Between the ultrasound a few weeks ago and last week's first birthing class, those little doubts I haven't yet talked to Mom about are starting to grow. In fact, doubts and what-ifs chase me into sleep.

Doubts that I'm doing the right thing.

What if something happens to the baby?

Doubts that I can handle this.

What if I screw up so epically the baby—my child—will hate me forever?

I haven't had a decent night's sleep in weeks, and it's taking its toll. And from everything I've read, having a baby means many, many more sleepless nights. My first-semester report card showed the worst grades I've ever gotten, and even Monica is losing patience with the number of dropped dishes.

And the sacrifices—the ones I've been so sure I am willing to make—are starting to grate. Every time I have to give up something, the resentment and bitterness grows.

Then there's the Fergusons. I can't help but remember how they were at Christmas. Even though Roger married my mom, they have fully accepted Mom and me into their clan. I even got a card with some cash from Russel and Miriam for my birthday next week. And it wasn't a generic card—they'd left a note asking me about the robotics team, about school, about things that show they are truly taking the time to get to know me. If my mom's husband's parents can adopt us into their family so fully, surely a couple who truly want a baby will do as much.

Monica's words flash through my brain. *Being a good parent means doing what's best for your child.* Am I, at not quite seventeen years old, what's best for the baby? Arguments—perfectly valid, logical arguments—could be made that maybe I'm not. Maybe a successful couple, one who truly wanted a child and would do all the things that parents should, would be what's best for the baby.

There's a strange car in the driveway, so the next couple to be interviewed must already be here.

It's a perfectly nice car. Not as sleek or fancy as Jim and Janice's was. Nothing pretentious, which I appreciate. Here's me being positive. No irrational reactions to alliterative names. A faded presidential election sticker on the back bumper makes me pause. Political affiliation doesn't have to mean anything.

"Be open-minded, Ben," I tell myself. I pull my gloves off to press the doorbell.

This time it's Maxie who answers the door. Her baby bump

is more obvious than ever, distorting the *Yuri on Ice* T-shirt she's wearing. "Hey," she says.

"Hey."

I haven't had much of a chance to speak with her since the birthing class. I don't think she's hiding from me anymore, but I've been busy enough and tired enough that I'm probably oblivious. I think I now have a better idea of what she's going through. To some extent, I understand why she wants the whole thing to be over.

"We're about to get started," she says.

I look at my phone, checking the time. "Didn't you say two P.M.?" It's only one forty-five.

"They got here early."

And clearly no one is going to wait on me, not when they'd rather I not be here at all.

I shrug out of my coat and pry off my shoes. I definitely don't want to miss any of the discussion.

The couple at the table are older than Jim and Janice. These two are easily the same age as Maxie's parents. They sit stiffly and barely react to my presence. They don't even acknowledge Maxie, either. Maybe Mr. Jacobson gave them a heads-up that I'd be here after the awkwardness of the last interview.

My knee starts to bounce as the uncomfortable silence continues to build.

Maxie pops her knuckles.

Mrs. Jacobson taps her nails on the tabletop.

Mr. Jacobson clears his throat.

The couple sit unnaturally still, hands folded in front of them. They remind me of one of those old-fashioned photos where no one smiles. Everything about them is sepia-toned too. From her faded brownish-red hair to his muted brown shirt, and their matching pasty complexions. The illusion is so strong, I almost jump when the man shifts in his seat, proving they are not, in fact, an old photograph.

Mr. Jacobson clears his throat again, then says, "Thomas, Brenda, thank you for meeting us here. I guess we should get started, yes?"

Thomas and Brenda. No alliteration, which I'm kind of happy about.

The couple nods. Thomas says, "The sooner the better. It's a long drive back and we'd like to make it home before dark."

"Where's home?" I ask.

A muscle tics in Mr. Jacobson's jaw, but he doesn't say anything.

"Near Ogden. It's a small town west of Oshkosh."

I review the mental map I have of Wisconsin. I know Oshkosh, of course, but have never heard of Ogden. I open my mouth to ask another question, but Mr. Jacobson steps in before I can say anything. I'm not sure if he's worried about what kinds of questions I'm going to ask or if he's got his own list of questions. Given the backwards nature of the last interview, I'm going to make sure we at least get to ask the lion's share of the questions.

"Why are you pursuing adoption?" Mr. Jacobson looks from Thomas to Brenda, including her in the question.

Thomas answers. "We've not been blessed with children of our own. For years we've waited to make a family, to have children we can pass on the family legacy to."

"Family legacy?" Maxie's mom asks.

"The farm. We have a small dairy farm. It's been in the family for over a hundred years, passing from father to son each generation. Brenda and I have waited as long as we could before taking drastic measures. I can't let the legacy die with me."

I have so many questions. *So many.* Like, what if the baby isn't a boy? Would he be okay passing the farm to a daughter? And what if the kid doesn't want to be a farmer? With Maxie's and my genetics, it would be more likely that the child would be drawn to computers or math or engineering, rather than cows. Despite my many questions, I manage to keep my mouth shut, even if I do have to remind myself to keep an open mind.

"So you don't have any other children? Do you intend to have more?" Maxie's mom asks.

Thomas shakes his head. "One will be sufficient."

Sufficient? It's not like he's picking up a hammer at the hardware store. Would it kill Thomas to not treat the potential adoption of a baby like a simple tool purchase?

"How about cousins? Any other children in the family?" Maxie's mom asks.

"No," Thomas says. "I have no siblings, and my own cousins moved away years ago."

I look at Brenda to see how she feels about Thomas doing all the talking. Sure, his cousins are gone, but maybe Brenda has a few relatives worth mentioning. She doesn't seem too put off that he's monopolizing the conversation, though.

Mr. Jacobson asks a couple more questions about the town of Ogden, the school there, while I try to figure out what I don't like about these two.

Maxie shifts in her seat, like she's trying to stretch her back. Thomas's eyes stray to her, his lips twisting.

I straighten up. I can't decipher the meaning behind the sneer, but it definitely doesn't seem like a good sign.

I listen for a few minutes longer as Thomas tells us about the challenges faced by local farmers, and how it's about time politicians stepped up to protect small-town Americans. When he stops for a breath, I jump in, completely ignoring Mr. Jacobson's warning look. "What do you think makes good parents?" It's the same question I asked Monica, and I want to see how Thomas will respond.

"Discipline," Thomas says without missing a beat. "Routine. Strong family values."

Don't get me wrong. I don't object to discipline and routines. Routines and discipline have always grounded me, giving me guidelines and boundaries that comfort me. Even the parenting classes I've taken have emphasized the importance of both routines and discipline. And family values *sounds* all right, but after reading about the number of "family value" organizations and their anti-LGBTQIA+ stances, policies, and lobbying, the words are a bit of a trigger. I know what they mean to me, but what do they mean to these guys? And the cool, superior way he says the words makes it sound more like dangerous rhetoric than good parenting tips.

"How would you respond if your child came out?" I ask. "If they tell you they're gay, or lesbian, or bisexual?"

The sneer is back. "Ridiculous question."

"Why is it ridiculous?" I ask the question, but the answer is obvious. I wonder if he's aware enough to recognize the truth.

"It's a bunch of horseshit. All these supposedly queer people making a stink. Throwing their private business into everyone's faces. Boycotting companies, claiming discrimination at every turn. Taking over the media. All a result of bad parenting and a lack of discipline."

That's what I thought.

"We'll raise the child right. Limit television and internet." His eyes shift back to Maxie and her *Yuri on Ice* T-shirt. "Avoid all those foreign influences."

Even Maxie's parents seem uncomfortable at this, shifting in their seats.

"I think we've heard enough," I say.

Thomas's brows rise nearly to his receding hairline. "Excuse me?"

"We're done here. There will be no adoption. Not now, and certainly not to you." I stand up.

"Who are you to make that decision?"

"I'm the baby's father, and I'm gay. No way in hell will I let any baby, especially my own, be raised by a bigot like you."

Thomas sputters. Mr. Jacobson stands, and I'm prepared to stand my ground. He surprises me, though. "Ben is right. It's time for you to leave. It's a long drive back, and I think you'll want to get started."

Thomas and Brenda huff and grumble their way through grabbing their coats and leaving the house. As soon as the door closes behind them, I spin to face Maxie.

"I thought I could come in with an open mind and make sure the best interests of the baby are met. But I can't. Those people, they are not what is best. They're bigots." I look at her parents. "And if these are the types of people you are interviewing, I don't trust you to find someone acceptable. I tried to be open-minded, but I can't. I'm keeping—no, not keeping, raising—I'm going to raise the baby and I'm going to do whatever I need to make it happen. I tried, Maxie, I did. But I'm not going to play along anymore."

No one says anything as I storm out of the house.

CHAPTER 28

March comes in roaring like an angry lion. And with it comes one more thing I need to worry about. The SATs.

Back when we were all still talking, Maxie, Mo, and I registered to take the test on the first Saturday in March. That gave us plenty of time, we'd assumed, to go through all the prep materials, training guides, and even take some of the SAT preparation classes offered at the community college. We'd had a plan. Then . . . stuff happened.

I swear, every minute of every day since the beginning of October has been filled. Between school, work, robotics club, and birthing and parenting classes, I've had more things to do than I've had time to do them. So when in the hell was I supposed to prepare for what is, arguably, the most important test in my life? Maybe if I cut an extra couple hours of sleep out a night—though I was already down to only five or six hours—I'd have managed something. But that kind of planning requires that I actually remember the test in the first place.

"You'll be fine," Mom says, patting my knee as I dig through my backpack to recheck for the fifth time that I have the pencils and calculator I need.

"I can't believe I forgot. I'm going to fail this test and I'll be stuck bussing dishes at Greco's for the rest of my life." I pat my pocket to make sure my state ID is still there.

"It's not a pass-fail test, Benny." Mom brakes at a stoplight. The windshield wipers beat against the glass in a near-futile battle against the raging rain. "You'll do fine. And if your score is lower than you want, you can make sure you review the practice materials before retaking it this summer."

"That's not as comforting as you think," I mutter. Thunder crashes in the distance, matching my mood. Mom accelerates through the light, reminding me that I still need to take my road test. I'm probably the only seventeen-year-old with a car who isn't clamoring to get his license. There simply hasn't been time.

I watch the clock. The test starts in twenty minutes, which should be plenty of time for us to get to the college campus where it's being held, get checked in, and get settled. But still I watch the clock and compare it against the ETA on the GPS app on my phone.

We pull into a parking lot across the street from the testing building. I do one last recheck on my pencils, ID, and calculator. I make sure my jacket is zipped, then pull the hood up.

"Good luck!" Mom calls as I swing open the door and duck into the rain. "You've got this!"

I wave at her and run through the downpour to the main entrance where I see a handful of other people congregating. Rain pelts my face, and I pull the hood down a bit. It's not much protection, but it's better than nothing. The problem is, my visibility is shot. Two steps from the door, I crash into someone else who's reaching for the door handle. I end up with a bony elbow to my gut, and my backpack lands in a puddle with a splat.

"Shit!" I snatch it up, more worried about the calculator inside than the fate of whoever I hit. I try to brush the water off my bag, hoping nothing has soaked through the material.

"Ben?"

I stop my frantic brushing to squint against the rain. It takes a second for me to recognize Mo underneath a broad red umbrella. "Oh, hi," I say.

Things have been better—not good by any means, but better—between Mo and me since I confided in him. He hasn't gone out of his way to ignore me, but we haven't exactly gotten back to normal. It's like the animosity is gone, but so is the friendship. We're essentially acquaintances now.

"Hey." He tilts his umbrella so it covers both of us. "So, you ready for this?" he asks as he pulls the door open.

"Not at all," I admit. "You?"

"Yeah," he says slowly, examining me. "I've taken the practice test several times and scored well. I hope that translates to the real deal."

I flinch.

He notices. "Your practice tests didn't go well?"

I snort. "What practice tests? I completely forgot about today thanks to all the crap I'm dealing with."

He closes the umbrella, eyes never leaving me. "You haven't prepared at all? Did you at least go through one of the workbooks?"

"Nope."

"But, Ben, this is too important to screw up."

"I know. Believe me, I know."

"What are you going to do?"

"I guess I'm going to take the stupid test and hope I do better than I think I will."

We join the line of students waiting to check in. Halfway up the line I see a familiar figure with wildly curling hair. "Maxie."

Mo looks past the twenty or so students between Maxie and us. "She doesn't look so hot," he says.

I look closer. Mo's right. Her skin is paler than usual, and her face is tight. "Probably the rain. It's cold enough to make anyone clammy."

Mo nods but I can tell he doesn't agree with me. Not that I blame him. I don't agree with myself either. She looks like she's sick.

By the time we make it through the line, check our bags, and enter the classroom where the test is being administered, I've lost track of Maxie. It's open seating in the room, and I check on Mo. I don't want to sit by him if he doesn't want me to, but I don't want to not sit by him in case he takes it personally. And should we sit near Maxie? I know I'm overthinking it. There are a few other familiar faces, and I wouldn't be obsessing over the seating arrangements for any of them.

Mo nods to a row in the center of the room. Relieved that he made the decision, I follow him. Halfway down the aisle I see Maxie's huddled form. Up close her face is paler than I'd thought, and she's massaging her temples.

I stop by her seat and tap her shoulder. "Hey, you okay?"

She looks up at me, her eyes darting from me to Mo. "Yeah, I have a headache. I took some Tylenol earlier. Just waiting for it to kick in."

Then the three of us stand around, watching each other awkwardly for a long minute.

The test proctor clears their throat at the front of the room, reminding us to take our seat for the first test.

"Well, good luck," I say. I move up the aisle a few spots and take the first empty seat I find. Mo ends up two seats in front of me. A minute later, the proctor explains the rules and agenda for the day. Then I break open the first test booklet and start the reading portion of the test.

A couple hours later we take a break. I consider finding my backpack so I can grab a snack, but my stomach roils at the thought of food. The first tests went okay. The problem is, I can't afford *okay*. I need to excel. I'm not quite as worried about the math sections that are coming up. I'm definitely more in my comfort zone there versus the reading and writing bits. I barely finished the sections before time was called, because I found myself rechecking and analyzing the information more than was necessary.

I see Mo in line for the restroom.

I look for Maxie in the crowd, but don't see her ugly sweater or untamed curls anywhere.

Maybe I should grab the granola bar out of my backpack after all?

There's a gasp and mumbling from the longer line at the women's restroom. The crowd waves and undulates and for a second, I wonder if they're doing the wave or something equally ridiculous. Then the crowd parts, and I see two girls lowering a third to the floor.

"Maxie!" I rush forward. "What's the matter? What happened?"

"She started swaying. I thought she was going to faint," the taller of the two girls says.

Maxie cradles her pregnant belly. "There's something wrong."

I drop down next to her. "What? With the baby?"

"I don't know. I hurt." Her voice trembles.

"What's going on?" Mo squats next to us.

"She's sick or something." I reach out to offer some kind of comfort, but stop before making contact. What if I make things worse?

"Should we call nine-one-one?" Mo asks. He rests his hands on Maxie's shoulders, no hesitation.

"I . . . I don't know." My brain is moving a hundred miles an hour, and I can't pull my thoughts into any kind of logical order. Variables, theories, and questions scroll through my head like code, but I can't pull out any single data point.

I look around the lobby. There's got to be someone who can help. A teacher. A parent. Hell, even a custodian is a better choice than me.

An adult, the middle-aged lady who handled registration earlier in the morning, bustles to us. "What's happened?"

A minute later, the lady places a call to emergency services, and she and Mo help Maxie up off the floor and to a bench along the edge of the hallway.

Not sure what I can do to be of any kind of help, I follow along. "You're going to be okay. Everything is going to be fine," I tell Maxie. I keep repeating the words, even though I don't know if I'm lying or not.

I'm not even sure Maxie hears a word I say. She's got one arm wrapped around her belly, her other hand pressed over her eyes.

Mo and I stare at each other over her head. His eyes are as wide as I suspect my own are. I don't know when I've ever felt this helpless.

A single tear trails down Maxie's ashen face. "I'm sorry, Ben," she says.

My helplessness morphs into full-blown panic. "What?"

"I think—" Her voice cracks. "—I think there's something wrong with the baby. Am I going to lose the baby?"

My brain stutters to a stop, and my lungs seize.

As a little kid I loved the merry-go-round. I loved the way it felt when it spun, faster and faster, the force of it pulling my body away from the center. It was exhilarating. It was fun. In middle school, I learned about the theory of centrifugal force, and I then had the physics definition for that feeling. That's how I feel now, caught up in a demonstration of centrifugal force. But it's not like the merry-go-round. It's not fun. It's not exhilarating. It's terrifying. It's nauseating. The merry-go-round is spinning, faster and faster, and faster still, and I'm barely hanging on and everything around me is a blur.

The baby.

Maxie might be losing the baby.

All of this, every decision, every action over the last five months, is for nothing.

And Maxie. What will happen to Maxie?

I can feel my fingers slipping off the merry-go-round handle. One bump, one misstep, and I'll be flung to the ground in a bone-shattering crash.

I cross my arms over my chest. I taste blood and realize I've bitten my cheek. I try to breathe through the panic.

"Ben."

The sounds around me echo weirdly—both booming loud and indistinctly muted.

"Ben."

People shift and merge around me, not registering as anything more than a blurry kaleidoscope of colors along the periphery.

"Damn it, Ben, move!" Suddenly everything snaps into focus. Mo jerks me back in time to let a couple of paramedics through.

They ask Maxie questions even as they prepare to take her

away. The symptoms she shares with them don't do anything to calm me down. Headache. Abdominal pain. Shortness of breath. Fuzzy vision.

The paramedics get her situated on the gurney while at least forty students stand huddled around us.

"I need to call my mom," Maxie says while they cover her with a sheet of some kind.

"We'll call her from the hospital," the older of the two paramedics says.

"I'll call her," Mo offers. "Which hospital?"

The paramedic names a hospital, but I miss it while I try to figure out what to do.

The lobby doors have barely closed behind them before it registers that Maxie's gone. "Shit! I need to go. I've got to— I need my bag." I swing around, scanning the crowd as though my backpack will suddenly appear.

"All right, people, excitement's over. We need to get back to the test." The test proctor beckons everyone back to the room.

I spin around, almost running in the opposite direction. I need to get to the hospital. Maxie . . . the baby . . . I have to be there.

Mo's barely a step behind me.

"The test is starting," the registration lady says, ignoring our demands for our stuff.

Is she out of her mind? She expects me to take some stupid test? While Maxie is being rushed to the hospital? "I have to go."

"If you leave, you can't come back. You'll have to sign up for a different testing date."

"Fine," I say.

Mo echoes my answer.

"Wait, what?" I turn to him. "You can't go. You need to finish the test."

"No, I need to go to the hospital."

"Look, Maxie's carrying my baby. I need to be there."

"And you are my best friends. I'm not going to abandon you both to take a stupid test."

"But—"

"Besides," he says, "how are you going to get to the hospital? It'll be at least an hour for your mom to get here and get you to the hospital. If we leave now, we'll only be a few minutes behind the ambulance."

Damn, I hadn't thought of that.

"I drove myself, so my car is in the lot."

"Wait a minute. When did you get a car? And you already have your license?"

He shrugs. "A lot has happened the last few months."

The reminder of all the things I've missed stings, but it's negligible amid the worry over Maxie. "Are you sure you want to ditch the test? Maxie will understand if you stay."

"I'm not going to abandon my best friends." His dark eyes are serious when he says, "Not again."

I swallow against the emotion threatening to overwhelm me. I don't have time for it, so I push it back. "Okay. Let's do this."

Something settles over me, like the last piece of a puzzle finally in place. We turn to the registration lady. "We need our bags. Now."

CHAPTER 29

Thankfully, Mo pays attention. While I have only the vaguest idea of which hospital the paramedics mentioned, he's able to plug it into his phone and get directions.

I stare at my phone, half wishing someone else would be available to make this call. But Mo's driving, and there's no one else around. I take a deep breath before dialing.

"Hello?" Maxie's mom says carefully. No doubt she sees my name on the caller ID, but since I don't make it a habit to call her—I've never called the main line, come to think of it—she's probably a little confused.

I clear my throat. "Ah, hi, Mrs. Jacobson. I don't know if anyone has called you yet, but, um, Maxie is on the way to the hospital."

"*What?*" And now the confusion is gone, replaced by panic. Honestly, it's the most emotion I've heard from her in a long time. "Why isn't she at the SAT? What happened?"

"She was at the test," I tell her. "But something was wrong, and well, they called an ambulance. Now she's on the way to the hospital."

"Was there an accident, or is it the baby?"

I lick my lips. "The baby, they think."

I hear shuffling noises on her end of the call and the slamming of a door. "Which hospital?"

I barely get the name of the hospital out before she disconnects the call.

"She's going to be okay, right, Mo?"

The logical part of my brain knows that Mo doesn't have any more information than I do, so he can't actually tell me anything. But the logical part of my brain is definitely not running the show right now.

"I'm sure she'll be fine." A wave of rainwater erupts next to me as Mo plows through a particularly deep puddle. "She's tough," he adds.

To distract myself, I examine the interior of Mo's car. I'm not positive, but I think it's a Honda Civic, the same kind of car as mine. Except, unlike mine, his has clearly left the driveway over the last couple of months.

"When did you get your license?" I ask.

For a second I don't think he's going to answer. After a long pause, he says, "Early January. Got the car last month." He looks away from the road briefly. "Did you get your license yet?"

I shake my head. "Not yet. Been too busy. I got a car for Christmas, though."

"Really? But you don't drive it yet?"

"Busy," I remind him. "It looks like this one, actually. It's a seven-year-old Honda Civic."

"Really? Same. Well, the Civic part is the same. I think this one is a couple years newer."

"How weird is that?"

"Right? So weird." I missed a lot the last few months with the distance between Mo and me. Sure, we've still had classes together, and we've still seen each other several times a week for the robotics club, but I feel like it's been ages since we've been together. And while it's possible that Mo's only lowering the shields between us temporarily for Maxie's sake, I don't think that's the case.

"I'm sorry," I blurt out.

"You don't have to—"

"I do. I lied to you and kept things from you. I didn't mean to. Not at first. Then it kept getting bigger and bigger, and I didn't know how to talk about it. Then when the whole school found out, I panicked."

"I get it," he says after a moment's hesitation. "I think I got it at the time, but I was so mad. You've never lied to me before, never kept something from me. I didn't know how to get past it."

"Did you get past it?"

"Eh, mostly. Now I think I'm just disappointed. We had all these plans, you know? And now none of them are going to happen. You're passing up the summer academy, you're going to be too busy being a dad to hang out like we used to, and you'll probably be stuck locally for college because there's no way you're taking a baby with you to Boston."

He sighs as he turns into the hospital's visitor parking lot. "I'm trying not to be selfish. Trying not to think about how all of this is messing with *my* plans. It's hard to say good-bye to that future we've been planning for years."

I don't say anything. It's not like I disagree with him. But somehow it feels wrong to agree. And if Maxie is losing the baby, then all of this goes away.

Nausea rolls over me like a tidal wave, so hard and so strong I almost throw up.

Holy shit.

I didn't.

I can't.

For a flicker of a second, the briefest, tiniest portion of a nano-second, the thought that Maxie might lose the baby is a relief. I could go back to my normal, everyday life with the knowledge that I did everything I could. That I stepped up.

Oh, Jesus. I'm stuck on the edge of the merry-go-round again, dizzy and light-headed. Along with an extra dose of shame and queasiness.

Mo clamps his hand around the back of my neck and pushes my head down until my forehead touches my knees. "Breathe, Ben, breathe."

But I can't breathe. I can't inhale. I can't exhale. I'm stuck in a weird stasis as sparkling lights dance and swirl around me, sucking the oxygen straight out of my lungs. Choking noises come from my throat as I try, and fail, to suck in a breath.

"C'mon, Ben. You're freaking me out." Mo pounds on my back.

I'm going to pass out. I'm going to suffocate. I press my fisted hands against my chest in a vain attempt to get some much-needed air. My muscles lock and I start to shake.

"We need to get inside. We need to see Maxie." Mo's voice cracks on the words.

Maxie.

Maxie, with her wild curls and blue eyes.

Maxie, with her clever brain and love of female-focused sci-fi.

Maxie, who's pregnant, pregnant with my baby.

My head begins to clear, and I gasp in a breath. "I'm okay," I say weakly, but the words are true.

Mo exhales heavily. "Oh, thank God."

I shake my head to get rid of the last of the fog. "Let's go. We need to see Maxie."

Mo and I rush through the automatic door of the emergency room, chased by icy rain and thunder. Our wet running shoes squeak on the polished floors as we rush to the lady at the front desk.

"We're here for Maxie Jacobson. She was just brought in. Is she okay?" I demand, slapping my hands on the counter in front of us.

"Are you family?" she asks. While her tone is professional, she absolutely knows we're not family. For one, I'm a pasty redhead and Mo's got the darker skin and hair of his northern Indian heritage.

"No, but—"

"I'm sorry," she says, and I think she means it, "but I can't discuss it with anyone not family."

"She's pregnant," I say. "The baby's mine. Is that close enough to make me family?"

She shakes her head. "No, I'm sorry," she repeats.

The doors swoosh open again, and Maxie's mom rushes forward. She barely blinks at the sight of Mo and me before she addresses the lady behind the front desk. "Maxie Jacobson? I'm her mother."

The front desk lady clacks away at a hidden keyboard, then nods. "Someone will be right up to take you back."

The three of us hover by the front desk while Maxie's mom waits to go back. I don't think they'll let Mo or me back too, but I can't figure out what to do next.

When you're in a hospital, there's never any doubt where you are. The artificial silence, the overwhelming smell of disinfectant, the almost physical anxiety that presses in on you.

"You should go home," Maxie's mom tells us. "There's nothing you can do here."

"I want to make sure she's okay." I hug myself, tucking my trembling fingers into my armpits.

"You've done enough already, don't you think?" She doesn't look at me, and the venom in her tone chills my blood. We both know she's not talking about me calling to let her know. No, she's talking about the pregnancy.

The pregnancy is my fault. Which means this thing, whatever it is that's happening to Maxie, is my fault. Maxie is here because of me.

She's right. I should probably go. But I can't make myself do it. I need to be here, for her and the baby, even if there's nothing I can do for her. Maybe knowing that there are people here for her will help.

A male nurse steps around a corner. "Family for Maxie Jacobson?"

Maxie's mom hurries toward him.

"We'll be waiting out here. Can you let us know what's going on?" I ask.

She hesitates for the tiniest second before continuing to the nurse but doesn't acknowledge my request.

Mo and I hunker down in two pastel-green seats in the waiting room. My knee bounces uncontrollably, and I've bitten my fingernails down so far they bleed.

After an agonizing period of time, which according to the clock on the wall is actually only fifteen minutes, I jump to my feet. Jittery restlessness, like I've had two too many shots of espresso and three bags of cotton candy, prickles at my skin and nerves. I check the clock. "How long should this take?" I demand, whirling to face Mo.

He's leaning forward in his chair, elbows planted on his knees, hands clasped between them. "I have no idea. They probably have to do some tests."

I pull out my phone. To call someone or research something, I have no idea.

My thumb dances over the phone icon and the internet browser. Who to call? What to ask? I need to do something. A quick round of eeny, meeny, miny, moe decides me.

I select my mom's contact info. Her phone rings several times before going to voice mail. Mom *never* doesn't answer her phone, and she decides today, when I think I might need her more now than any other time in my life, is a good day to ignore the incoming call? I disconnect before the message finishes, then immediately call the number again.

"You have reached Eliza Ferguson, I'm unable to—"

"Why? Why? Why is she doing this?" I jab at the phone again.

I don't know why I do what I do next. I really don't. Without putting too much thought into it, I hit another contact on my phone. After two rings he picks up.

"Roger, I . . . I need you."

CHAPTER 30

Roger rushes through the emergency room entrance. His face is red from the cold, and the rain has flattened his hair. He swipes his sagging bangs out of his face even as he charges across the room to me.

After he hung up to head over, I started cursing the impulse to call him. Seeing him now, I don't understand why it feels like a weighted blanket has been pulled off my shoulders. "I'm sorry—"

He grabs me up into a hug before I can finish my apology. His jacket is chilly and damp, and despite that, something warms inside of me.

"Are you okay? What happened?"

"I'm fine," I mutter into his rain-soaked collar.

He pushes me back, hands still gripping my shoulders tightly. "Maxie? Have you heard anything?"

I shake my head. "Where's Mom? Why isn't she answering her phone?"

"She and her girlfriends met for a movie. You know she turns her phone off at the theater."

I don't notice right away that my fingers are digging into the sleeves of his coat. When I do, I loosen my grip and try to pull away. "You didn't have to come here. I shouldn't have called—"

"Ben, stop." He cups my cheek, angling my face so I'm forced to make eye contact. "It's okay. I'm glad you called me. I know it's not easy for you to understand, but I'm going to be there for you. I want you to be able to come to me. We're family now. That's part of the deal."

I nod, not sure what to do with those words. Part of me, the part that's kept me from getting too close to the men in my mother's life, warns me that these are just words, something Roger says because he feels like he has to because of my mom, not because he means them. Another part of me, one that desperately wishes the words to be true, remembers what Roger said during the argument with Mom. *I hope one of these days Ben will let me get to know him better, and that we'll build a solid relationship.* This might really be what Roger wants.

"Thank you," I say softly, the words wispy.

"Let's take a walk. Maybe find a soda or bottle of water or something." Roger looks at Mo. "You want something to drink?"

"Sure."

I look from the front desk to Roger. I don't want to miss anything, but the idea of moving, of using up some of the restless energy buzzing through me, is tempting.

Mo waves his phone at me. "I'll text you if someone comes out with news," he says, once again proving he knows me too well.

"Thanks," I tell him, unable to really express the gratitude I feel.

Roger claps me on the back, urging me to a set of doors with signs indicating bathrooms and vending are to the left. "What's going through your head right now?"

"I don't know," I admit. "Too much. A lot of noise, a lot of thoughts, kind of bouncing and twisting inside my head."

"Can you tell me what happened with Maxie?"

In halting words, I explain.

"And you left the test, knowing that you'd have to retake it later? Are there going to be any consequences for that?"

I don't pick up any judgment in his words, but beyond that, I don't know how to interpret his questions. Does he think I'm stupid for walking out of the test, even knowing there's nothing I can do for Maxie here at the hospital? Does he think it's a waste of time, a decision that's going to cost me even more of my future than I've already had to sacrifice?

"I'm not sure. I'll have to retake the tests for sure. I may not be able to apply to some of the schools as early as I'd planned. Beyond that, I have no idea."

He swings his arm over my shoulders. "It may not mean much to you right now, but I'm really proud of you. It can't have been an easy decision."

That's the thing. It was an easy decision. So easy. In fact, I'd barely thought about it. I only did what I thought was best. And Roger saying he's proud of me means more to me than he or I could possibly have guessed.

"It's Maxie, you know?" I offer as explanation. "She's my best friend, and seeing her sick like that . . . I had to do something. Even if there's nothing really for me to do."

"You're a good friend," Roger says.

And those words, words that should have been comforting and supportive, nearly destroy me. "I'm not," I say, my voice hitching.

"I'm not a good friend. I haven't been a good friend in months, not to Maxie, not to Mo. Not to my friends on the robotics team."

"You've been going through a lot," he says. "You need to give yourself a break. Sometimes we have to focus on the big things just past our fingertips, and sometimes that means the other things, while still important, have to take a back seat. It's human nature, Ben, not a character flaw."

I can't believe I used to think he wasn't very bright.

For the first time, I actually think he'll understand the thoughts and emotions running through my head better than Mom would. Then I remember the horrifying, absolutely unforgivable thought I had in the car on the way to the hospital.

"You shouldn't be nice to me. I don't deserve it."

He stops our forward progress with a touch to my arm. "You do deserve it, Ben."

The temptation to tell him, to confess my fear and shame, is a lot. I'm not Catholic, but the idea of cleansing my guilt through confession and penance appeals in ways I can't describe. But I can't. What if I share that momentary flash of relief and Roger condemns me for it? What if he's so appalled, he goes straight to Mom and she decides not to help me with this custody case?

Or, a little voice whispers in my head, what if he understands?

It's too much to hope for. I shake my head and resume the walk to the vending machines.

It sounds like Roger sighs, but I don't look back to make sure.

I dig in my pocket for some cash when we reach a dilapidated Pepsi machine. "I've got it," Roger says, pulling out his wallet. He pulls some bills free and some other kind of paper flutters out. I squat to grab it, my fingers stilling when I touch the glossy paper. It's a picture. Maybe half the size of a playing card, it's a snapshot someone took at Mom and Roger's wedding. We're seated at a table with Mom at the center, a beaming Roger on her right, and me on her left. Roger's got his arm across both Mom's and my shoulders, and they look happy. I don't remember the picture being taken, but I'm smiling.

We look like a family.

I pick up the picture, but I don't hand it back to Roger.

I swallow and look up at him. "I'm scared." It's the first time I've said the words out loud. The first time I've admitted them to anyone.

"Of what?" Roger asks. "Walk me through it. It might help. It certainly can't hurt."

I hesitate.

"Anything you say stays between us, okay?"

I take the leap. "What if I can't do it? What if I give up everything I've worked my whole life for, and I mess it up?" I think back to my mom's story about her father. "What if I end up resenting the baby? What if I decide the sacrifices aren't worth it?"

"Those are fair questions." His voice is full of gentleness and understanding, and it's too much. The pressure behind my eyes builds, and it's all I can do to hold back the tears. "So let me ask you, what if you can't do it?"

The matter-of-fact way he says this helps rein in my emotions. "Huh?"

"What if it is too much? Isn't it better to figure that out now rather than later? You just turned seventeen, Ben, and no matter how prepared you think you are, you won't be ready for the reality."

"So you don't think I can do it?"

"That's not what I'm saying. If anyone could make it work, I think it's you. You're smart, you're determined, you're capable. The focus and dedication you've already put into rearranging your life proves that you are willing and able to make it work. You can do anything you put your mind to. But parenthood is tough. It's tough whether you're seventeen, or twenty-seven, or even forty-seven."

"Then you think I should do it?"

"That's not what I'm saying either. I'm saying there's no shame in changing your mind. There's no shame in realizing that a baby might be better off with parents who are not you. There's no shame in recognizing the best way to be a parent is to do what's best for the child, even if what's best for them isn't you."

He waits a minute, until I meet his gaze completely. Then he says, "But, Ben, it doesn't matter what I think. It doesn't matter what anyone else thinks. Those who'll judge you don't matter, and those who matter won't judge."

"Did you really misquote Dr. Seuss?"

He shrugs, grinning. "Hey, the dude was smart, and it fits."

Roger nods to a padded bench next to a water fountain halfway down the corridor. I settle in next to him and cross my feet out in front of me. I stare at my shoelaces, not quite sure what to say next.

Roger leans forward, bracing his elbows on his knees. "Have you talked to anyone about this?"

"Sure. I mean, Mom and I have talked a lot about the legal stuff, and the planning and preparations. We've talked about the logistics, I guess you could say."

"Yeah, but that's all the practical stuff, the plan of attack for getting custody, right? But what about the other angles?"

No, because discussing the other options might have given Mom the idea that I'm open to those other options. I don't need any sliver of doubt in her mind, no matter how much doubt is in mine. "I'm not—or I wasn't—considering any other angles."

"I think that's what scares your mom the most about this."

I keep my eyes glued to my shoes. This feels important, and if I look at Roger, the whole thing will fall apart. "What's she afraid of?"

"Your tunnel vision. That focus. It's a great thing when it comes to getting your schoolwork done, or your robotics projects. It's what's going to make you a successful adult. But she's nervous that your focus is so narrow you're not seeing the whole picture."

"What part of the picture does she think I'm missing?"

"A realistic view of what it will mean to be a parent. Not only the day-to-day stuff like diapers and midnight feedings, but the worry and stress. You think you understand what you're giving up, but do you? In a few months, you're going to have a baby, a full school schedule, and a job. You think you're losing sleep now by trying to do everything, how do you think it will be in a few months when you have a baby? You probably won't have time for the robotics club or any other extracurricular activities. You're as good as giving up on MIT or one of the other universities you're looking at."

I open my mouth to object. I'm not going to give up the baby because I might have to find a different college program.

Roger holds up his hand. "That's only one option, though. And if it's the right one for you, the one you are determined to go with, your mom and I will support you. You know that. She's worried that you're not going into it with your eyes open. And that you've got blinders on when it comes to the other options."

"What other option? The adoption?" I snort. "If you saw the couples Maxie's family has been talking to, you'd understand. No. Just no."

"Can you honestly tell me you're giving the couples a fair shot?"

I open my mouth, *yes* nearly tripping off my tongue before I stop. "I may have been a bit prejudiced against the first couple I met. They were probably okay, but they were so . . .

condescending, I couldn't like them. But the second couple, they *were* awful people. Bigoted and racist. No way would I want any kid to be stuck with them, let alone mine."

"If the right couple came along, would you still be so set against the adoption option?"

My knee starts to bounce. "I don't know." I strain to get the words out through my spasming throat.

"What's holding you back?"

My stomach twists. For a moment I'm not sure I can put it into words, and it feels weird to be talking about it with Roger, of all people. Then I think about the picture in his wallet, and the driving lessons, and the car that's still parked in our driveway even though I haven't gotten around to getting my license. I think about his excitement for me when I came back from the robotics tournament with a measly fifth place, and how thrilled he was for me when I received the acceptance into the Vaucanson Summer Academy. I think about how he didn't hesitate to rush to the hospital this morning because I called in a panic.

Is this what it's like to have a father?

"What if"—I stop to clear my throat—"what if they grow up thinking they weren't wanted, or that they weren't enough for their biological parents to stick around? I . . . know what that's like, and it sucks. I can't do that to another kid."

Roger's brows lower and his eyes widen in understanding. "Ben—"

"You know what, it's fine." I plant my hands on the bench on either side of my thighs and push myself up.

He grabs my elbow, pulling me back down. His eyes are soft with something like pity. I hate it. "Ben, is that how you feel?"

I shake my head. "Mom—"

"You and I both know your mom would move mountains for

you, and has loved you, and will love you, forever. But it's not the same, is it?"

I look away because I actually want to burrow into Roger and accept the comfort and understanding he's offering simply by being there. But my nerves are too close to the surface right now, and the wrong word, the wrong movement, will be even more painful because of it.

"I . . . I know I'm not normal. I'm not the same as everyone else. I'm more comfortable with equations and mechanics than I am with emotions and feelings. I've always been that way. Mom gets me, but sometimes I know it's a lot for her to deal with. It's not fair to expect someone else to have the same tolerance as she does. But after a while, it hurts, you know? I've had four different father figures in my life. One died before I was born. Two left us without a backward glance, or even a phone call to stay in touch. Until the whole baby thing, I hadn't seen or heard from James or Paolo. And you—"

I swallow back the rest of my words. I peek up at Roger to gauge his reaction. I don't want to upset him, not after he's gone out of his way for me today. He doesn't seem angry, though, and that's almost worse.

"Go on, what about me?"

Because he sounds calm, and because his hand on my arm is strangely comforting, I say, "Are you and Mom going to divorce?"

He flinches, the first sign of surprise I've seen from him during this whole discussion. "No, of course not."

"I've heard you fighting."

"People fight, they argue and get frustrated. But we work through it. And hopefully, we're stronger on the other side of it."

"So you're sticking around?"

"You couldn't get rid of me."

"Good," I say. Then, "Roger?"

"Yeah?"

"If—if you and Mom do split up, can you . . ."

"Can I what, Ben?"

"Will you stay in touch with me? Please?"

Roger drags me to him, wrapping his arms around me. "Of course. I told you, you couldn't get rid of me. Even if things don't work out between your mom and me, I promise to be there for you."

We sit there for a few moments, until it starts to feel awkward. My face is tight and itchy from dried tears, and my stomach still jumps queasily. Roger lets me pull away a bit. I don't leave the bench, but I do need a little distance.

"Stay there," Roger says, standing and reaching for his wallet. He hustles to the vending machine again and feeds some cash into it. A minute later, he's back with two cans of Pepsi. He hands one to me before popping the tab on his.

"Did you know I'm adopted?" Roger asks.

I roll the cold Pepsi can between my palms as I stare at him. "What?"

"Yeah. My biological mother was young, only nineteen when I was born, and an addict."

"But you look just like your dad," I say.

"She—her name was Sylvia—was my dad's sister, actually. He and Mom hadn't been able to have kids themselves, so when it became clear that Sylvia wasn't going to be in any position to raise a child, they adopted me. I met her a few times when I was a kid. Called her Aunt Sylvie and didn't know until years later that she was my birth mother. She died before I graduated high school. She'd had an undiagnosed heart condition. Because her heart condition is often genetic, I had to have some tests done. That's when they told me."

"You didn't know you were adopted before that?"

"Oh, I knew I was adopted. They didn't hide that. They just didn't tell me Sylvie was my birth mother."

"What about your father, your biological one? Did you find out who he was?"

"They didn't know."

"And you didn't feel, I don't know, rejected? And before you found out about your aunt, didn't you wonder why you were put up for adoption?"

"Of course I did. And even after I found out about Sylvie, I wondered why it was so easy to give me away. And I wondered who my bio dad was and if I had any other family out there. But I also knew, deep down to the absolute core of who I am, that my parents love me, and that I have the best family in the world. I knew—know—that I'm loved completely, and I've had the best life."

He takes a drink of his Pepsi, but I can tell he's not done yet, so I wait. "I was really mad at my parents when I found out about Sylvie. I felt betrayed, like they'd lied to me for years. I was about your age at the time. And I was mad at Sylvie. Angry and hurt. How could she have given me up? And how could she interact with me in that aunt role so easily? Do you know what my dad said?"

I shook my head, though I had an inkling.

"He told me that giving me up for adoption was both the hardest and easiest decision Sylvie had ever made. She almost didn't do it, because even before I was born, she loved me. But she knew she was not in a place to take care of a child, and she knew she couldn't give me what I deserved. Sometimes, my dad told me, being a parent means putting the child's needs first, no matter how hard it might seem, and no matter what you have to sacrifice to do it."

They aren't new words. Mom had said something similar. Monica had said something like it. But when Mom said it, I thought she'd meant sacrificing things like which university I'd go to, or the dip in my GPA, or committing time to Greco's instead of robotics. Like those sacrifices were the price I'd have to pay to do what I thought was right. When Monica said it, it felt like actual parenthood goals. But now, with Roger sharing his story, it feels different. Heavier. More meaningful.

That weight, that meaning, is a pressure on my chest, because part of me really doesn't want to do what I need to do. But it's also a release, a freedom, because I know in my heart, it's the right thing to do.

Assuming, of course, the baby and Maxie are okay.

CHAPTER 31

My phone buzzes even as Roger and I walk back to the waiting room with a soda for Mo. We round the corner and find both Mr. and Mrs. Jacobson huddled close together near the front desk. It looks like Maxie's dad is getting a briefing from her mom.

I rush forward. "How's Maxie?"

Roger stands behind me, hands on my shoulders. I think that's the only reason Maxie's mom answers me. "She'll be okay."

"And the baby?"

Her mouth tightens. "Fine."

By this time, Mo's reached us as well. "What's wrong with her? What happened?"

Maxie's mom takes another look at Roger. "It looks like pre-eclampsia."

Mo's eyes widen. "That sounds serious."

I mentally flip through the pregnancy and birth research I've accumulated over the last few months. "Preeclampsia is a pregnancy complication characterized by high blood pressure," I recite. "What are they going to do for her? It's too early to deliver the baby, right?"

"Maxie will be put on bed rest for the next few weeks to give the baby more time to develop. In about four weeks, the baby should be far enough along for a safe delivery." She turns to her husband. "Let's go back to her. The rest of you"—she looks at Mo and me, her gaze completely avoiding Roger—"should head home now. There's nothing you can do for her."

We watch as the Jacobsons disappear behind a door.

"She was right about one thing," Roger says, stepping back from me. "There's nothing more we can do here. We should head home. Mo, do you need a ride?"

Mo shakes his head. "My car is here."

Roger looks to me. "You coming with me or Mo?"

Any other day, hell, even four hours ago, I'd have gone with Mo, no question. I'm feeling a little shaky now, and something about Roger steadies me. I bite my lip, glancing at Mo. Our reconciliation, or whatever we call it, is new and I don't want to mess that up.

"Go ahead," he says. "My mom's going to kill me for skipping out on the test. Better not to have an audience."

Roger and I are quiet on the ride home. Mom's car is in the driveway when we pull up.

She's waiting for us in the living room, face drawn tight with worry.

"Mom," I say before she can ask any questions. "There's something I need to tell you. Can we go to the kitchen?"

Because the kitchen is where we make plans, and I've got some big plans to put into motion.

. . .

Mom sits on one side of the table, and I'm on the other. She's poured us both tea. I still don't like tea, and, honestly, I'd probably hurl if I tried to eat or drink anything right now.

I don't wait for her to ask any questions. "Did you tell the Jacobsons that I'd give up on getting custody once I realized what all is involved?"

Mom stills, the teacup she'd lifted pausing halfway to her mouth. "Excuse me?"

"I overheard Maxie's dad telling one of the couples they interviewed that the only reason I was involved is that you assured them that if they let me participate in the process, I'd come to my senses sooner rather than later, and we could avoid the whole legal custody battle thing."

Mom doesn't say anything, but she puts the teacup down.

"Is that why you've been so supportive? Because you think I'll drop the whole thing? That I'll look at the summer camp, or the colleges, and decide the sacrifice is too much?"

"Ben," she says. "It's not what you think."

"Isn't that what everyone says? Did you tell the Jacobsons I'd back off?"

"I said it."

I thought I'd be too emotionally drained from the day I've had for anything Mom says to hit me so hard. I was wrong. So wrong. I feel like she's sucker punched me in the gut. I suck in a breath, trying not to show how much the words hurt.

"I lied, Ben."

"No kidding. Telling me you'd support me in this—"

"Not to you. I lied to the Jacobsons."

"You—what?"

She reaches across the table and takes one of my hands between hers. "I needed to buy some time. If we put too much pressure on, they would have dug in their heels and kept you out of everything. They would have fought us every step of the way. I needed you to be a part of the process. Some of that was so that if things did not go our way, you'd have a chance to assure yourself that the baby would be cared for. Other parts I needed you to see. You needed to see the baby as a person, as a reality, not as some kind of theory. You needed to see what Maxie was going through, so you'd understand exactly what she's had to sacrifice for your baby. You needed to see the human experience. Because, Ben, I don't think that's what you saw, not at the beginning. And if you are going to do this, if you're going to be a father, you need to see all that."

She's right, of course. Didn't I have the same thought during the ultrasound? That there was a real, live baby involved, not some theoretical project. I nod. "Okay. I guess I can see that. So you aren't secretly hoping I give up?"

She closes her eyes. "I won't lie to you. I'm worried that you're not seeing the whole picture. I'm worried you're not being honest about your reasons. But I'll be there."

"And Roger?" I ask.

Her face softens. "And Roger. And Miriam and Russel. We've got a whole family to back us up."

"I really like Roger," I admit.

"I'm glad. He loves you, you know. He's been stealing all your parenting books so he'll be able to help out. I think he's excited to play grandpa."

"I don't want my baby to feel like his father abandoned him. I know what that's like, and it sucks," I say in a rush. "Growing up, I felt like all the father figures were always leaving us behind. I hated it. Hated knowing I wasn't enough."

Her hand squeezes mine and her eyes fill with tears. "Oh, Ben."

"I know it wasn't really about me, but that's how it felt. You kept bringing in these men, men who acted like a dad for a little while, but they weren't, not really. And then they kept leaving."

"Benny." The tears welling in her eyes start to fall.

"I'm not trying to make you feel bad," I say. "I wanted to be honest, is all. Everything I told you before is true, but this is part of it too."

"You have to know, none of that is on you. It wasn't anything you did or didn't do, anything you said or didn't say. I should have done a better job of talking to you about it. You never seemed to react. You never said anything, and I let myself believe it didn't affect you. I should have known better. I, more than anyone, know how much you keep inside."

"If it helps," I say, "I'm getting past it. Talking to Roger has helped. And seeing all the things that James and Paolo have been doing for me helps. I think maybe I've had better fathers than I knew. I don't think I gave them enough of a chance."

"I'm not sure it helps. I'm happy to hear it, of course, but I think it will be a while before I forgive myself for putting you through that. I don't regret them, but I should have spent more time making sure you understood everything."

"Mom, here's the thing. I need you to know I can do it. I can be the father this baby needs. I need to know you believe me when I say I'll do whatever it takes—sacrifice whatever I have to—to make sure my baby is healthy and happy and wanted."

"I do believe it. Ben, I've watched you these last months. I've seen your determination and your commitment. Your hard work. I've been so damned proud of you. I know you can do it. I know you can do anything you put your mind to. But, Ben, I've also seen the stress and the worry. I've seen the disappointment when you realize that your future won't look the way you'd planned. I wanted that future for you. The future where you'll be successful and challenged. And I'm afraid. I'm afraid that, no matter how many books you read, you'll be unprepared for what parenthood entails. No one knows what's involved until they experience it, and no amount of planning and research will tell you exactly what to expect. So, yes, I believe in you, Ben. I know you can do it."

"Do you think I'll be a good parent?"

Her smile is not a happy one. It's almost bittersweet. "I know you are going to be an amazing father. You already are. And your child will grow up healthy, and happy, and wanted."

"Okay. And a good parent does what's best for their child, no matter the cost, right?"

"Right." She draws the word out until it's almost a question.

For once, my knee doesn't bounce, and I'm not compelled to chew my fingernails. I fist my hands, take a deep breath. If I don't say it now, I don't know if I'll ever be able to.

"Mom, we need to make a new plan. I'm done fighting."

CHAPTER 32

"Well, how does it feel?" Roger grins at me from the passenger side of my Civic.

"Are the pictures always so terrible?" I slide my thumb over the little square that shows I should have taken a minute to smooth down my hair before the photo was taken. The hair is the least of the problems, though. "Am I cross-eyed?" I demand, turning to him. "How did I not know?"

I do not appreciate Roger's unnecessarily gleeful chuckle. "You're not cross-eyed. It's a rite of passage. Your driver's license photo should always be awful. Mine makes me look like a mug shot after a 'People of Walmart' compilation." He pulls out his wallet to show me.

I snort. Yeah, it's terrible.

Finally, *finally*, I'd made time to take my driving test. Mom says that because Roger is the one who taught me to drive, he deserved to be the one to take me to the testing facility. It feels right, somehow, to share this moment with him.

The license is just step one in my plan. The timing isn't the best. It's not a prerequisite for the other stages, but it's given me the confidence boost I need. The meeting I have scheduled—I check the time display on the Civic's dash—in two hours has me alternating between determination and terror. It's the right thing to do. The perfect solution. If only everyone else could agree.

Roger slips his license back into his wallet. He swaps the wallet for his phone. "Lean in," he says, angling his body over the center console. He holds his phone up. "We need a picture."

I shake my head.

He nods. "It's a big deal, we need to commemorate it. Besides," he adds, "your mom made me promise." He waggles the phone. "Come on."

I sigh, secretly pleased. Not that I really want to have my photo taken, but it's nice to have a *moment*. To share this moment. To have Roger make this moment special. "Fine," I huff. I scoot over and lean in until my shoulder touches his.

Making a bracket with his free hand, Roger says, "Hold up your license and smile."

I do as instructed.

"Say *seat belts save lives*."

A snort escapes and I smile despite myself. He's ridiculous.

"Perfect." He taps the screen and his cell phone snicks.

He angles the device toward me. The image on the display shows two grinning faces. Mom will love it.

"All right, enough mushy stuff." Roger sits forward and snaps his seat belt. "Home, Jeeves." He shoots me another grin. "I think I'm going to like having a chauffeur."

I roll my eyes but fasten my own seat belt before starting the car.

"You ready for this?" Roger asks after we've gone a couple

blocks. He knows my plan, and while he and Mom say they support my decision, it's clear he recognizes that it might be rough on me.

"I think so. It's the right thing to do, and I really hope the Jacobsons will agree."

Roger pats my knee. He doesn't assure me that it will work out, which I appreciate. I may have shifted my priorities, but Maxie has the final say, and she is still heavily influenced by her parents. And based on what I've seen so far, my plan doesn't look exactly like their vision. Will they be stubborn and narrow-minded, or will they recognize the compromise I'm offering?

"Are you sure you don't want your mom and me there? You don't have to do this by yourself."

"I know," I say. I slow to a halt at a stop sign. I take a moment to watch his expression. "I think I need this. I need to show them, and myself, that this is what I want, that I'm looking out for the baby's best interests. That I'm being a good parent." My voice cracks and I blink against the pressure behind my eyes.

"I get it," Roger says, and I believe him. "Just to make sure you understand, that it's clear, your mom and I are very proud of you. So proud."

His words don't do anything to loosen the tightness that's developed in my throat, but it lightens something in my chest. "Thanks," I croak out.

I drop him off at our driveway before heading the six blocks to Maxie's house.

I don't see the distinctive yellow car in the Jacobsons' driveway yet, but I park on the street anyway. Never has the walk to the front door felt so daunting. Probably because for the first time I don't have righteousness and a backup plan behind me. If I don't like what is said or what Maxie and the Jacobsons decide, I still have some legal steps I can take to make my claim. But here, just by bringing the option up, I'm essentially letting go of some of that claim. And if the Jacobsons don't agree . . .

Maxie meets me at the door. Cocking her head, she peeks over my shoulder. "Did you drive?" she asks.

I shrug out of my jacket, hanging it on the coatrack by the door. "Yep. Finally got my license today."

"Cool," she says, stepping back. There's no denying now that she's pregnant. It looks as though she's trying to smuggle a basketball underneath the NOTORIOUS RBG T-shirt stretched over her belly.

"How are you feeling?" I ask her. She's been out of the hospital for two weeks with orders to take it easy. So no school, no outside activities. I stopped by to see her the day after she was released from the hospital, but I was only allowed to say a quick hi and drop off the flower arrangement Mom said was mandatory. While she looks a lot better today than she did then, it's easy to tell she's not up to 100 percent.

"I'm okay," she says. "Serious case of cabin fever. Sleeping a lot."

"And the baby's okay? No problems?"

Her hand strays to her baby bump. "Doctors say everything is looking good for now. We're monitoring my blood pressure and I'm barely let out of bed, but everything seems to be on track."

Maxie's parents are already sitting at the dining table, coffee cups in front of them. Dark circles bag underneath Mrs. Jacobson's eyes, stark against her wan complexion. I've never seen her look so exhausted. It's the same way Maxie looks after a late-night study session before a big exam. My stomach twists, a queasy, greasy sensation I can now identify as guilt. Or maybe shame. Because for the first time since any of this started, I realize the toll it's taking on Maxie's parents. For the last six months I've held them

up as the villains, intent to keep me from what I wanted, and punishing Maxie for her mistake. Not that I'm willing to empathize
completely. I don't think I can entirely forgive them for the way
they've treated Maxie through all of this. How much happier, or at
least more settled, would Maxie be if her parents had behaved
more like Mom and Roger? That kind of understanding and support might have made all the difference.

The sound of tires on concrete and the muted rumble of an
engine interrupt my thoughts. My heart picks up its pace. Maxie's
parents stand up. Maxie crosses her arms over her belly. This is it.

I hold my breath, counting the seconds.

Three . . . four . . . five . . .

How far is it from the driveway to the door?

Eight . . . nine . . . ten . . .

Maybe thirty feet at a sedate pace? Shouldn't take more than
twenty seconds, surely?

Fourteen . . . fifteen . . .

When the doorbell finally chimes, all four of us in the house
let out a deep breath. This moment feels significant to me. Maybe
they're picking up on that? Or maybe they also recognize that this
could be the answer we've been waiting for?

Mrs. Jacobson swipes her hands down the thighs of her tan
pants and steps forward. I didn't plan it, but somehow Maxie and
I end up standing shoulder to shoulder on one side of the living
room when Maxie's mom opens the door.

I must admit I pay extra attention to the expressions on Maxie's
parents' faces when they see Monica and her wife standing on
the porch holding hands. Lisa is at least half an inch shorter than
Monica, and her curling golden-blond hair, clear blue eyes, and
pale skin scream Nordic princess. I've never seen or heard anything from the Jacobsons that seems particularly homophobic,

but after meeting the other couples over the last few months, I've begun to question what I thought I knew about them. If they are taken aback by two women holding hands on their porch, they don't so much as blink to show it. Mrs. Jacobson holds the door open, inviting Monica and Lisa in.

"Hello," Monica says, holding her hand out to Mrs. Jacobson. "I'm Monica Grant, and this is my wife, Lisa."

Again, I watch for reactions from Maxie's parents. Mr. Jacobson comes over, resting his hand on his wife's waist, and offers Monica his hand. I let out a slow breath and relax my shoulders a bit.

The adults go through a quick round of introductions, but Lisa's bright blue eyes focus mostly on Maxie. She reaches out both her hands to take Maxie's. "Hello, Maxie. I'm very pleased to meet you." I haven't had much opportunity to interact with Lisa. I've seen her a couple of times at Greco's, but not enough for more than saying hi in passing. Where Monica is dynamic and confident, Lisa seems softer, quieter maybe.

"Hi," Maxie says softly.

"We should all have a seat," Mrs. Jacobson says. "Can I get anyone coffee? Water?"

I notice a big difference between Monica and Lisa compared to the other couples who were interviewed. The first being, they don't eye Maxie like a commodity. When Lisa asks about Maxie's health, it doesn't come off as a buyer evaluating a brood mare. She seems genuinely concerned about how the pregnancy is progressing, and how Maxie is feeling. When Monica talks about their house, she isn't using it as a yardstick to measure her wealth. There's no condescension, just a warm, generous couple.

"How long have you been pursuing adoption?" Mrs. Jacobson asks.

"We started discussing it six years ago, and officially began the process four and a half years ago."

Mrs. Jacobson frowns. "That long?"

Monica and Lisa look at each other; a thousand unspoken words pass between them before Lisa speaks. "It can be difficult for a same-sex couple to contract with an agency."

"I see." I can't identify the expression on Mr. Jacobson's face, but Maxie, who I've known long enough to read, relaxes. "Why do you want to adopt?" he asks.

Monica squeezes Lisa's hand. "The simple answer is because we want a family." She pauses. "No, that's not quite right. We want to complete our family. We're already a family but being parents has always been important to us. We would love a son or daughter."

"What makes you think you'll be good at it?"

She narrows her eyes at me, and by the way everyone else is gaping at me, I've clearly said it wrong. I shake my head. "I didn't mean it like that." I struggle to find the right words, but they're floating in my mind like dandelion fluff in a summer breeze, and there's no way I'll be able to pluck one from the air with my fingertips. She relaxes, and I think she maybe understands.

"We have a lot of love to give. We want to be able to share that love with a child and with each other. Motherhood—or parenthood if you prefer—is an amazing thing." She looks at her wife with a gentle smile. "Lisa is one of those people who you just know is meant to be a mother."

Lisa beams at her.

I ask the other question that's been plaguing me for months. "What do you think makes a good parent?" Somehow I know these two—unlike the other couples we've seen over the months—will get the answer right.

"Being a good parent means doing what's best for your child. It means loving them, supporting them, guiding them. It means hugs and discipline and nutrition and being there for them. It's not only fulfilling their physical needs, but also their emotional ones." She breaks off and clears her throat.

"And you're not worried that the baby you adopt won't be related to you, you know, genetically?"

Lisa shakes her head, a look of exasperated fondness that's so much like my mom's crossing her face. "Not at all, Ben. There's so much more to family than the blood connection. My parents were well off but couldn't be bothered with their kids. My brother and I were looked after by a nanny most of our childhood. When we graduated high school, and then college, my parents didn't even attend the ceremony. But Pamela, our nanny—the woman who raised us and loved us and showed us every day that we were special—she was sitting front row for both, cheering and shouting louder than anyone else. Monica and I still go to Pamela's house once a month for Sunday dinner and I'm even godmother to Pamela's granddaughter. Pamela was more my parent than either of my biological parents."

Her gaze is unfocused, and for a moment I wonder if her mind is on something else. "That's what I want," she says softly, her eyes coming back to me. "I want Sunday dinners and graduation parties. I want potty training and play dates."

Maxie's mom blinks suspiciously bright eyes. I don't know if it is Lisa's words or the longing even I can hear in her voice that draws the reaction from her. Even Mr. Jacobson clears his throat.

Maxie's hands tremble as she grips the edge of the table. "Yes," she says.

"Yes?" I ask, holding my breath.

Mr. Jacobson blinks quickly. "Maxie, we should—"

Maxie shakes her head. "No, Dad. This is right. *They* are the right ones."

Mrs. Jacobson reaches across the table and covers Maxie's hands with hers. "Are you sure?"

She swallows heavily, eyes steady on first her mother, then her father. "Yes. I want Monica and Lisa to adopt the baby."

"Okay," her mom says.

Lisa's breath catches and she clings to Monica's arm. Monica's lip wavers, but other than that, her face is neutral. It's almost like she's afraid to even hope. After all the misses and rejections, I guess I can't blame her.

"Okay," Mr. Jacobson says.

Suddenly all five sets of eyes are on me.

This is it. Once I take this step, there's no going back. This is the moment I've been fighting against for six months. The moment I've spent orchestrating for the last two weeks. This isn't how I expected things to turn out back in October. Or even back in January. I should feel some kind of reluctance or hesitation, shouldn't I? Some doubt?

"Yes," I say.

The tension in the room drops as everyone relaxes in their seat.

"But—" I begin.

And just like that the tension ratchets up a notch. I rush to get the words out before we're suffocated by it. "I want an open adoption. I want—no, I need—the baby to have the ability to know me, to meet me if they want to."

I turn to look at Maxie, wanting her to see how important this is to me. "I know it's not necessarily what you wanted, what you planned. I just . . . I just need to . . ."

"I get it," she says softly. "I—I can agree to that."

Monica leans forward. "Does this mean—"

"Everyone agrees," Mrs. Jacobson says.

Lisa's breath catches on a sob. Monica, teary-eyed, pulls her close. She meets my eyes. "Thank you," she says. "Thank you."

It's not the end of it, of course. There are still details to work out, lawyers to get involved, contracts to be signed, but for now, having settled on the direction we're to take, relief settles in.

CHAPTER 33

The air-conditioning in the Madison convention center ball-room is not up to the challenge of the unseasonably warm April temperatures and the four hundred students participating in the Wisconsin State High School Robotics Competition. Sweat drips down the side of my face, an irritation I barely notice as the awards ceremony approaches the top placements.

Madison West High School is announced as the fourth-place winner. Their twelve-person team lines up at the front, accepts their trophy, and poses for a group photo.

Mo shifts in place, looking half asleep. Percy has his hands in his pockets, staring at the floor. Mr. Rose watches the ceremony with appropriate attention. Mitch and Anna and the new guys are bored out of their minds. I know this because they've each mentioned it at least once. They don't understand why we have to wait through the whole ceremony and act excited for the winners when we didn't place.

"Good sportsmanship," Mr. Rose says simply.

Am I disappointed that we didn't win? Yeah, of course I am. Do I blame myself? Maybe a little. We actually placed higher this year than in previous years—just missing out on an award. Part of me can't help wondering: if I hadn't been so distracted all year long, might we have done better? Granted, there's more to the competition than the programming I did. Which is exactly what Mo said when Percy muttered under his breath about my "half-assed" dedication to the team this year.

It's nice having him in my corner again.

Placing would have been nice—especially with the club on the chopping block for next year. Mr. Rose has been working with some of his contacts to secure a private grant to keep the team running.

My phone buzzes in my pocket.

I ignore it. Mr. Rose has very strong opinions about personal devices being in use during a school event.

The buzzing in my pocket stops.

The announcer's voice calls out the third-place team, Middleton Lutheran High School.

The buzzing starts up again.

Damn it. I grab my phone to check the display. When I see Monica's number, I almost drop the device.

I hit the green button to accept the call. "Yeah?" I whisper. I duck down a little in a useless attempt to hide the fact that I'm talking on my phone.

Mo glances at me, brows raised. I ignore his silent questions. There's only one reason why Monica would be calling me, especially today.

"It's time," Monica says, and the excitement in her voice is completely contagious.

"Now? I thought they wanted to wait another week?"

"Well, the baby has changed the plans. I know you're at your tournament today, so we weren't going to call until you got back, but Maxie's been in labor most of the day, and it seems to be progressing quickly now. So if you want to be there, you'll need to head out ASAP."

"Shit!"

Now the whole team is glaring at me. I may be speaking a little louder than I think. Whoops. "We came in the team van, I have no way to get there."

"Gio should be there any second," she says.

"You sent Gio?"

"As soon as we knew you'd likely need a ride." There's a voice in the background. I hear muffled sounds, then Monica says, "Hey, I've got to go. But tell Gio to haul ass so you can be here in time."

I lean past Mo and tap Mr. Rose on the shoulder. He looks over. "I've got to go," I say in a low voice. "Maxie."

Mr. Rose nods at me. "We'll bring all your bags. Give Maxie our best."

I nod before pushing and weaving my way through the crowd of students, trying to find the closest exit. I trip over more than one equipment tub and backpack. At one point, I nearly take out a trio of girls from one of the Green Bay schools. "Sorry," I mutter, grabbing one of them to steady them.

I finally reach the exit. As soon as I clear the door, I sprint for the main entrance and parking lot.

My phone vibrates in my hand. I forgot about it in my dash from the arena. I guess it's a good thing I haven't lost it somewhere along the way. Gio's name flashes on the display. It stops buzzing a second before a honk sounds from in front of me. A familiar black Toyota idles at the curb.

I jump in, barely taking time to hook my seat belt before urging Gio to haul ass.

"I guess it's happening, huh?" Gio says.

"So it seems." I grip my phone in my hand. I don't want to chance missing any calls or communications. "I can't believe Maxie's been in labor all day and no one told me."

"Everyone knew how important this tournament is for you. Besides, from what they told me, labor and birthing take a long time."

I grunt.

"How'd it go today? How'd you guys do?"

"Meh." I rock my hand in a so-so gesture. "How long is the drive to get there?"

"A little over an hour," he says. "How are you feeling about this? Honestly, Ben. This is different than you'd planned."

I've had a lot of time over the last five weeks to come to terms with my decision. I've had a few moments of doubt, sure, and more than a little guilt. The what-ifs are a constant struggle. But I know, deep down, this is the right thing to do. It's the best thing for everyone.

The Jacobsons had no objections to approving the private adoption by Monica and Lisa. I think they were just happy to have it settled without the threat of a custody battle later. But Maxie has spent some time with Monica and her wife, and seems to genuinely like them. It helps that Monica and Lisa are not bigots, and they did not treat the whole thing like some kind of financial or business arrangement.

I worry sometimes that people will think that I've given up, that I can't handle it. Or that I've decided a child isn't worth the sacrifices they'd require.

I talk to Mom about it sometimes, and she reminds me that

what others think of me is none of my business. It's on them, not on me. I don't know if I always believe her, because how can it not matter? Then I remember Roger's butchered Dr. Seuss quote about those who matter not judging, and those who judge not mattering.

But these moments of doubt and shame are rare.

"I'm feeling good about it," I tell Gio in answer to his question. "I'm glad I did what I did. I don't think I'd have been as content with this decision if I hadn't taken the steps I did. But this feels *right*."

"Good. I'm happy to hear it."

We ride in silence for a while. Where once it was awkward, we've spent enough time riding in cars together that it feels natural and comfortable.

A little while later he says, "I've got news today, too. Nothing as big as this," he says, waving his hand at the road ahead of us, meaning, I assume, the baby and not the interstate. "But something pretty big for me."

I turn as much as the seat belt allows, so I can watch his expression. I'm never going to be good at reading people, but I'm getting better at reading him. I'm getting a hint of . . . pride. Pride and anticipation. "Yeah?"

"I talked to my mom."

I grab his sleeve. "Really? About school?"

He bites his lip, but it's not enough to hide his grin. "Yep. I sat down with her and explained that I'm more interested in culinary school than journalism, and that I'm going to be pursuing that instead."

"And how did she take it?"

He shrugs. "She wasn't happy, but when she realized I was serious, and that I wasn't going to back down, she accepted it. Reluctantly. There were a couple of compromises."

"Like what?"

"Since I'm already enrolled at UW–Madison, I'll start there in the fall like planned. I haven't applied to any of the culinary schools yet, and that will take time. I'll start the gen ed classes, get a few of those out of the way while I research what's available. There's a local community college in Madison with a decent culinary arts program. I'm going to see if I can take a class or two there while I research and apply at some of the bigger culinary schools."

"That's amazing."

"I'm not going to lie, I'm pretty psyched about it. It also means I'll be spending more time in the kitchen with Pops, so someone else will have to take over my front-of-house duties." He winks at me.

"Not a chance," I say. I know he's not serious—but the thought of it . . . no way. I've cut back my hours at Greco's, but I still go in a couple times a week. "Seriously, though, I'm really proud of you. This is a huge step."

"Yeah, well, it needed to happen. It's thanks to you, by the way. You're what gave me the kick in the ass I needed to face my mom."

"*Me?* What did I do?"

"You really can't figure it out? Ben, watching you work so hard for what you wanted, and not backing down from the fight be-cause it would be easier, is a total inspiration. If you could face your parents, the school, everyone, and work more hours than any other sixteen-year-old—"

"Seventeen."

"—seventeen-year-old I've ever met, then I can sure as hell face my mother."

Emotions lodge in my throat, and I don't know what to say. I feel the heat of a blush creeping up my neck. "I didn't—"

He reaches over and grabs my hand. "You did. You didn't let anyone's opinions sway you from your course. Not when you were doing what you thought was right. You inspired me to do the same, even if the stakes aren't quite the same."

"Well, that's good. I mean cool. Or whatever." Damn it, someday I'll be able to talk smoothly. At least I hope so.

"Or whatever," he agrees.

He keeps ahold of my hand as the miles pass. It's nice.

"So, I have a question for you," Gio says a little while later as he merges onto I-94. "Now that you're not as busy with the baby-related stuff, and you've reached the end of your robotics season, do you think you'll have a little more time for other things?"

"Like what?" I glance at the time display on my phone. Still more than half an hour to go.

"Like dating."

I drop my phone. "What?" I refuse to acknowledge the squeak in my voice, and try to keep it together as I reach to the floorboards to retrieve my phone.

His lips quirk, but he keeps his eyes on the road. "Dating, Ben. You know, going out with someone. Some kind of activity. Maybe some kissing."

"*Kissing?*" Okay, so there is no denying the squeak this time.

Gio chuckles. "I'm totally messing this up, but this is so much fun. I guess I need to be a bit more direct before your face burns from the strength of your blush. Ben Morrison, would you go on a date with me?"

I gurgle.

"Maybe that was too formal. Let's try this. Ben, I like you, and I'd like to spend time with you to see where this can go."

I sputter, and the words I know I should say don't come out.

Now Gio looks worried. He takes a hand off the wheel, reaches for me, but pulls back again before making contact. "Hey, look, if you're not into it, I get it. I don't want to pressure you."

It sounds like he's kicking himself. I finally force the words out. "I'm into it. I'm *so* into it, you have no idea. Yes. Let's do that. The dating and kissing and whatever."

This time when he reaches out, he takes my hand and doesn't pull back.

Gio and I hurry into the maternity ward of the hospital. For some damn reason, the only open parking space we could find was practically two blocks away. We jogged the whole way, so when I cross into the waiting room, I'm huffing and puffing like we just completed a timed mile run in gym class.

The last time I rushed into a hospital, I was terrified. This time, excitement pushes my steps.

"Maxie?" I wheeze, coming to a halt as soon as I see someone in the crowd I recognize. I find Mom sitting between Roger and a table covered in magazines. There's also a pair of yellow balloons dancing happily above a yellow-and-white teddy bear in Roger's lap.

"The last update said any time now," Mom says. "Maxie's mother, Monica, and Lisa are back with her."

I'm in time then. Thank goodness. I sink into the open seat next to Roger, only then noticing a couple of familiar people in the room. Mr. Jacobson is parked on the other side of the seating area, face pale and foot tapping. As much as I don't really like him or how he's dealt with everything, it's obvious he cares about Maxie.

"Hello, Gio," Mom says, standing up to give Gio a hug.

Gio lets himself be pulled into her embrace. "Hey, Eliza. Today's the day, huh?"

She smiles. "Looks like it."

"Pops?" Gio asks.

Mom nods to a hallway. "Gift shop. Got some inspiration from this one." She tilts her head to Roger.

I take the seat next to Roger, and Gio sits next to me. My knee immediately starts to bounce. The whole row of interconnected chairs shakes to the same rhythm.

Gio reaches over and grabs my knee, stilling the movement. "Relax. Everything's going to be fine."

Over the last several weeks, Mom has said the same thing. Even Maxie, who's been going stir-crazy during the mandatory period of bed rest, has said the same thing. But the preeclampsia scare was, well, scary.

Until this is over, until the baby is born, and until I know that Maxie and the baby are safe and healthy, I don't think I'll be able to relax.

Paolo strides into the waiting area with arms full of flowers and balloons. From the look of it, he's bought the gift shop out.

"Did you get enough balloons, Pops, or do we need to find a party store?" Gio asks.

Paolo waves this aside. "We have a lot to celebrate." His eyes stray to Gio's hand, which still rests on my knee. "Do I need more balloons?"

My face burns, but Gio scoffs. "That's a little extra, even for you."

"Took you long enough." Paolo smirks.

This time it's Gio's turn to blush. Before I can revel in that, a beaming Monica bursts into the waiting room. "It's a girl!"

The door to Maxie's room is open, but I hesitate at the threshold. I need a second to calibrate my emotions. There's a part of me that has been afraid that when the time comes, when I see the baby for the first time, I'll change my mind. That I'll regret the decision I made.

But walking into that room, I know immediately that I made the right call.

Lisa holds the little girl, her cheeks damp with tears, her smile broad and happy enough to be seen from space. Her eyes never leave the red-faced baby in her arms. Monica stands behind them, her chin hooked over Lisa's shoulder. She's got one hand on Lisa's hip; the other trails along the baby's swaddled form.

They're in their own little bubble of love and don't seem to notice anything else except the baby and each other. Their joy and pride are so thick in the air I can practically taste them on the back of my tongue.

It's almost as if everything Maxie and I have gone through is worth it for this moment.

Maxie and I created a life. That life—that little girl—is helping two women I've come to care about complete their family. While this is an ending of sorts for Maxie and me, it's only the beginning for Monica, Lisa, and their new daughter.

I look to the bed where Maxie is lying, face pale and curls barely contained in a sloppy knot at the top of her head. Her gaze is fixed on Monica, Lisa, and the baby. And I think, just for a second, that Maxie isn't as content with this as I am.

I ignore the others who have followed me in. Even though the room is now crowded with friends and family, all ready to congratulate the new parents or to check on Maxie, my concern at the moment is 100 percent Maxie.

I want to help her, but I don't know how. How do I make it easier for her to let go? Through all of this journey, she's been so strong. I don't think I recognized, even when she told me, how hard this has been for her.

I lean over the edge of the bed so I can whisper in her ear, "Look what we did, Maxie. Look at their family." I nod toward Lisa and Monica. "It may have been the result of questionable decisions, and it was hard, but look at what we did. We created that life, Maxie, but that baby isn't ours. I don't think she ever has been. Look how happy they are, how perfect. That's thanks to you." For once, I think I actually have the right words.

She grabs my hand and squeezes. Her voice shakes as she whispers back, "I know you're right. I didn't think I would feel like this. It'll be fine. I'll be okay."

We both ignore the unspoken *eventually* at the end of her sentence. I look around the room. It hasn't only been Maxie and me, though. Maxie's parents lived with this every day. Mom and Roger. Even James and Paolo.

"Have you decided on a name yet?" Mom asks Monica.

Monica and Lisa share a long look before turning back to us. "If Maxie doesn't object, we were thinking of Pamela Maxine Grant," Monica says.

Maxie's smile wobbles a bit at the edges, but it's genuine. "That's beautiful. That's fine with me."

I look around the room, at the friends and family surrounding us. In this moment, amid the smiles of joy and tempered grief intermingling with balloons and flowers, I know without any doubt or second-guessing that I've made the right choice.

This is right.

This is family.

ACKNOWLEDGMENTS

Books are rarely created in a vacuum, and this one is no exception. Huge shout-out to the individuals who made *Unexpecting* possible. Thank you to my amazing critique group: Stephanie Scott, Vanessa Knight, and KD Garcia. Your friendship, support, and feedback have made all the difference! Thank you to the Chicago North Romance Writers, whose enthusiasm for this story is matched only by their generosity. An energetic and hysterical brainstorming session with them led to the perfect title for this book. Thank you to Eileen Rothschild and Lisa Bonvissuto and the team at Wednesday Books for seeing the potential in this story and making the dream of a lifetime come true for me. Thank you to Saritza Hernandez, literary agent extraordinaire, for being the best advocate a girl like me could have. Thank you to my JABB girls—Ana, Barbara, and Berenice—for showing me that the line between friendship and family is a really narrow one. And last but not least, thank you to my mother, the woman I admire most in the world, for always being in my corner.